OUTLAW WEST OF THE PECOS

The Memoirs of H.H. Lomax

Book 7

PRESTON LEWIS

WOLFPACK PUBLISHING
— EST 2013 —

OUTLAW WEST OF THE PECOS

For Harriet,
On Our
Golden Wedding Anniversary

INTRODUCTION

As far as scoundrels, H.H. Lomax may finally have met his match in Judge Roy Bean. So, it goes in the seventh volume of *The Memoirs of H.H. Lomax*, where Lomax not only meets the frontier legal legend, but also the deadliest gunman in the violent history of Texas. Along the way, Lomax claims to have matched wits at a distance with three governors and two presidents, even though none of them ever heard of him.

Outlaw West of the Pecos covers the shortest time span of Lomax's memoirs published to date, an eight-month period between July 1895 and February 1896 when the frontier was narrowing, and civilization and religion were challenging the old ways and traditions, ranging from consuming whiskey to enjoying prize-fights. Lomax is caught in the middle of these shifting values, usually siding with tradition no matter how destructive to society.

As with past Lomax volumes, his story follows the history as best I can reconstruct it from afar. Sometimes his chronology is skewed, but that is not unusual for someone recalling events decades earlier. A couple claims struck me as false, but investigation showed Lomax was actually correct. The first was his description of early gun control legislation enacted by Texas. Despite its reputation as a state of rugged, gun-toting men, Texas had restricted the open and concealed carry of weapons as early as the 1870s. The second assertion was that both

Judge Roy Bean and John Wesley Hardin sought biographies on their—in one case colorful and in the other murderous— lives. Once again, Lomax's recollections proved accurate.

Part of the back story of this tale is Lomax's references to Oscar Wilde, the Irish poet, and playwright who toured North America in 1882. According to Lomax, he served Wilde as a bodyguard on part of that tour. Though I found no references to Lomax in a quick exam of the historical record from that time, I did discover a selection of Lomax papers referencing his time with Wilde, and I am editing them for a future volume in the Lomax memoirs.

Wilde is important in this story because of his acquaintance with Lilly Langtry, the British socialite, actress, and mistress of noblemen, including the Prince of Wales. Judge Roy Bean had a long-distance crush on the Jersey Lilly, as she was known, and found in Lomax a vicarious connection to the beautiful actress. That friendship between the actress and Wilde helped Lomax survive better than most his court encounters with the infamous Law West of the Pecos because of Bean's fascination with Langtry, who spelled her first name as Lillie. The judge, however, misspelled her name as Lilly, naming his saloon "The Jersey Lilly" in her honor. For consistency, if not accuracy, I used Bean's spelling since this account is set in Texas, not Europe.

If this is your first encounter with *The Memoirs of H.H. Lomax*, I will refer you to the introductions of previous volumes for background on Lomax, his family, and his outlandish adventures across the Old West. At his death, he left an extensive body of recollections written in pencil on Big Chief tablets. As my schedule allowed, I have researched those memoirs over the last quarter of a century and published select reminiscences since 1996. That experience has been entertaining as Lomax had a different, often irreverent, perspective on the people and events of the frontier. Generally, Lomax possessed a knack for being at the wrong place at the wrong time, but somehow survived, partially on cunning and largely on luck with a smattering of wit thrown in.

Outlaw West of the Pecos marks the first occasion I've found that Lomax wore a badge for a time. Though he did clean up the streets of El Paso, it was not quite how he expected. That, however, is part of the charm of the vagabond H.H. Lomax, and why I keep publishing his memoirs. As I've said before, he may not have won the West, but he sure made it fun.

Preston Lewis
San Angelo, Texas
December 21, 2021

Chapter One

While I never intended to wind up dangling from the last car in a westbound Southern Pacific passenger train as we approached the Pecos River gorge, bad things always found me anytime I passed through that godforsaken country people called Texas. Nor did I have plans to stop in Langtry, Texas, but I did, and the sporting world was a better place because of it. By the time this chain of events had finished, I'd been dragged multiple times before the wisest judge in the history of the Old West, roomed across the hall from the worst lawyer—and that's saying a lot—whoever walked the face of the earth, outwitted two presidents and three governors, wound up in a cage with a bear drooling over me for his next meal, fed an African lion before he ate me and wore a badge while cleaning up the streets of the meanest town in Texas.

All of this resulted from an unfortunate railroad accident when an ace slipped from my sleeve during a friendly Southern Pacific smoking car game with four Texas cattlemen, who fancied themselves fine poker players but weren't nearly sharp enough to spot me palming cards and manipulating the pasteboards that left me a couple hundred dollars ahead. I was grinning and shaking my head at my fine luck, and they were scratching theirs as bewildered as if beef prices had fallen to zero after they had cornered the market. Then the ace of diamonds fell from my coat sleeve. They grinned. I frowned. They stood up from the makeshift card table. I reached for my winnings, but a beefy, callused hand grabbed mine and yanked it away from my greenbacks.

"Not so fast, Lomax, if that really is your name," said the one called "Tiny" for his beer-barrel girth.

"That's my name, and that's my money," I challenged, letting my free fingers slip toward my side and my revolver.

Before I touched iron, another rough hand grabbed my wrist and yanked it upward, freeing a king of diamonds that fell in my lap from inside my coat. Claude pumped my hand with his powerful grip, shaking my arm, my shoulder, and my entire torso. "What else have you got hidden on you, Lomax?"

"Nothing," I protested, hoping they didn't pull off my boots and find the five hundred dollars I'd deposited between the socks and the soles.

"Card cheat!" shouted Joe Beedy, the dumbest and ugliest card player I ever saw with his bent nose, crooked teeth, crossed eyes, and moth-eaten mustache. Until Beedy's outburst, the accusations had been a private matter, but now everybody in the smoking car turned and glared at me like I had done something wrong. "Card cheat!"

"Sore loser," I spat back as Beedy, and Tiny lifted me to my feet. I tried to shake myself free, but their grips tightened.

The fourth player, Merritt, slowly pushed himself from his chair. He sported thick black hair, a thin black mustache, tight lips, and bug eyes, which bulged with rage. He reached across the table and grabbed my lapels, yanking me halfway across the playing surface. "You know what we do with cheaters and horse thieves in Texas?"

"Make 'em honorary citizens and give 'em a parade?" I shot back.

"We hang the sons of—"

"Watch your language," shouted another voice from the opposite end of the car.

I saw the uniformed conductor striding down the aisle.

Merritt released my lapels and turned around to face

6

the train man. "He was cheating at cards. I don't take kindly to that."

"And the Southern Pacific doesn't approve gambling on board."

I cleared my throat to get the conductor's attention. "These gentlemen insisted I play."

"You looked like easy pickings," Beedy said, "and we—" He hesitated, forgetting what he intended to say.

The conductor shook his head. "You're disturbing other passengers."

"He's a cheat," Merritt said.

"We're nearing the High Bridge," the conductor replied.

Tiny grinned. "That gives me an idea, boys."

The railway employee continued, "From the bridge, it's fifteen miles to Langtry, where we stop for water. We'll kick him off there. If you fellows create any more trouble, I'll drop you off as well and tell Judge Roy Bean you boys tried to rob another passenger."

"Yes, sir, Mr. Conductor," Tiny answered. "I think we'll all step outside on the platform to cool off."

"I'm fine where I am," I replied.

Tiny grinned and yanked me into the aisle. "Let's head out back, boys."

The quartet escorted me out the back door and squeezed beside me on the narrow platform, pushing me against the railing as they shut the door behind us. The clackety-clack of the rails accompanied the whistling wind as the huffing locomotive pushed itself down the tracks, leaving wisps of black smoke in the scorching June air.

"You ever seen the High Bridge over the Pecos River?" Tiny asked me.

I shrugged.

"It's two thousand feet long and three hundred feet tall," Tiny said. "You need a good look at it." With that, Tiny shoved me against the back rail and two of his compatriots grabbed my calves and hoisted me headfirst over the back. Then two more sets of hands took hold of my calves and left me dangling above the iron, my head bumping against the greasy coupler, my Colt sliding from my holster and bouncing off the ties and over the iron rails. My hands fell toward the creosoted ties, and I knotted my fists to keep my fingers from dragging.

"Here comes the bridge," Merritt cried.

The train braked and started across the rickety wooden structure the Southern Pacific called a bridge. From my angle, the bridge looked like a skeleton of toothpicks held together by prayers and good intentions.

"Hell, just drop him and get it over with," Merritt suggested. "Not even the buzzards will find him out here."

"By the time he bounces off all the wood supports, there won't be enough of him left to feed an earthworm," Claude said.

I didn't know whether they intended to drop me or just scare me, but I was petrified watching the ties flash by just inches from my head and feeling my ankles sliding from my boots.

My inept card-playing associates noticed too and laughed. "His boots are—" started Beedy, who again forgot what he was about to say.

I slipped closer to the ties, my shoulder bumping against the greasy iron coupler as my boots lost their grip on my feet. The train hit a bump and jolted me a tad more out of my boots. I tried to grab the railing to keep from falling but couldn't grip the iron bar. Another bump and I'd be skidding along the ties and over the rails and into the timber trusses and beams, my only consolation being that I might damage the bridge so that the whole train would collapse with me into the Pecos River gorge.

Just as I figured my time was over, I heard a commotion on the platform and felt another pair of hands grab my gun belt.

"What the hell are you fellows doing?" cried the conductor. "Do you know the amount of paperwork I'll have to fill out if we lose a passenger? Pull him back aboard the train, or I'll file murder charges against you in Langtry. Judge Bean loves to try murderers."

"Yeah," answered Claude, "he'll fine us for every cent we've got, then let us go."

"I'd pay double whatever he fines us, just to see Lomax dead," Merritt said.

Slowly, they pulled me back over the rail and stood me up between them. I remained dizzy, my knees mushy and my brain foggy.

"Take him inside," commanded the conductor, "and if I have any more trouble from you, I'll kick all of you off in Langtry." My savior stared at me as I got my balance. "You look a little puny, fellow. Are you okay?"

"I'll be better once I get out of Texas."

He looked to the west, where you could just see the glint of the afternoon sun on the Rio Grande. "Mexico's worse." He opened the door into the smoking car and motioned me inside. He followed me, and my assailants trailed behind him.

I sat down in my chair, regretting I had ever picked up a deck of cards and even sorrier over the fact one of them had escaped my sleeve. The conductor told the four cattlemen to take seats on the other end of the car. He escorted them there and exited into the adjacent car, returning shortly with my two valises. I was aiming to visit San Francisco, but this unplanned stop in Langtry, Texas, would delay my intentions. I watched the passing landscape and couldn't imagine an uglier piece of God's green—in this case, brown—earth. Dry arroyos snaked between rocky hills peppered with prickly pear, juniper, and mesquite. Ugly as the desolate countryside was, I doubted a tree stout enough to hang a man stood within a hundred miles of me. I liked that.

Shortly, the train slowed, and the engineer cut loose with his steam whistle announcing the approach. What I saw was a scab of a gray clapboard town hugging the railroad track, the depot on the north edge of the tracks and beyond it a few scattered buildings, including one festooned with signs proclaiming Judge Roy Bean as a notary public and justice of the peace. Other clapboards named the place THE JERSEY LILLY and advertised cold beer. The biggest sign of all hovered over the steps leading to the shady front porch, reading LAW WEST OF THE PECOS. On the far side of the building, I could see a variety of animal cages and, most curious of all, a black bear chained out in front of the saloon.

As the train pulled up to the depot platform, the conductor announced a stop of twenty minutes to take on water. He said the engineer would toot the whistle five minutes before time to depart, and all travelers should start back if they didn't want to be left behind in Langtry. He warned everyone curious about seeing Judge Roy Bean not to buy anything from his honor with a large bill as the esteemed jurist was slow to give change. Most passengers got off to see the frontier curiosity, including my card-playing pals who accompanied me and my carpetbags with the conductor toward the seat of justice west of the Pecos.

As the crowd strode to the Jersey Lilly, a pot-bellied man with a white beard over a red bandanna and a Mexican sombrero came out waving a brown bottle of beer at everyone. He walked over to the black bear and gave him the drink. The bear took the bottle, put it between his teeth, and yanked off the cork, spitting it out, then tilting the container to his mouth and gulping down the amber liquid.

"There's plenty of beer for everyone," the old man called, waving his arms inviting the passengers in to sample his wares.

As we approached Judge Roy Bean *and* Judge Roy *Bear*, as I called the pet, the conductor called the magistrate. "Judge, we've got a card cheat here." He pointed at me.

"Yeah," said Tiny. "He had cards up his sleeve."

"That's not true," I protested, dropping my bags, and intending to defend my honor. "There was only one card up my sleeve. The other fell from my coat."

"He's a card shark, just the same," Merritt interjected. "We should've thrown him off the train on the High Bridge."

Bean nodded. "I wish you had because I'd have gotten five dollars for conducting the inquest and then fined him whatever he had on him for disturbing the peace."

"Not guilty," I cried.

"That'll be determined by this court of law," the honorable judge said. "I've got a trial scheduled later this afternoon between trains. I'll add him to the docket." Bean studied me.

I smiled, confident of my acquittal since I doubted

10

my accusers would stay to testify against me. Without witnesses, I was as good as a free man.

"He's a mangy-looking animal. Did he eat axle grease for breakfast?"

I swiped at the lubricant smeared on my face after my close brush with the coupling and the railroad ties.

Bean shook his head and waved his arm like my legal case was insignificant. "Now, tell me, boys, any news on the Corbett-Fitzsimmons fight?"

The conductor shrugged. "Nothing's been settled as far as I know, or at least it hasn't appeared in the papers. They're still arguing over details and who's the real champion."

"I was hoping for a fight. That's the biggest news around here since Oscar Wilde's trials for sodomy and gomorrahmy."

My ears perked up. I had been Wilde's bodyguard a decade earlier during part of his tour around the west. Without a doubt, Wilde was the strangest fellow I ever met anywhere, including Texas.

"I'm surprised, Judge," said the conductor, "that you would follow the trial of a reprobate like that."

Bean grimaced. "Any friend of Lilly Langtry is a friend of mine. I named my town after her, and you'll see her portrait inside my courtroom."

"Don't you mean saloon?" The conductor grinned.

"Half and half," Bean said, "and now I must attend to the customers in the saloon half." He looked at me. "Don't try to escape, fellow, as your trial will start this afternoon."

I smiled, knowing I'd soon be walking free, either vindicated by the court or catching the next train out of town.

"I'll make sure he doesn't," said Beedy behind me.

Instantly, I saw a brilliant flash and felt myself collapsing into a tunnel of darkness.

When I came to an hour later, I slowly opened my eyes, squinting into the glare of the late afternoon sun. I rubbed the knot on the back of my head and gradually figured out I was propped up against the iron bars of a metal cage. Flashes of light darted through my brain as I lifted my throbbing skull. Tiring of the effort, I stared at my waist and realized I was wearing my long johns only. Not only were my clothes missing but also my boots and certainly the five hundred dollars I had hidden there. Damn if Texas wasn't a lawless hellhole.

Then things got worse. I gradually lifted my head and saw I had a companion in the cage—Judge Roy Bear. I looked at him. He eyed me, then licked his lips with that red tongue. I licked my lips, trying to intimidate him back, but my tongue and throat were as parched as the West Texas landscape around me. The bear and I stared each other down for a half hour until the judge himself came out carrying a coffee can and looked us both over.

"Bruno must like you, fellow," Bean announced.

"How's that?"

"He hasn't eaten you for starters. He takes to some folks okay and dines on others, but it's time for his evening treat and I need to get you cleaned up for trial." Stepping to my corner with the coffee can, Bean tipped it over my head, just as I looked up, drenching my face in honey. Barely had he finished slathering me with the bee sweets than Bruno was atop me, licking me with a tongue as rough as sandpaper, his breath smelling like death warmed over.

"Why'd you do that?" I sputtered between Bruno's licks.

"To clean the axle grease off your face. You should be presentable at your trial."

"What about my clothes and boots?"

"Your long johns and socks are fine. Did you know I found near five hundred dollars in your boots? Illicit gambling winnings, I suspect."

I twisted my head toward Bean, annoying Bruno, who growled, then continued to lick my face. "That's my money, fairly earned. I want it back."

The judge stroked his white beard and nodded. "You'll get it all back, less fines and court costs. That's a promise as honest as the law west of the Pecos. What's your name, fellow?"

I twisted my head to look the judge in the eye, but Bruno took his paw and moved my chin to more easily lick the rest of the honey from me. "The name's Lomax, H.H. Lomax."

"Only known one other Lomax in my life, Andy Lomax, a Texas Ranger with the El Paso battalion."

Shoving Bruno's jaws aside, I looked up at Bean, the fast movement making my brain flash with daggers of light. "Andrew Jackson Lomax, is that his name?"

Bean nodded. "I believe it is."

Letting out a heavy breath, I sighed. "He's my brother."

"It's a shame you didn't turn out as decent as Andy," Bean replied, spinning about, and walking away. "I'll see you shortly."

I looked as bewildered as Bruno, who hesitated a moment, then resumed licking the sticky honey and railroad grease from my face and neck. When he finished, Bruno returned to his corner, and we sat there like two wary prizefighters eyeing each other.

A half hour later, one of Bean's men—a constable or a bartender—came for me and led me barefooted and long-johned into the building, a lengthy structure with a hall down the middle. On the left stood an open door into the sparsely stocked store he kept, but we turned right into his courtroom and bar about fifteen by thirty feet in size, with a bar on the east side of the room and a pool table in the center. Gazing over the messy straw-strewn room from behind the bar hung a portrait of the great English actress Lilly Langtry. Behind his liquor counter sat Bean on a stool beneath Lilly's smile while a Mexican man fidgeted on an empty beer keg at the end of the bar. Six men eyed the Mexican as the judge spoke.

"Gentlemen of the jury," Bean intoned, "you see before you a meskin accused of horse thievery. Do your duty to the laws of the great State of Texas."

The men nodded, leaned their heads into a tight circle, then one stood up and spoke. "Your Honor, we've reached our verdict. We find the defendant guilty of being meskin."

Bean banged his gavel on the counter. "So acknowledged and please remain for our next trial." He turned to the defendant. "Having been found guilty, you are hereby sentenced to return the missing horse and pay a fine of twenty dollars, fifty dollars should you be unwilling or unable to return said steed."

The convicted horse thief nodded. "*Gracias, Señor Frijol,*" he said, as he stepped away from the keg.

While Bean wrote out the verdict and the punishment, his associate directed me to the bar near the judge. I saw a missive on the counter with the seal of the governor of Texas, the honorable Charles A. Culberson, at the top. I twisted the letter around and read the governor's complaint about the justice of the peace not submitting fines from his court, a duly recognized agency of the state, to Austin for deposit in Texas accounts. In a scribbled hand, Bean had responded, "You take care of Austin, and I'll take care of Langtry. Otherwise, go Oscar Wilde yourself!" It was signed "Judge Roy Bean, Law West of the Pecos."

When I finished reading the missive, I put it back in place only to discover Bean staring at me. As he swung his gavel at the letter, I yanked my fingers away, barely in time to keep them from being crushed. "Hands off, Lomax. That's official government correspondence."

"My apologies, *Señor Frijol*," I said.

Bean banged the gavel. "It's Bean, not *frijol*. That's meskin talk. You're American. Talk American and take the witness stand."

I stood there bewildered. "Witness stand?"

Bean pointed with the gavel to the perch the horse thief had just abandoned. "The keg, go sit on the keg."

Walking across the straw-strewn floor, I realized how dirty the courtroom was. I'd seen stables and even outhouses that were cleaner, but I kept my assessment of his housekeeping to myself as I took my place on the stand, feeling odd sitting there in my long johns and my sock feet. I hoped justice was blind in Langtry.

The honorable judge turned to the six men who would decide my fate. "Gentlemen of the jury, you have before you H.H. Lomax accused of cheating at poker on the Southern Pacific westbound this afternoon. I have looked through the statutes of the state of Texas, and I have found no law saying it is illegal to cheat at cards. It may be unethical, unchristian, and uncalled for, but it's not illegal. So, that complaint is dropped. Instead, I'm charging H.H. Lomax with carrying a concealed weapon."

"What?" I cried. "I entered Langtry without a weapon at all, having lost my revolver during an unfortunate incident atop the High Bridge."

"You admitted to hiding a playing card up your sleeve and another in your coat? I heard you say so myself," Bean shot back.

"But a playing card?"

"Back when this county teemed with Chinamen building the railroad, I once saw a celestial fling a playing card like a saucer clipping another Chinaman's pigtail as easily as if he had cut it off with a butcher knife?"

"A playing card, Judge? Are you crazy?"

"Are you questioning the authority of an official of the great State of Texas?" Before I could answer, he continued. "Indeed you are, and I am holding you in contempt. Now then, gentlemen of the jury, fulfill your obligation to the State of Texas."

"Don't I get a lawyer?" I asked as the jurors convened.

"There aren't any lawyers in Langtry, just the law. And don't forget, I *am* the law."

The sun-bronzed fellow I took to be the jury foreman spoke next. "Your Honor, we have reached our verdict."

"Very well, then. How do you decide?"

"We the jury find the defendant guilty as charged."

"This is the greatest legal wrong in the history of the State of Texas," I cried.

"Another outburst and I'll add a second contempt charge to your list of crimes. You best keep quiet for your own good."

I sat there fuming, but silent.

"Okay, for carrying a concealed weapon, I'm fining you fifty dollars. There's a seventy-five-dollar fine for contempt of court. I'm tacking the five-dollar inquest fee I would have received from the county had you fallen from the high bridge."

"I've got the money, so I'll pay the fine and leave on the next train," I offered.

"No, sir, I'm also incarcerating you for the next ten

days to teach you respect for the laws of this great state. That'll be another ten dollars a day for a jail boarding fee."

"What?" I sputtered. "Before I leave here, you'll have all my money?"

Bean grinned at me. "That's a good thought, Lomax. Now I want you to strip naked."

I was as bewildered as a rat at a cat convention. This magistrate struck me as a lunatic, but I jumped down from the keg and unbuttoned my long johns.

The judge slammed his gavel against the bar top. "Not in here, not in front of Miss Langtry," he shouted. "She's a lady. Go out in the hall and throw your union suit and socks back in here."

I hesitated.

"Move or I'll tack another contempt charge onto your bill."

Bolting out of the room, I did as ordered, standing in the hallway making sure that Lilly's lifeless eyes didn't see my nakedness. Now I hoped not only that justice but also Langtry was blind as I questioned my future in Texas. I stood there maybe ten minutes before I heard Bean call me from the front porch. Slipping just my head outside the doorway, I saw him sitting on a burro with a double-barreled shotgun pointed my way.

"Come on out, Lomax. Let's go for a walk."

"Where?" I wanted to know.

"To the river to bathe."

"I need my clothes," I pleaded.

"I don't have any shackles," Bean answered.

"What's that got to do with my clothes?"

"I've found I don't need shackles for naked men. Now come on out or I'm fining you another hundred dollars."

Damn if Bean wasn't right. As soon as I stepped outside, my hands dropped to my groin and stayed there all the way to the Rio Grande. We walked past the tracks and beyond the more numerous buildings on the railroad's south side, where folks had built their homes and stores to put some distance between them and the law west of the Pecos. As I ambled through town with the double-barreled shotgun pointed at my back, some men and women giggled, but most made the sign of the cross over their breast. "*El camino de la muerte*," cried one woman.

Bean translated for me, "The walk of death."

I suppose it was a half mile or less from his courtroom to the ledge overlooking the Rio Grande River, but it seemed like forever, me being naked and barefoot and trying to miss the cactus and thorns that littered the trail. At the canyon's edge, Bean pointed me down a path that led a hundred and fifty feet to the water's edge below. I followed it and Bean's instructions to wade out to an island that appeared to be an acre or more in the middle of the river. Bean followed me; the shotgun always pointed at my back.

"This island is neither Texas nor Mexico. Nobody's certain who has jurisdiction, so if I shoot you, I won't be prosecuted by me as law west of the Pecos or anyone else. Now if I *do* shoot you dead, and you float away, make sure you land on the Texas side of the river so I can get my five-dollar fee for handling the inquest."

I emerged from the water on the island and Bean came close enough that I could've grabbed the scattergun's barrel, but I feared he'd earn five dollars if I did. He reached in his britches pocket and tossed me a bar of soap.

Catching it, I asked, "What's this for."

"It's soap. Don't you know how to take a bath?"

"I do, but why do I need one?"

"Every man needs to be clean on his wedding day."

"What?"

"You're getting married when we return."

Stunned, I looked from him to my naked flesh. At least I was already dressed for my wedding night.

CHAPTER TWO

Stepping waist-deep into the cool brown waters of the Rio Grande, I remained bewildered about my impending marriage. I soaped and lathered myself and wondered if it might have been healthier to have tumbled off the High Bridge and taken my chances on the way down to the splat. The honorable judge kept his shotgun pointed at me the whole time I washed away the dirt, grease, soot, and any honey that Bruno may have missed during his supper. I had been booted from the train with five hundred dollars, but my count I was down two hundred and thirty from that, so the day had been costly with yet a couple hours until dark.

After ducking my head in the water and scrubbing it, I felt as clean as a whorehouse pussycat. As I emerged from the river, Bean slid off his burro and tossed me a saddle blanket for a towel. "Cleanliness is next to godliness," he apprised me.

"Are you God west of the Pecos, too?" I asked.

Bean snorted so hard that he choked and dropped his shotgun at his feet. I considered grabbing it and escaping, but I had no clothes. He finally caught his breath. "You might say that, Lomax. You've got more humor in you than your Texas Ranger brother. He's a straight-shooter if ever there was one."

As I continued drying, Bean tossed aside his sombrero and started undressing. After his comments about sodomy and gomorrahmy, I fretted about his intentions.

He removed every item of clothing except for the red bandanna around his neck. Bean then strode toward me, his pale skin bloated like he had already died. Coming opposite me, he extended his hand. Not sure what he wanted, I hesitated.

"The soap," he said, "give me the soap."

I handed the clump cleanser to him, and he marched past me into the waters and started bathing himself. "At least once a month I take a bath," Bean informed me. "I want to be at my best if Lilly Langtry ever comes to town. What do you know of her?"

With his back still to me, I edged toward the shotgun, figuring to pick it up and shoot him or march him back through his village naked with me in his clothes. "She's an English actress or something," I answered as I reached the donkey. I tossed the saddle blanket back atop the animal and bent down to grab the judge's shirt. It would dwarf me like a tent, but it was better than walking nude back through Langtry.

"She's not just an actress, she's the most beautiful woman God ever created. It's a shame God made her English rather than Texan. Wouldn't you agree? You saw her portrait in the Jersey Lilly."

As I lifted the judge's shirt, the odor of salty sweat, West Texas sand, and grime's unknown assaulted my nose. Bean may have bathed once a month, but he sure didn't launder his clothes that frequently. I tossed it aside and picked up the shotgun, deciding I'd plug the judge and escape naked into Mexico.

"She's not only beautiful," he said, "she has a voice like a songbird."

With the hammers already cocked, I leveled the weapon at Bean's back, figuring I didn't have to take careful an aim with a scattergun. I pulled the twin triggers, gleeful that the shotgun's blast would be the last bird tweet that he ever heard. Instead of a blast of powder, all I heard was twin metallic clicks as the hammers fell on empty chambers.

Without looking back at me, Bean called over his shoulders, "It's empty, Lomax. You lack your brother's honor. Andy would never shoot a man from behind, especially not an officer of the law. Anyway, wouldn't you agree that Lilly Langtry is the most beautiful creature God placed on this earth?"

I dropped the weapon on the ground. "I can't say, having never seen her in the flesh, though I knew a fellow a dozen years ago that believed her beauty was perfection, the same guy you read about recently, Oscar Wilde."

Bean spun around and looked at me, his eyes as wide as the Pecos River gorge. "You're, you're not one of them sodomy and gomorrahmy fellows, are you?"

"Why, judge, how can you say that about a man that's just a couple hours away from his wedding?"

"But you knew Oscar Wilde, the poet, aesthete, and author?"

"I did indeed, the oddest fellow I was ever around. I guarded him during part of his tour a decade ago. Strange duck, he was, but he filled meeting halls to lecture a little about the beauty of the world but mostly about himself."

Bean barged out of the water and came straight for me, his sun-bronzed face a stark contrast to the pinkish-white flesh of his jiggling belly. "I want to shake the hand of the man who shook the hand of the man who touched the fair hand of the Jersey Lilly." He grabbed my hand and pumped it so enthusiastically that both of our bodies bounced up and down. Fearing injury, I yanked myself from his grip.

"What did he say of the fair Miss Langtry?"

I never paid much attention to Wilde's comments about the Jersey Lilly, though one stuck in my mind about the crown prince who had taken her as his mistress. "She was courtesan to an English nobleman who said he had spent enough on her to build a battleship, then Langtry responded he had spent enough in her to float one."

Bean's face clouded and his mouth twisted into a snarl. "Such crudeness would never defile Miss Langtry's lips." He knotted his fists and lifted his arms, like an overweight and over-the-hill prizefighter, to threaten me. "Take it back!"

Shrugging, I realized how foolish we must look,

standing there naked and talking about a woman neither of us knew and possibly coming to blows over that same female. "I'm telling you what Oscar told me. If you don't believe it, find him and punch him in the face."

Bean scowled. "I would if he weren't in prison."

"And across the Atlantic," I reminded him.

The judge strode past me, jerked the saddle blanket from the burro, and dabbed himself dry enough to start for home. He tossed the blanket on the donkey and then quickly dressed, erasing the result of his just-finished bath. As he put on his shirt, he moved the red bandanna aside for a moment, but long enough for me to spot a ragged purple scar encircling his neck. Someone had tried to lynch him years ago. He climbed aboard his burro, then pointed to his weapon on the sand. "Hand me my scattergun, would you, Lomax?"

I retrieved the shotgun and offered it to him. "Why do you even carry an unloaded gun?"

"So, folks'll think I'm in charge of things." He yanked the cannon from my grip.

"How about loaning me the blanket for the return trip to the Jersey Lilly?"

"No shackles, remember? Besides, it'll give your new bride a chance to see what she's marrying into." Bean pointed to the trail. "Let's head back to the courtroom."

"Don't you mean saloon?" I challenged as I stepped into the cool waters of the Rio Grande and crossed to the Texas embankment.

"It's a courtroom when I've got more legal matters to attend."

So, I emerged from the river, climbed up the embankment, then started through Langtry, naked as the day I was born. I kept my hands below my waist, humiliated by the experience, especially when people applauded. One Mexican woman shouted, "*Sobreviviste al rastro de la muerte!*"

"Why are they clapping?" I asked Judge Roy Bean.

"As the *señora* said, you survived the trail of death, but everyone knew you would!"

Even more perplexed than before, I almost scratched

21

my head until I realized I should keep my hand where it was for modesty's sake. "This is some kind of prank, then? They knew you wouldn't kill me?"

"You're catching on, Lomax. Maybe you have your brother's smarts after all." I stumbled crossing the railroad tracks and flung my arms aside to keep my balance, drawing stares and snickers from the handful of spectators before I could re-manacle myself. Reaching Bean's porch, I rejoiced and started up the first step, but Bean stopped me.

"Follow me around the back. Enter by the rear door. I don't want the innocent Miss Langtry to see you like this."

She's not that virginal, I thought but kept my feelings to myself. We marched around the building, which had a wing in back.

Bean pointed to a door on the back of the building. "You'll find your clothes inside. Get dressed and meet me in the courtroom. We've got additional legal matters to resolve."

I went inside, glad to be out of sight of Langtry and its inhabitants. My hat, trousers, shirt, and coat looked like they had been brushed and my long johns and socks had been washed. Even though we had been gone but an hour, they had dried in the withering desert heat. I figured Judge Roy Bean could've benefited from his own laundry service as my clothes, even after the honey bath and Bruno's licking, had not reeked as much as his outfit. I took my time dressing, fearing my impending wedding and hoping it just might be another joke that Bean was playing on me. Finally, I stepped outside and walked around to the front of the place, climbed the steps, and entered the front door, turning to my right into the courtroom or barroom or whatever Bean considered it at the moment.

As I walked in, I could've sworn the portrait of Lilly Langtry smiled at me as she peered over Bean on his stool behind the counter. Six men littered the room, two playing pool on the table in the center of the space and the rest drinking beers at tables around the perimeter.

The jurors had departed, but as soon as Bean saw me, he picked up his gavel, banged it against the bar, and announced, "Court is now in session, Judge Roy Bean, law west of the Pecos, presiding." He shook the gavel toward the beer keg at the end of the bar. "Take the witness stand, Lomax."

Nodding, I doffed my hat to show my respect to the judge and Miss Langtry behind him, moving into place as ordered and playing along. "Yes, your Honor."

"As duly elected and appointed judge of Val Verde County, Texas, I am charging and convicting you of assault with intent to kill in the cowardly ambush of this officer of the great State of Texas this afternoon along the Rio Grande."

"What?" I screamed.

"Order, order in the court," Bean cried, pounding his gavel on the bar for emphasis.

"You are hereby fined one hundred dollars."

I stammered. "Wha ... what? You told me yourself the island was of uncertain jurisdiction."

"That's true," Bean shot back, "but I was standing in Texas waters when you pulled the trigger of the shotgun."

"I appeal," I cried.

"Appeal denied," Bean shouted. "The conviction stands as does the hundred-dollar fine. You best shut up or I'll hold you in contempt and fine you again."

Releasing a slow breath to cool my anger, I nodded.

"Next, you are being charged with two counts of public indecency."

My jaw dropped and my mouth flew open. I was as perplexed as a Texas Republican on election day. "Two counts?"

Bean nodded. "One count for going naked to the river and the other count for returning naked to the courtroom."

"But you ordered me to undress! You forced me through town both ways."

"Following the order of a legally constituted officer of the court is no excuse for breaking the laws on public decency. You are convicted on both counts as I saw you on each occasion, each a horrible insult to the propriety and dignity of Langtry, Texas, and its good citizens."

I stood up stunned at this travesty of justice, intending to protest my legal railroading with the six customers in the saloon, but they ignored me, drinking their beers, and shooting pool. I calculated my fines from my first and second court appearances. The total came to four hundred and eighty dollars. At least I still had twenty bucks remaining, perhaps enough to buy a revolver and plug the judge before I left town and began a life on the run.

"I appeal my convictions," I cried.

"Your appeal is denied," Bean said, then cut loose with a shrill whistle. "Juanita. Juanita, your groom awaits."

I turned to look and instantly a Mexican woman about twice my age, weight, and girth entered from the hallway. She wore a yellowed dress with gaps between the buttons and carried a bouquet of sotol stalks that screened her face. Fortunately, I had lost my revolver, or I would've shot one of us because this marriage would not last.

For the solemnity of the occasion, the drinkers put down their beers and stood up, placing their hands over their hearts, and the pool players straightened and placed their cues at their sides like infantrymen at attention. I could've sworn that Bean was humming the wedding march as he cracked open his shot gun and inserted two shells, then clicked the barrel back in place, cocking both hammers and pointing the weapon at me.

I looked from the shotgun to Lilly Langtry, smiling at me from behind the justice of the peace, then at my bride, whose hips were wide enough to block sunshine at dawn. As she neared, I briefly glimpsed her face. She had all her teeth plus a button nose and dark, alluring eyes. She may have been cuter in her younger years, but that was a century and a ton or more ago.

Stunned and speechless, I stood there. She stopped before me, grabbed my arm, and pulled me in front of the grinning justice of the peace. I could've sworn that Lilly Langtry winked at me from her portrait. If I had been drinking, I would've accepted it as my imagination, but I hadn't had a shot of whiskey or a beer in a week. My bride inserted her arm in mine, and we stood before the son of a witch that planned on hitching us.

Bean removed his sombrero and smiled at my bride. "*Te ves hermosa hoy, Juanita.*" He paused, then patted the shotgun which lay across the bar pointed at me. "Doesn't she look beautiful today, Lomax?"

I nodded, fearful to do anything that would cost me my last twenty dollars or earn me a belly full of buckshot.

Then Bean recited the holy bonds of a man and woman in marriage and read our vows, turning to Juanita, and asking her if she accepted me as her lawfully wedded husband.

"*Si*," she said.

He turned to me and asked me if I took Juanita as my lawfully wedded wife. Before I could answer, he spoke on my behalf. "You do. Now, by the powers vested in me by the great State of Texas, I pronounce you man and wife. May God have mercy on your souls." He paused but a moment. "That'll be five dollars."

The drinkers and billiard boys clapped and whistled, then returned to their beer or pool table.

Because of this shotgun wedding, I realized the cash I'd brought to Langtry had shriveled to a mere fifteen dollars.

On top of that, my new wife yanked her arm from mine and immediately began wailing and speaking in Spanish so fast that I had no idea what she was saying.

"*Quiero el divorcio. Quiero el divorcio. Quiero el divorcio,*" she kept repeating.

Bean crowned himself with his sombrero and shook his head. "She says, you don't love her and never have. She wants a divorce."

Juanita nodded.

I just shrugged. "Fine with me."

Bean smiled. "Sometimes, through no fault of either party, marriages just don't work out. By the authority vested in me by the State of Texas, I hereby declare this marriage dissolved now and forever more. That'll be fifteen dollars."

Now I was broke, not a cent to my name, with ten days of Langtry custody ahead.

Bean dug into his pocket and fished out two dollars, handing them to Juanita, who bolted from the room. I never saw her again, though sometimes when a spot of shade came over Langtry I wondered if she was out and about.

Once my former wife departed, Bean pushed his shotgun aside on the counter and took pencil to pad, and finished the legal paperwork required for my short-lived marriage and sudden divorce. "By my calculations, Lomax, your fines, and jail costs total right at five hundred dollars, the amount we found in your boots. I suggest you avoid any more trouble, or you may wind up in the penitentiary. That would shame your brother's good name, him being a Texas Ranger."

I fumed and could feel the anger reddening my face.

"To show you there's no hard feelings, Lomax, let me offer you a shot of whiskey." He slid off his stool, and turned around to the shelf behind the bar, pausing a moment to gaze at Miss Langtry.

Seeing my chance, I grabbed Ben's shotgun, cocked the hammers as I pointed it at his back, and yanked the twin triggers. Instead of a boom, I heard the same metallic trick I had listened to on the river island. I cursed, knowing I'd seen him put a shell in each barrel. They must have been defective. I cocked the hammers again and pulled the triggers again. Nothing but a metallic clank.

"Damnation," I cried.

My bartender judge turned around and smiled as he put a jigger on the counter and filled it with cheap whiskey. "Shoot me all you want. I put hulls from shells fired years ago in the barrels." Setting the amber bottle on the counter, he grabbed the twin barrels of the scattergun and gently pulled it from my grasp. "Enjoy your drink because you'll be bunking with Bruno tonight in the cage outside. We don't have a jail, so that must do, but remove your clothes—"

"No! I'll not be fined again for indecency."

"—except for your long johns and socks, of course. No reason to fine you anymore, Lomax, because you're broke." He placed the shotgun behind the backbar, then grabbed the whiskey bottle and walked around the counter. Coming close enough that I could smell the rankness in his clothes, he patted me on the shoulder. "Let's sit and have a drink, Lomax. You need to relax."

He escorted me to a table, but I was in no mood to talk and sat sullen and bewildered. After multiple questions went unanswered, he turned to his other customers. "Did any of the papers off the train bring any news about the prizefight?"

The pool players put down their cues and grabbed chairs, joining us at the table, as did one drinker. A lanky red-haired cue man speckled with freckles spoke first. "Before we talk about the fight, Judge, let me tell you that was the most beautiful wedding I ever saw." Then he elbowed me in the ribs. "And don't think you're the first fellow that's tried to dry-gulch the judge with his own shotgun. That's why he never loads it with anything that can hurt him."

"Yep," said the heavyset beer drinker. "He's outwitted fellows a lot smarter than you."

"What about the fight, boys? Any news?" Bean asked.

The short pool player said, "I saw a Dallas paper off one train and they're hoping to host the fight. The promoter thinks he can pull it off in Texas, but he's got everyone riled up all the way to the governor."

Bean snickered. "I've got correspondence on the bar there for Governor Culberson. Need to send it out tomorrow. He wrote to me."

"Why, would he be writing you?" Red asked.

"He complained that not enough of my fines were reaching him in Austin. Like I've fined Lomax here five hundred dollars today. The governor had nothing to do with that. Why should he be getting any of the money I raised here in Val Verde County?"

"Tell them what else you told him, Judge," I offered.

Bean grinned. "I told him to go Oscar Wilde himself."

Two of the three fellows laughed, though I doubt the heavyset fellow understood.

"Now back to the fight," Bean continued. "What else did the papers say?"

"This promoter Dan Stuart's planning a fistic carnival, hoping to schedule multiple fights, culminating with Gentleman Jim Corbett and Fighting Aussie Bob Fitzsimmons for the undisputed heavyweight championship of the world."

Bean laughed. "That'll be a kick in the ass to the governor. I wonder if he's writing letters to every judge in Dallas complaining they're not sending him enough fine money."

After taking a deep gulp of his beer, the pudgy fellow nodded. "The Dallas Pastors Association is already protesting the planned match, demanding that the barbarity end for the benefit of civil society."

I shook my head. "I don't understand these preachers, always butting into other people's pleasures. Seems to me they would support boxers beating the hell out of each other. Isn't that their life's work, scaring hell out of people?"

"Have another drink, Lomax," said Bean. "That's profound."

I passed on the offer. If I was going to be sleeping with Bruno, I wanted to have my wits about me.

The fellows kept sharing their opinions on the match, everybody supporting Corbett over this kangaroo of a boxer from Australia. I didn't care who won because I had to figure out a way to get my money back and escape Langtry.

As a joke, I added a bit to the discussion. "I hear Lilly Langtry is quite the boxing fan. She loves seeing half-naked men fight each other, almost as much as she loves floating battleships."

Judge Roy Bean scowled at me while the three customers just scratched their heads, uncertain what the navy had to do with boxing and the esteemed actress. After a blank-faced pause, they resumed their conversation on the championship and pugilism as a manly art.

The discussion gradually seeped away like the daylight, and Bean arose to light four kerosene lamps while the pool players resumed their games and the heavyset fellow departed to be replaced by a trio of new drinkers.

As a Val Verde County prisoner, I reminded Judge Bean that my jail fee included meals. He departed, returning a half hour later with a bowl of cold beans and a tin cup of frigid coffee. An hour after supper, Bean told me to leave my clothes in the back room where I had found them and meet him out by Bruno's cage.

Ten minutes later, I found the judge waiting for me. "I gave him a tin of honey, so he shouldn't bother you. Just don't make any sudden moves or step on one of his paws. He's a mite touchy about those things." Bean unlocked the padlock on the chain that secured the door and motioned for me to crawl inside.

I would've wished for a shotgun if it would've done me any good but climbed inside to my corner of the cage as Bean locked it back up. Judge Roy Bear eyed me from across the cage as I leaned back against the iron bars. Then Bruno walked over and laid his head on my lap. I stroked the ears of the only friend I had in Langtry, resolved that I would get out of this mess and make Judge Roy Bean pay to boot.

CHAPTER THREE

The following morning at dawn before the day's first passenger train arrived, Judge Roy Bean poked me through the iron bars. "Wake up, Lomax," he said, "and put on these clothes."

Groggy, I roused and nudged Bruno aside, the bear snorting, but never lifting his head.

"Change clothes," he repeated.

"I'm not walking through town naked again," I replied, rubbing my eyes.

"Put these on before the train gets here."

The esteemed judge gradually came into focus in the early morning gloom. He shoved clothing piece by piece into the cage, a sombrero, a serape, pants, pullover shirt, and two bandoliers. To the west, I heard the faint shrill of the train whistle.

Shaking my head, I crossed my arms over my chest. "What's this about?"

"It's too early to give Bruno a beer, so I need something to thrill any passengers expecting a show. Do as I say, and I'll cut your sentence in half," he said.

I hesitated.

"If you don't, I'll double your jail time."

He convinced me. I pulled on the tan pants with a rope for a belt, yanked the shirt on, slung the ammunition belts on, threw the serape over my shoulders, and plopped the sombrero atop my head. When I finished, Bean offered me a canteen of water and two cold tortillas for breakfast.

"What's this about, Judge?"

"Your new name is Claude Bawls, but you're known all along the Rio Grande as the 'Gringo Bandito,' the most feared outlaw in two countries."

"Are you insane?" I cried.

"No, but I'm working on it. Now don't you say anything, let me do the talking. Hide your face beneath the sombrero. All I want you to do is snarl or growl when I poke you." He paused. "Oh, I forgot something." Spinning around, he scurried back into his saloon.

As I sipped warm water from the canteen, I felt Bruno stir behind me. After swallowing two health swigs, I reached for the tortillas on the cage floor but discovered the bear had found them first. Judge Roy Bear was eating my breakfast. The train whistle grew louder and closer as the sun cracked the skyline with shafts of light, which sent long shadows inching across the desolate landscape.

Bean darted out of the saloon to our cage, carrying my empty holster and a cane.

"Hitch up your holster. You should look mean and dangerous."

"I'm hungry," I answered.

"What about the tortillas I brought you?" He shoved my gun belt between the bars.

"Bruno ate them."

"You need to be quicker on the draw," Bean answered, looking west down the Southern Pacific tracks. "The train's a coming."

I buckled the empty holster around my waist and serape, then yanked the poncho from beneath the gun belt and leaned back against the iron bars. No sooner did I get comfortable than Bean poked me with his cane. I shoved the walking stick aside.

"Growl and snarl," he commanded.

"Grrrrr—"

"Louder," he cried.

"GRRRRRR," I grumbled.

"That's better."

Removing the sombrero, I glanced westward and saw

31

the train belching smoke and steam as it neared Langtry. Putting the broad-brimmed Mexican hat back on my head, I tugged it in place to hide my face and my shame from the arriving passengers. Approaching the station, the locomotive braked so the three passenger cars halted opposite the depot platform. As the locomotive took on water, the travelers poured out of the railroad coaches like ants streaming from a disturbed hill toward the saloon.

"Where's the beer-drinking bear," cried the fellow in the lead.

Peeking through a hole in my hat's crown, I saw Bean remove his sombrero with a sweep of his arm, then bow to the gathering spectators. "Welcome to Langtry," he cried as he straightened and placed his straw crown atop his head. "I am Judge Roy Bean, law west of the Pecos. Unfortunately, Bruno does not drink before noon, but today he has a more important job."

"What's more important than beer?" cried a wiseacre in the crowd.

"Protecting your lives," Bean answered as he adjusted the red scarf around his neck, then pointed to the cage with his cane. "Bruno is guarding the most feared outlaw in two countries, Claude Bawls, better known as the Gringo Bandito."

"If he's so feared, how come I've never heard of him?" shouted a spectator.

"Yeah!" spat another.

"Because even the Texas Rangers are afraid to mention his name for fear he will come after them. I've heard that even the devil himself won't speak his name because the Gringo Bandito is too mean for a room in hell."

The crowd hushed as Bean tiptoed toward me. He slid the cane through the cage and poked me softly.

"Grrrrr," I answered.

Then he stabbed me in the ribs with his walking stick. "GRRRRR," I growled.

Several women and even a few men gasped at my snarl.

"But don't you fine folks worry," Bean continued,

"Bruno will protect you during your brief stop in Langtry. While it may be too early for my bear to have a beer, there's plenty for you." The crowd scurried inside. I thought the show was over, but through the hole in my sombrero, I saw a woman approach and stand beside the cage.

"You poor thing," she said, as she slowly slipped her hand between the bars and grabbed the crown of my sombrero, lifting it from my head.

I squinted as I looked into the soft eyes of a petite woman dressed in black like a widow, her face covered by a black veil, obscuring her features, save for a few tufts of auburn hair that tumbled from beneath her hat.

She spoke with a gentle lilt. "There's good in all of us, Mr. Bawls, and who wouldn't take some wrong turns in life with such a profane given name as Claude Bawls. It is an offense unto the sanctity of God. Know that I will pray for you and your salvation."

"Thank you, ma'am," I said, embarrassed that Bean's prank had fooled this godly woman.

"Even now, I am saddened that I am going through a divorce. My husband is as good as dead to me and me to him, but our suffering is small compared to yours." She dropped the sombrero in my hand and stroked my hair with her fingers. "So many men to redeem and so little time. Do you read?"

I nodded.

She removed her hand from the cage and bowed her head, silently mouthing a brief prayer for me. "I have asked for forgiveness for your wickedness, Mr. Bawls, and for mercy upon your soul."

I figured she should've been praying over Bean, whose wickedness exceeded mine by a trainload. "Thank you, ma'am."

She turned and walked back to the train, Bruno and I looking at each other with perplexed eyes. The shrill locomotive whistle cut through the morning air to announce the impending departure. Passengers scurried out of Bean's bar, several complaining the beer was neither cold as promised nor cheap. The last handful of customers ran by grumbling that the judge had either short-changed them or not given them change at all. It was hard to feel any sympathy for them over a few cents when I had been fined five hundred dollars and caged with a bear. The last angry customer bolted from the saloon toward the depot, climbed the platform, and reached the departing train just in time to jump on the steps of the last passenger car.

Shortly, Judge Roy Bean came out and congratulated me on playing my part so well as the Gringo Bandito.

"It ain't happening again," I informed him, "unless you reduce my sentence to time already served, and I sleep in a bed at night rather than in Bruno's cage."

Bean nodded at the bear. "You hear that, Bruno? Lomax doesn't care for you. Of course, if he hadn't divorced Juanita, he would've had a warm bed to sleep in."

"There wouldn't have been any room if Juanita was on the mattress."

Bean nodded. "You've got a point." He scratched his chin. "Rather than reduce your sentence by half, I'll let you out as long as you promise to get in the cage and play the part of the Gringo Bandito for every passenger train for the next nine days."

I nodded.

He stuck his hand in the cage, and we shook on our new agreement.

Over the balance of my sentence, I became the main topic of conversation in Langtry, even bigger than the proposed Corbett-Fitzsimmons fight, though state officials in Austin had confirmed that prizefighting in Texas was a bigger sin than pride, greed, wrath, envy, lust, gluttony and even sloth combined. The way Judge Roy Bean embellished the Gringo Bandito's reputation, I had robbed trains; shot two judges in the back with a shotgun; thrown a Texas Ranger off the High Bridge; stolen enough horses to outfit two regiments of cavalry; walked naked through towns in the States and Mexico, daring people to stop me; stolen more cattle than all the railroads in the country carried in a year; single-handedly faced down an Army of Mexican soldiers, escaped from two prisons and a Baptist revival; and had buried enough stolen gold throughout the Southwest to buy off every politician—save possibly Roy Bean himself—in the country for the next century. Yes, Bean was building me up to be the most feared outlaw ever west of the Pecos. I didn't care, as I no longer roomed in the cage, nothing against Bruno, except for those times each day when passengers arrived.

Other than when the trains arrived, I had freedom to do whatever I wanted around town. Nights I slept on a feather mattress in the back room, and I got to know Sam Bean, the judge's youngest son, who had his father's larceny in his heart, but not the temperament to implement his schemes with the flair and audaciousness of his father. Sam brought me my supper each night, but I suspected he was eating most of it before he delivered it to my room.

During the late morning and early afternoon train stops, Bruno remained the star, drinking a bottle of beer after prying the cork free with his teeth while I remained caged for the duration of the train stop. But if Bruno overslept or got too woozy to walk, he'd stay in his cage with me so Bean could display the Gringo Bandito and relate all the sordid things the outlaw had done. No scofflaw in the Old West ever committed more wicked misdeeds than the infamous Claude Bawls, an outlaw whose very mention would've sent terror coursing through the veins of the bravest of men, were it not for the humor inherent in the name itself.

One afternoon halfway into my ten-day sentence Bruno entertained the fresh passengers off the El Paso-bound train, I rested in the corner of my cage in the shade from a blanket the judge had ordered his son to put over the top of the enclosure to give me a little relief from the glaring sun during the train visit. Apparently, Sam had taken a disliking to me since Bruno now favored me more than him. Even Bean seemed more amused by me than his own son. I confirmed Sam despised me when he delivered a canteen to my cage. I thanked him for his courtesy, then took a swig and spat out vinegar.

That afternoon in the blanket shade I gazed through the hole in my sombrero just in case Sam tried to pull another prank on me when I glimpsed a black shadow coming my way. As my eye focused, I realized the silhouette was a woman dressed in black. She stopped at the cage and spoke with a familiar, high-pitched voice. "Mr. Bawls," she said softly, "I have something for you and your soul."

Inching the sombrero off of my head, my eyes adjusted slowly to the afternoon glare, and I saw the same woman who had pitied me during my first performance as the Gringo Bandito. Her face remained veiled, but she handed me a small book with a pimpled black leather cover. I took the tiny volume from the lacy fingers of her black gloves and read the tiny gold lettering on the front: NEW TESTAMENT.

"This will help you get right with God and yourself, Mr. Bawls. No man is as bad as you have been described—"

She was right on that count.

"—and no man is beyond redemption."

Nodding solemnly, I responded, "Thank you, ma'am, I fear the stories have been exaggerated far beyond the truth or even the possible. I shall endeavor to turn my life around." Through the blur of her veil, I thought I detected a smile.

"I predict great things will be possible for you *if you repent.*" She reached into the cage and stroked my hair again, then patted my cheek.

She perplexed me, as I had never encountered a female preacher.

"Are you a woman of the cloth?" I asked.

"Heavens no," she replied. "I run a boarding house in El Paso. I just see weaknesses in men and desire fervently to set you fellows on the right path. I failed to get my former husband to see the light, so I divorced him. Since then, I've been in mourning for losing a husband not to death, but to drunkenness and debauchery. I could not abide living with his wicked ways."

Uncertain what to say, I just nodded.

"No priests in El Paso would give me absolution for

my divorce, so I went to San Antonio to see if any there might view my plight any differently. They viewed my sin of divorce more seriously than my husband's shortcomings with women and liquor. I have resolved once I get home to put aside my mourning clothes and resume my life without the church's forgiveness, though I have vowed to help other men in place of my former husband. You are my first, though I have a boarder whose sins equal yours, and I will attempt to steer him straight. Odd thing, he's a preacher's son. Can you imagine that?"

"No, ma'am. Perhaps his father beat the hell out of the boy, but it grew back in the man."

"Tsk, tsk, tsk, I fear you have spoken a truth about all men," she answered as the train whistled five minutes before departure. "I must go now, but remember it is never too late for any man, yourself included, to redeem himself."

"Truer words were never spoken," I offered, then thanked her for the Testament a final time as she scurried toward the depot ahead of the throng scampering out of the saloon with their lukewarm beers, their pocketbooks short-changed and their tales of being served or swindled by a frontier legend. Once the train chugged out of sight, Sam brought Bruno back to the cage, unlocked the chain latch, and let Bruno in for a nap, the black bear having consumed his daily quota of beer. As Judge Roy Bear crawled past me, I could smell the alcohol on his heavy breath.

Sam started to re-chain the cage and re-snap the padlock, but I shoved open the door and forced myself out. "I'm not staying with Bruno except when the trains arrive." I stood up and brushed off my pants with the testament.

"Pa should've made no such deal with you, not after you tried to kill him, not once, but twice."

"You realize, don't you, that you're talking to the Gringo Bandito, the meanest, fightingest varmint ever to come through these parts."

"You're nothing but a card cheat that can't keep from getting caught." He draped the chain around two iron bars and snapped the padlock shut.

Walking away from Sam, I lifted the Testament and opened to the middle of the little book and mouthed words like I was reading. As I passed the steps leading into the saloon and courtroom, I heard the judge call my name, sort of.

"Claude," he cried, "come here a minute."

I spun about and angled up the steps, climbing into the shade of the overhang. "I take it you're a man of letters, reading a book like that. Didn't you say you knew Oscar Wilde?"

"Indeed I did, but it's been a dozen years or more ago."

Bean motioned for me to sit on a stool. "He knew Miss Langtry, but wasn't he an author?"

Taking a seat, I replied. "He fancied himself a writer, but I never read anything of his. I heard him lecture enough to doubt anything he wrote would be understandable."

"So, you know a bit about publishing?"

I played coy. "Maybe a tad."

"You ever thought of writing a book?"

"Can't say that I have. Not sure anyone would be interested in what I had to say."

Bean hesitated. "I'm getting up in years."

"You don't say."

He nodded and pulled up a rocking chair opposite me. "I'll be seventy-one next year. I don't have many years left, that's a fact, hard as it is to believe."

"That's hard to believe, about as unlikely as me arriving in Langtry with five hundred dollars in my pocket and within hours being broke and sleeping in a cage with a bear."

"Just fulfilling my duties as the law west of the Pecos."

Clearing my throat, I studied the judge. "You are to the law what rustlers are to ranching."

Bean grinned. "You have a way with words, Lomax."

"And you have a way with the law, tying it in so many knots that even Moses couldn't untangle the Ten Commandments after you got through with them."

Bean threw out his chest, patted his palms against

his knees, then leaned forward in his chair. "God and the law work in mysterious ways, Lomax. I'm glad you recognize that."

"I got a five-hundred-dollar lesson in the law from you, Judge."

"You keep flattering me, Lomax, and we might work out a business arrangement that would get us what we both want."

"What is it you want, Judge?"

"I'm getting up in years like I said, and I want people to remember me."

"Then buy a granite tombstone, not one of those wooden ones with painted name and dates on it. After a few years, the lettering's faded and unreadable, assuming no one took the marker for firewood. You can't burn granite."

"I fear my boy Sam'll buy the cheapest he can find, pocket the savings. He's just turned twenty-one, but's got a lot of growing up to do."

"He don't care much for me."

"Sam don't cotton to people smarter than him."

I figured the judge was flattering me, trying to convince me to help him out. Hoping to get my money back, I took my time answering him, stringing him along. "I suspect Sam enjoys eating out of your feedbag more than he does filling his own."

"Maybe so, but I want a book about my life, one that'll tell how I brought order to the most lawless corner of these United States."

I held up my hand. "Wait a minute, Judge. I think better when I've got a full stomach. You haven't been feeding me that well."

"I give you the same plate as Sam and the others get at my supper table."

"Then maybe you ought to let me dine with you so I can make certain I'm getting all the grub I'm due."

"About the book—"

I held up my hand for silence. "Not another word about it until after supper. Don't we have another train to work in forty-five minutes?"

"The eastbound, yes, and Bruno's too loaded to drink anymore, so we'll need to do the Gringo Bandito."

"I figured as much. Now, what's new on the prize-fight?"

Bean grimaced, scratched his white beard, and shrugged. "Nothing sounds promising. Corbett and Fitzsimmons are only fighting in the papers, throwing more ink than punches at each other. It's a pitiful state of affairs when men can't settle a title in a manly way, or as manly a way as possible with the Queensberry rules requiring gloves."

"Any idea where it will be, Judge?"

The old man shrugged. "Who knows? Some Texas official, the comptroller of public accounts, whatever that is—"

"Probably the guy you should share your fine revenue with," I suggested.

Bean scowled, then continued. "—said that prizefighting was definitely illegal in Texas, and anyone engaged in promoting or taking part in such an activity would be fined and jailed."

"He's just trying to get votes from the church crowd."

"Yeah, the sporting press is saying the same things, but the daily newspapers are riding high and mighty, stirring the clergy up. Austin pastors are claiming fights squander time, waste money, and subvert morals, leading to intoxication, gambling, and, worst of all, lewdness."

I grinned. "So, Miss Langtry would approve of prize-fighting, the lewdness I mean."

Bean glared at me like I had struck his momma with a pound of raw liver. "Don't defame Miss Langtry, Lomax, or Sam'll be eating all your supper."

"So, no one knows where the fight will locate or even if it will come off at all."

"That's about the size of it, Lomax, and there's nothing we can do about it, not when we're fighting every preacher, politician, and Baptist in Texas."

A distant train whistle interrupted our conversation.

"Into your clothes and cage, Gringo Bandito." Bean eased up from his chair, grabbed his cane, and escorted me to Bruno, removing his padlock key and opening the lock and the gate for me to enter. "Let's continue our talk at the supper table."

I put the outfit over my clothes and crawled to my corner. "Only if my plate is full," I said as he chained and locked me in with Bruno. The bear was sleeping off the joy juice so the judge would blaspheme the Gringo Bandito for this edition of Southern Pacific passengers.

When the train stopped to take on water and mail, the travelers spilled out like beans from an overturned jar. Bean regaled them with the tales of the dastardly doings of Claude "Gringo Bandito" Bawls, the meanest man on the frontier, and I played my part, growling twice when he poked his walking stick at me, then he struck them with the inflated charges for their drinks. The passengers grumbled about the exorbitant prices and Bruno's failure to bend an elbow for them but climbed aboard the train anyway as none of them wanted to be stranded in Langtry and face the improbable justice that had made Bean famous.

After the train disappeared on its eastward journey, Sam came out to unlock me from the cage and feed Bruno. He was grumbling to himself because he hated I had been invited to dine with him and his father. I smiled as I crawled from the cage and removed the Mexican clothes.

"Is it true, Sam, you will be dining with me and your pa for supper?"

He ignored me, locked the cage, spun around, and marched back into the saloon.

I retired to my room, then joined the judge and his son in the back room of the house where the *señora* who did his cooking had left three bowls of Menudo and a stack of tortillas smeared with mashed black beans.

The judge seated me across the table from him, and we picked up our earlier conversation, much to Sam's annoyance.

"I don't want to be forgotten," Bean said, "and I need some-one to write a book of my life."

"Little I can do about that," I answered. "I've never written a book."

41

"You're the closest thing we've ever had to a writer to stop in Langtry, other than a few newspapermen who are nothing but hacks."

"Having no interest in writing a book, I can't write one for you, but perhaps I can find someone who can."

Bean's eyes widened. "Go on."

"There's bound to be a writer in El Paso that could do it."

"Why not in Austin or San Antonio?"

"Because I want to find my brother if the Rangers haven't assigned him to another post."

Bean nodded.

"Of course, it'll be a five-hundred-dollar fee plus two hundred for expenses."

Sam snarled, but Bean grinned and nodded. "That's possible once you've finished your sentence. We must follow the law."

I grinned because I had found a way out of Langtry, Texas. Finally!

CHAPTER FOUR

A week later, when my sentence expired, Claude "Gringo Bandito" Bawls disappeared from Langtry. I discarded the Mexican outfit I had worn, shaved, and put on my own clothes, never more to be identified as the Gringo Bandito; at least I thought so at the time. However, Judge Roy Bean had done such a good job of embellishing his nonexistent legend to hundreds of eastbound and westbound passengers that the imaginary bandit lived in the fears of gullible citizens throughout the Southwest for years.

In the evenings after the last passenger train had passed through and the combination judge and bartender had overcharged them for his stale beer, Bean and I sat on the porch outside his saloon, enjoying the shade and fanning ourselves with our hats, as we talked about his desired biography. Sam scowled at me for convincing his father to return my five-hundred-dollar fine, plus another two hundred of the family's assets for expenses in finding an author and publisher for his desired book.

"You can't trust him, Judge," Sam frequently muttered under his breath.

I found it odd that Sam called him "Judge" instead of "Pa," but the blistering desert sun had probably baked all the sense out of his brain.

"Lomax is a *lépero*, one of the rabble, a common thief," Sam said several times.

With a wave of his arm, Bean dismissed his son's comments. "He's smart enough to have arrived in Langtry with five hundred dollars. No matter how he earned it, that's more than you ever came up with on your own, Sam. Besides, he's a lettered man, unlike the two of us. Beyond that, he's a handshake away from Lilly Langtry through Oscar Wilde. That's closer than you or I ever got to Miss Langtry, so behave yourself around Lomax."

"Yeah," I added, "or I might send the Gringo Bandito looking for you."

Sam skulked off, his tail between his legs, and the judge told me the story of his life. Born poor in Kentucky, he left home at sixteen, taking a flatboat to New Orleans to find a job, but all he found was trouble, so he escaped to San Antonio, then to Chihuahua where he opened a trading post but killed a Mexican desperado who tried to rob his place. To avoid a murder charge, he fled to San Diego, California, where he got in a duel over a young Mexican lady and was arrested for attempted murder. By his telling, he was a favorite of the *señoritas*, who smuggled him knives in tamales so he could dig his way out of his adobe cell.

Bean next fled to San Gabriel and tended a saloon, until he fell for another *señorita*, claimed, and abused by a Mexican army officer. In a second duel, Bean killed the soldier, but the deceased's friends captured him. They left him atop a skittish horse and bound beneath a tree with a rope around his neck. When mount finally ran out from under him, the lariat almost strangled him, but the branch and the rope gave enough that he could stand on his tiptoes to gasp occasional breaths until the young maiden cut the noose and rescued him. He survived with a ragged purple scar on his flesh from the rope burn, the reason he always wore a bandanna.

He next moved to New Mexico where he spent a few years during the Civil War, then retreated to Texas with other sympathizers, challenging the Union blockade by hauling cotton from San Antonio to Matamoros, where he loaded it onto British ships in exchange for supplies badly needed by the Confederacy. After the war he settled in San Antonio, marrying a Mexican woman, and producing four children, Sam being the youngest. His attempts at various businesses failed as the firewood he sold was cut without permission from a neighbor's land, and the milk he produced from his dairy was watered down. Even the beef he butchered came from unbranded cattle he found. Then he turned to tending bar in San Antonio, but a neighbor grew weary of his questionable practices and subsequently bought him out for a thousand dollars on the condition that he leave San Antonio for good.

With that money, Bean moved to the Rio Grande, first to Vinegaroon and then Langtry. Having failed at everything else, Bean like other men in his situation took up the law, getting appointed as justice of the peace and producing such unconventional rulings along the Rio Grande that he was either King Solomon in a sombrero or a typical judge lining his own pockets every chance he got. At first, he called himself "the only law west of the Pecos," but he soon changed that to "law west of the Pecos," adding a dash of legitimacy to his otherwise debatable interpretations of the law. Texas Rangers along the border welcomed the judge, even if his rulings were dubious because it allowed them to get judicial decisions locally rather than having to ride a hundred and twenty miles to Fort Stockton, the nearest other court.

I had to admit Bean had led an interesting life, though no more so than my own, but I wondered how much was true and how much was as cockeyed as his legal rulings. Also, I didn't know if I could convince anyone to write his biography. I sure didn't plan to do it, though it gave me my first idea of one day writing about my own adventures in the West.

"Don't mean to brag," Bean would conclude his stories, "but I think there's plenty of fodder for a good book there of how I changed the West and brought law and order to the Rio Grande between El Paso and Brownsville. Wouldn't you agree?"

I nodded. "It sounds like good grist for a writer's mill, but who knows if I can find someone to write it."

"And I don't want a tawdry dime novel that makes

me out to be a frontier freak, but a respectable book on my life."

"It depends on what you pay the author, what kind of result you get."

Bean shrugged. "I don't intend to pay the writer. He can have all the profits. I just want my name held in high esteem for posterity."

Now I shrugged. I doubted that was possible, but what did I know? "Don't forget to include how you tamed the Gringo Bandito."

The judge snickered. "I'm surprised I haven't received a telegram from the Texas Rangers inquiring if I wanted them to take Claude Bawls into custody." Bean pointed to the depot, and the poles strung with wire. "Isn't the telegraph amazing? Those copper wires can inform us within seconds of things happening throughout Texas and in the lesser states of this nation. Of course, the railroad over charges for its services—"

"Like some courts fine an innocent fellow five hundred dollars."

Bean looked as surprised as a puppy catching his first cat and realizing she had claws. "It's the difference between commerce and the law," he explained. "You'll get your money back when you leave town."

"Plus two hundred more, remember?"

"I ain't forgot."

"And I need a revolver."

"You arrived in Langtry without one."

"That's because it fell out of my holster while I was dangling over the High Bridge."

Bean looked at me. "You know it's illegal now to carry a deadly weapon, either visible or hidden."

"I'm not a lawyer."

"Neither am I, but I am a judge, and I know it's against the law to carry any pistol or other weapon in public. The legislature said so several years ago."

Shaking my head, I replied, "I've sure seen a lot of weapons on the train and in Texas before I arrived here."

"Not everybody follows the law, but it prohibits rifles, shotguns, pistols, dirks, daggers, sword-canes, spears, and brass-knuckles."

"What about sling-shots and tomahawks?"

Bean tugged at his white whiskers. "I don't know that they're covered."

"What about hatpins or straight razors or playing cards?"

"I can't say, but I don't want you being arrested and being fined out of what I paid you."

Crossing my arms across my chest, I scowled at the judge. "I'll be toting more of my money than yours, and I intend to protect it from thieves or fine-happy judges. I'd hate for the Gringo Bandito to rob me of your two hundred dollars and end your dreams of telling the world about Judge Roy Bean."

The judge pondered my response, finally nodding. "You win. I've got a trunk of revolvers I've taken from dead men at inquests or live men in my courtroom. I'll have Sam pick one out for you."

"No, sir. I'll pick out my own because Sam will give me the runt of the litter."

"You don't trust, Sam, do you?"

"No! Do you?"

Bean provided no response, answering my question by his very silence.

"I plan on leaving day after tomorrow. You'll buy my ticket, of course."

"Didn't you have a ticket, to begin with?"

"It was in my coat pocket when I arrived, but not when you returned my clothing."

Bean twisted his head from side to side. "Sam," he said. "I'll cover your fare to El Paso, but no farther."

"It's a deal. Any more news on the fight?"

"Just bits and pieces. Four hundred Dallas businessmen have organized to work with the promoter to bring it to their city. They're thinking there's thousands of dollars to be made, especially if Dan Stuart can pull off what he's calling a fistic carnival, where there would be a match or two every day leading up to the showdown between Corbett and Fitzsimmons, but Governor Culberson's stuck his nose into it and is blowing snot everywhere.

That's why politicians are so slick."

I laughed. "Aren't you a politician? Don't you stand for election now and then?"

Bean harrumphed. "I'm a judge, not a politician."

"And a mighty fine judge, I might add,"

He smiled, even more so when Bruno wandered up. Sam had let him out of his cage, likely hoping the beast would eat me, but instead he sauntered up onto the porch and stretched out between me and the magistrate. We both dropped our hands and stroked his black fur. All three of us contented as the dusk finally drew a blanket of darkness over the land and brought a breath of cool air to the vast desert.

Come bedtime, I led Bruno to my room and had him stretch out on the floor beside my bed. He seemed pleased to be freed from the cage. I slept well, looking forward to escaping Langtry after one more night. My dream erupted though in the early morning with a sudden explosion and a deep growl from Bruno. I rolled off my mattress onto the wooden floor, the smell of gunpowder engulfing the room. Another shot exploded in the darkness, a flash of gunfire lighting my surroundings as I scrambled toward my empty holster, draped over a chair but came away defenseless. Bruno leaped to his feet, bolted for the door, and shoved it. I heard him growl again, then a scream and the clatter of an object falling to the floor. Another human screech ensued, then Bruno snarled again, and I heard the door slam shut. Bruno stood on his hind legs and slapped the door like he wanted to chase the assailant.

"Easy, Bruno. I'm okay. How about you?"

Judge Roy Bear ignored me, pawing at the door, eager to get out. I scurried to the tiny table in the corner and lit a candle, carrying it toward Bruno. He backed out of the way. By the door, I found a Colt revolver and three drops of blood. The assassin had lost more blood than me, thanks to Bruno's teeth. I grabbed the weapon and retreated to the table so I could set the candle down and check the load on the pistol. I released the cylinder and saw two hulls and four unspent rounds of .45-caliber ammunition. Snapping the cylinder back in place, I knew I would have four bullets to fend off my attacker if he came back. I dropped the weapon on my pillow and scooted the bed across the room to confuse the assailant should he return. Then I approached Bruno, calming him, and finally getting him to lie by the entry to make it harder for my enemy to get inside. I went to bed again, but sleep came in fretful spurts.

I suspected Sam was the attacker and come morning I confirmed my suspicions as he was wearing a blood-stained bandage around his right wrist. He didn't show up for breakfast, and he avoided me all day. At the breakfast table, I pulled his revolver from my holster and put it on the table in front of the judge.

"Look what I found last night, Judge."

Bean shook his head. "Sam's pistol. Where'd you find it?"

"He dropped it in my room when he tried to shoot me. If he'd been a better shot, you'd made five dollars on the inquest over me."

"Nah," Bean replied, "Not even Sam would pull a stunt like that."

"He fired two shots, but Bruno bit his arm. When you see him, he'll be wearing a bandage on his right wrist. Check it out. You'll find that the bites match up with Bruno's teeth."

Bean sighed. "Maybe you need to depart Langtry today. I don't know what Sam's up to, and I can't control him anymore."

"He's angered I'm leaving town with my five hundred dollars and two hundred of yours."

Shrugging, Bean huffed. "Maybe so. That boy's never been the same since his mother died, living off of me and not toting his load around here."

I pointed to the pistol in my gun belt. "I'm taking his revolver, but I intend to take some others from the trunk. Maybe I'll get arrested for carrying weapons, but I won't get robbed."

"Don't play any poker on the train with my money and stay in touch with me by telegraph or letter on finding me a writer and a publisher."

"Sure, Judge, but I don't want Sam involved in your business or knowing mine. I'll send telegrams when I've something to report. As code, I'll refer to cattle for books and ranchers for writers or publishers. I'll sign them GB."

"Gee bee?"

"Gringo Bandito," I replied.

Bean grinned and motioned for me to follow him. I trailed him into the saloon and behind the counter, where he unlocked a door into a storeroom, filled with kegs of beer and bottles of cheap whiskey. He pointed to a corner and a trunk with the key still in the lock. "There's the gun box. Help yourself."

When he stepped aside, I knelt, twisted the key in the padlock, and opened the trunk. There were sixty or more guns piled atop one another. I rummaged through them, finding a Colt.45 of the same model as Sam's with a matching five-and-a-half-inch barrel so I took it, then I discovered a Remington double derringer that would ride well in my pocket and a five-shot.32-caliber Smith and Wesson revolver with a three-inch barrel that would fit in my boot. As I was shutting the trunk lid, I spotted a six-inch dagger to carry in my other boot, so I grabbed it as I closed and locked the chest.

I checked the loads in my new guns, and all were empty. "Where's you ammunition?" I asked Bean.

"I don't keep it so people can't shoot me with it."

"What do you do with it?"

"I give it to Sam."

"So, he can shoot people, me specifically?" I asked.

A sly grin parted Bean's white whiskers. "That's how it worked out; I reckon."

"Where's my money?"

"I'll give it to you at the depot when I buy your ticket."

"I don't want any chicanery, you short-changing me right before the train pulls out."

Bean slammed his fists against his waist, standing there akimbo. "Now who would do such a thing?"

"The law west of the Pecos," I reminded him.

He lifted his right hand and tugged at his ear. "Maybe

on occasion."

I returned to my room and inspected my two valises. Someone—likely Sam—had rummaged through my belongings. Missing were a marked deck of cards and a loaded pair of dice, tools that occasionally even an honest man needed to hold his own at the gambling tables.

Come lunch time, I dined with Bean at his usual table, but Sam never joined us, nor had I expected him to after his failed assassination attempt. If he couldn't kill me while I was dead asleep, he stood little chance with me fully awake. As soon as we finished eating, the judge counted out seven hundred dollars for me, pushing the stack of bills my way.

"I decided it'd be safer to settle with you here rather than in the depot, where someone might see you were carrying a lot of cash and waylay you later on." I pulled fifteen dollars from the bills and slipped in my pants pocket, then pulled off my boots and split the money between them for safe keeping along with my weapons. Then Bean handed me a railroad ticket.

"I bought it so Sam wouldn't see us going to the depot together. He might realize you were leaving and do some damage. The next westbound should arrive ninety or so minutes from now. You might grab your things and head to the train station to avoid my son."

"Sounds good, judge." I put the ticket in my pants pocket with my spending cash.

"Call me Roy."

"Sounds good, Roy."

We both stood up and shook hands.

"I'm gonna miss you, Lomax, but you know who's gonna miss you more?"

"My ex-wife," I joshed.

"Not Juanita, but Bruno. Ever since he licked the honey off you, he's taken to you like nobody I've ever seen before. That's another thing bothering Sam. Bruno likes you better."

"I'll tell him goodbye before I head to the station." I reached across the table to shake Roy's hand. He clutched it firmly for a man of his years and wished me well. "Get

51

someone to write a book about me, and I'll include you in my will."

"Sam wouldn't like that."

"I know!" He winked at me.

I walked to my room, where I quickly grabbed my two carpet bags and marched around to the front of the saloon, where Bruno lounged in his cage. Spotting me, he arose. I stuck my hand in the cage and rubbed his furry head. He lifted his snout and licked my fingers.

"Goodbye, old boy. It's been good knowing you. Take care of the judge, will you? And watch out for Sam. I'm indebted to you for saving my life last night, but he'll carry a grudge against you for biting him." Patting him a final time, I then headed for the railroad. I heard him groan for a moment, but I didn't have the heart to turn around and look into his dark eyes.

At the depot, I took a hard-backed seat inside, where a soft breeze blew through the open windows. The afternoon was splotched with shade, and I wondered if Juanita was out and about looking for her former husband. The westbound was a half hour late, but I got on and seated as soon as the others bolted off to see the legendary judge and his beer-drinking bear.

After twenty minutes and interminable railroad whistles, the passenger car filled with rough men, nervous women, and a handful of fussy children. The locomotive lurched forward, and I began my first trip to El Paso. Within half an hour, the conductor came by to punch tickets. He took mine, then stared at me. "Don't I know you?" he asked.

I studied him. "Can't say we've ever been introduced." I then realized it was the same ticket-puncher that had saved me from my card-playing pals at the High Bridge.

"It's not like me to forget a face, especially among passengers," he said. "Seems like I saw you on a previous trip." He punched my ticket a couple times, then offered it to me.

Before I could grab it, he yanked it away. "Is there a problem?"

"Now I know it. You resemble the Gringo Bandito. I

saw him a week ago in Langtry. Fearsome looking character without an ounce of decency in him."

I scowled. "From what I hear, the bandito escaped and promised to take his revenge on the Southern Pacific for his capture. He's vowed to slit the throat of any conductor, engineer, fireman, or brakeman he encounters."

The ticket-puncher swallowed hard. "He's a mean one everybody agrees."

"Thank your lucky stars that I'm not him or you'd be dead and gone."

The conductor nodded, handed my ticket, and continued his journey down the aisle, but the rest of the ride to El Paso, he kept scratching his head and staring at me. I ignored him like I tried to forget I was in Texas.

It was the summer of 1895, and Texas had pretended it was a civilized state, passing the laws restricting the carry of guns and other weapons, and acting as if it was finally a respectable place to live. It wasn't before and it wasn't then, but the perception of respectability had driven the meanest of the Texas bad men to the city on the Rio Grande. For men on the run, El Paso offered refuge with Mexico just across the river and New Mexico Territory a quick ride from the city limits should the law get too hot and require an immediate change of jurisdiction. Texas Rangers Company D of the Frontier Battalion was headquartered outside El Paso and reputed to be the toughest group of Rangers ever assembled in Texas.

The four hundred miles between Langtry and El Paso spanned some of the most rugged, god-forsaken land on earth. Thirsty mountains pimpled with boulders separated dryer basins of rocky soil splattered with every type of thorn, thistle, pricker, and barb you could imagine on a plant. The scattered plants were not so much green as gray or even yellow once they had given up the ghost.

The Southern Pacific locomotive pulled us from water stop to water stop, quenching its thirst for liquid while the surrounding land stayed thirsty and dusty. With the open windows in the passenger car, the scorching breeze chapped our faces and lips, the grit and embers stung our flesh. The ride was crowded and tedious, even more so after dark when the train had to slow almost to a crawl with the visibility barely improved by the headlight atop the locomotive. Then there was a problem with the tracks that delayed us a couple of hours.

We reached El Paso about two-thirty the next afternoon. In the glaring sunlight, the town looked like a petrified dung heap deposited between an imposing mountain to the east and the Rio Grande to the west. We passengers were groggy and stiff from fitful sleep on the wooden bench seats. We stood up and gathered our belongings, me taking my two valises and working my way down the crowded aisles to the exit where the conductor awaited, a cocky smile frozen on his face.

As I approached him, he nodded, pointing at my nose. "I remember you. High Bridge, that's who you are."

"Sorry, but you've confused me with Claude Bawls."

"Claude Bawls?"

"The Gringo Bandito," I informed him as I stepped from the passenger car onto the platform. I stood in the stifling afternoon heat, panting for breath, and realizing the city was misnamed. It should've been called "Hell Paso," not only for the temperature but for the rugged population that was certainly bound for the netherworld upon their demise.

CHAPTER FIVE

El Paso drew to its hellhole every kind of scalawag, out-law, calico queen, buscadero, painted lady, rustler, road agent, sharp, conman, and lawyer, the worst crooks of all, to its dirty, sunbaked streets. Nowhere would you find so many criminals per capita short of an Earp family reunion or a convention of Democrats. Lawmen and outlaws traded places from day to day, depending on who the newly elected politicians preferred to do their sordid tasks, so you never knew who was upholding the law or breaking it. All a badge meant was the bearer, like John Selman or George Scarborough or Jeff Milton, had the authority to commit his crimes without fear of being jailed or brought to trial. Besides that, the police-men, marshals, deputies, constables, and Texas Rangers were as likely to kill one another as they were scofflaws, though as I think about it, they were often one and the same.

As I stepped off the train onto the depot platform on that July day in 1895, it was like walking into an oven. Behind me, I heard the conductor call, "Take care of yourself, High Bridge. You don't look tough enough to survive El Paso." I ignored his assessment and took a deep breath as I moved to the middle of the platform, dropped my two valises, and studied El Paso, trying to figure where to go next and if I had any chance at all of con-vincing someone to write and publish Judge Roy Bean's life story. I brushed the soot from my coat and trousers, then slapped my hat against my britches, raising a puff of more rail dust as the other passengers marched around me toward whatever depravity they desired. As for me, I was interested in finding me a glass of cool water—if cool even existed in El Paso—a decent meal since I had eaten nothing since dining with Bean, and finally a place to stay. I thought a hotel would cost more than I wanted to pay, so I figured I'd get a cheaper weekly rate at some boarding house until I could find a writer and publisher to ensure Judge Roy Bean's posterity. As I considered my next step, a brown bean of a shirtless boy, his baggy pants held up by twine suspenders, approached, peddling newspapers. "*Bienvenido a El Paso, señor. ¿Quiere comprar un periódico?*" he called, his white teeth glistening in the afternoon sunlight.

"How much?"

"*Un níquel*," he answered, his smile as innocent as a morning dew if El Paso had ever seen dew.

I tousled his mop of black hair. "A nickel it is." I reached into my pocket and pulled out the few bills I'd tucked there for expenses. Peeling off a dollar, I swapped the greenback for a copy of the *El Paso Times*. I studied the front page as I waited for my change, but the newsboy darted down the platform, escaping with a ninety-five cent profit.

"*Gracias*," he taunted as he jumped from the loading dock and darted around the depot out of sight.

Welcome to El Paso, I grumbled to myself, then glanced at the date on the paper and discovered it was two days old. My *Times* was behind the times. I tucked the news rag under my arm, picked up my valises, and walked to an empty bench in the shade of the train station. As the conductor yelled, "All aboard," I tossed my baggage on the seat and sat down to scan the newspaper for any advertisement that might point me to a decent room.

Like I figured, the hotel rooms were expensive, daily rates ranging from two dollars at the Hotel Phoenix to three dollars at the Hotel Pierson and three-and-a-half dollars at the Hotel Vendome. I scanned the rooms for rent and the boarding houses and settled on the Herndon House, which advertised a couple rooms for rent for three dollars a week. That was more in line with mine and Judge Roy Bean's budgets, and the proprietor, a Mrs. Williams, also advertised a dressmaking parlor. Any boarding house with a seamstress had to offer a sedate and safe room, as I didn't care for folks to find out how much money I carried. If a newsboy could steal my change, no telling what a real crook could do. All I had to do was find 207 East Overland Street and hope a room was still available.

Rolling up the newspaper, I arose, stuck the edition in my pants pocket with my spending cash, and grabbed my valises as the locomotive whistled and pulled away from the station. I asked a Texas and Pacific baggage handler where to find East Overland, and he pointed me downtown to a collection of stone buildings. I passed a dozen saloons and stopped to look inside, tempted to have a drink, but deciding if bartenders were half as crooked as El Paso's paper peddlers I'd be broke before sunset. What surprised me about each saloon was not a one sported gambling tables. I later learned the local do-gooders had demanded vice be eliminated, and the city fathers had outlawed gambling in all drinking establishments. Saloon owners had simply moved the gaming upstairs or into windowless back rooms so the busybodies couldn't see the sin. The local constabulary looked the other way while taking their bribes and payoffs. Yep, there were more hypocrites in El Paso than at a Republican rally.

And the streets handled the usual horse, buggy, and wagon traffic as well as two streetcar lines crossing the Rio Grande into Juarez and a surprising number of bicycles that weaved in and out of traffic. I'd seen the big front-wheeled variety of the pedal conveyance, but this was a lower rig with wheels of equal size. As I stepped off one curb, a bicycle almost barreled into me. The bicyclist screamed, and I cursed him as he sped away. He twisted about in his seat and shook his fist at me but collided with a stray dog and went head-over-handlebars onto the street. I didn't care if the rider survived, but I hoped the dog did as I had seen several other dogs, cats, and even a pig splayed dead in the street.

I finally found East Overland and walked to the address, a fine-looking two-story stone building that seemed respectable, though plenty of saloons dotted the area. The streets on both sides of the structure growled with men, many of them gruff types who'd never been to Sunday School a day in their lives.

Above the entry hung a small sign that said HERNDON HOUSE UPSTAIRS. I went inside and climbed the staircase, grateful for the breeze that wafted through the long hallway thanks to the open transom windows. At the top of the stairs, I spotted an arrow pointing to the office midway down the hall and headed that direction. I saw a sign that read OFFICE COME IN IF YOU ARE SOBER! I figured I was sober enough to kiss a prohibitionist no matter how ugly she was and not leave slobber on her lips. Dropping one valise at the entry, I twisted the knob, pushed open the door, grabbed my bag, and entered. As I kicked the door shut with the heel of my boot, I nodded at the lady sitting in the corner hand-sewing some lace on a calico dress.

"I'm here to inquire about a room," I announced, placing my portmanteaus gently on the floor, then pulling my dollar edition of The *Times* from my pocket. "This is the Herndon House, isn't it?"

She cocked her head, dropped her sewing in her lap, and studied me like we had met somewhere before, and she needed to place me. Dressed in a brown dress with a collar buttoned up her neck, she also wore an inquisitive stare. Brushing a lock of auburn hair from her forehead, she answered. "I don't want any trouble."

Though I didn't recognize her, the voice seemed familiar, a gentle lilt that matched her petite frame. "I'm looking for a room, not trouble."

She arose from her chair, placing her sewing on the table at her side, and then strode over to the desk, where she opened a drawer and lifted a small revolver, which she pointed at my gut. "Take another step toward me, and I'll have to shoot you."

I caught my breath and shook my head. If this woman was this tough on a potential boarder, I wondered how mean she'd be if I approached her with a complaint. "Ma'am, I was just inquiring about a room. No sense in getting riled about it. I've got cash to pay in advance."

"I've had enough bad men in this place without taking on another outlaw."

"Outlaw? What do you mean?"

"You're the Gringo Bandito."

Then my memory clicked like a telegraph key. This woman had given me the Testament when I was caged in Langtry. She had been wearing black and a veil over her face after her divorce. I remembered the red hair and the lilting voice.

"Now git," she said, "before I shoot." She cocked the hammer on the pistol.

"No, ma'am," I replied. "I'm H.H. Lomax, Henry Harrison Lomax, originally from Cane Hill, Arkansas. Occasionally I've been told I resemble this bandito, but I wouldn't know, never having seen him."

"I saw him in Langtry, caged like the animal he is, and gave him a Testament, hoping maybe he could change his life around."

"You are a blessed woman," I responded. "Perhaps we could go to church together one day and pray for his worthless soul."

As a slight smile broke her stony glare, she lowered the revolver and gently released the hammer on the weapon. "A woman can't be too careful with the type of men that scurry like cockroaches around this town. I'm Annie Williams. What brings you to this godforsaken land?"

"The Southern Pacific," I said, drawing a snicker from her. "Actually, I'm here looking for a publisher for an acquaintance of mine, who's interested in someone writing the story of his life, a fine book, not one of those cheap tawdry dime novels that corrupt the minds of our youth and put evil thoughts into the minds of men."

"Amen," she answered, then hesitated, scratching her chin. "So, you know something about getting books published?"

"A tad," I lied. "It's about linking a good story with a good printer."

"There are a half-dozen printers within blocks of here," she said as she placed the gun back in the desk and pushed the drawer shut. "But there's also a man residing here that's writing a book on his life, and he could use someone like you that knows how to do it. Maybe he'd quit pestering me and annoying my boarders."

I nodded. "That all depends upon whether a room is available, Miss Williams."

She blushed her cheeks for a moment matching the tint of her auburn hair. "Been years since I was a miss. I'm freshly divorced, not something I'm proud of, nor something God smiles on, but sometimes you've got to shed yourself of a man like a snake sheds its skin." She paused. "I'm sorry, that's my problem, not yours. Your need is a room, not a sermon."

"Our problems are in God's hands, Mrs. Williams," I replied, hoping to convince her that such a godly man as me could in no way be the Gringo Bandito. "I would love to see your accommodations."

"But of course, Mr. Lomax." She picked up a ring of keys from her desk. "Please follow me. You can leave your bags here, as the room is just down the hall."

I doffed my hat and followed her out of the office, then trailed her down the hallway to Room No. 1, a corner room overlooking Overland and Utah streets. She unlocked the door and pushed it open, letting me pass to inspect the lodging space. Annie punched a button by the door and electric lights came on, then another button on a wall plate and a ceiling fan whirled overhead.

"With corner windows, you can open them both and draw a little draft to ease the heat," she said.

I examined the furniture, lifting the spread over the feather mattress to find clean sheets and pillows. In addition to the bed, there was an oak chest, a washstand with a porcelain basin and water pitcher, a rocking chair, two cane-bottom chairs beneath a corner table, and a battered wooden trunk at the foot of the bedstead.

"There's a slop jar under the bed if you don't care to

walk to the end of the hall for the toilet, but you have to empty your own slop. Clean sheets are provided once a week. If you want me to change them, that's an extra twenty-five cents per week. I charge four dollars a week for a corner room. Regular rooms go for three dollars a week if you can't afford a corner. I require a week's deposit and payment in advance. That comes to eight dollars up front if you want the room, plus an extra quarter if you want me to change your sheets."

I wanted the room but stalled answering as I sat in the rocking chair and enjoyed the gentle breeze from the ceiling fan.

Impatient for an answer, Annie put her hands on her hips. "Though I don't approve of it, I let my male boarders keep their female friends overnight, as long as they are sober and quiet. I know how men are." She pointed out the Overland Street window. "The two blocks south of Overland between Oregon and Utah streets is 'the Reservation' where women of loose values peddle their wares. I advertise a dressmaking shop here so I can meet these fallen women and convert them to a more righteous life."

The more I delayed renting the room, the more she told me.

"I provide the room, but not the board as there's too much chance for a fire," she continued. "That aside, there's plenty of eateries and saloons where you can buy a cheap meal, though I'd avoid the tamales, as rumors have it some Mexicans use cats for the meat filler. Same with their chili."

Pushing myself up from the rocking chair, I nodded. "I'll take it," I said, deciding to sweeten the arrangement since she appeared to be a fine, God-fearing woman. "Perhaps we can even read the Bible together some evenings."

Annie smiled and clasped her hands over her modest bosom. "That would be wonderful. I've never had a boarder share scriptures with me before. Do you have a favorite verse?"

My deal-making soured with that question because I couldn't remember a verse my momma had taught me. "I love them all so much it's hard to pick just one."

Her grin parted wider than the Red Sea. "Let's go back to my office and complete the lease."

I tossed my hat on the bed, then marched past her, taking the proffered key to my new room, and sticking it in my pocket as I followed her down the hallway. Back in the office, she sat at her desk, pulled out a ledger from a drawer, turned to the middle of the book as she picked up a pencil. Then she wrote my name atop a clean page. "I collect rent on Fridays. This being Wednesday, I'll charge you a dollar for today and tomorrow. That plus the deposit and first week's rent comes to nine dollars, nine and a quarter if you want me to change your sheets."

"Do change the sheets," I said, pulling my traveling money from my pocket and counting out my single bills. "I'll need a few nickels to buy a newspaper or two." I slapped at the rolled newspaper in my other pocket. "This one cost me a dollar."

Annie looked up from her ledger, expecting an explanation.

"I arrived at the depot with no change. When I gave a newsboy a greenback, he bolted away without giving me change. On top of that, the newspaper was two days old. If I find that scamp, I'll wring my change out of him."

"Chicanery abounds in El Paso, corrupting even the young ones," she replied. "I run a respectable boarding house, but it can be a challenge. Overall, my boarders are decent folks. I've got a fireman, a hack driver, a laborer, a stenographer, a wool buyer, and even a lawyer, among our twelve residents, you making number thirteen. Hopefully, that's not an unlucky number for you or me."

Shrugging and not believing in superstitions, unless they came true, of course, I took the change from Annie, not bothering to count it since she would be my landlady.

"You're paid up through a week from Friday. I value boarders that pay up without me having to remind them."

"I saw your peashooter, Mrs. Williams, so I know you're serious."

She blushed. "Call me Annie, but you were the spitting image of the Gringo Bandito."

"Don't spread it around," I requested. "I wouldn't want someone shooting me for any reward on *his* head."

She pointed to the pistol at my side. "You look like you can defend yourself between the Colt on your belt and the one in your boot."

Annie caught me unprepared. "In my boot?"

"Men with something extra in their boot walk with a hitch in their gait, Henry."

I didn't admit it was close to seven hundred dollars in my boot that gave me a slight limp. "Just call me H.H. As for my boot, I believe in being prepared."

"You know there's state laws and local ordinances prohibiting weapons, don't you?"

"That's what I've been told, but on the walk from the station, I saw a lot of men carrying revolvers at their sides or walking with a hitch in their gait."

"In El Paso, the rules are enforced by whim. Most badges look the other way, but sometimes they use that as an excuse to arrest you."

"I'll be on my best behavior, Annie." I bent down and picked up my two valises as my landlady scampered around the desk for the door, opening it and following me to my new room. She pushed my door, and I marched in, tossing the valises on the bed by my hat.

"Hand me your pitcher," she said, "and I'll fill it with water in case you want to wash up some. There's traces of train soot on your face. You'll find a towel and face cloth in your top dresser drawer. I provide fresh ones when I change the bedding."

Grabbing the porcelain handle, I carried the pitcher across the room. Annie took it and turned. I closed the door all but a crack for her return. After removing the towel and cloth from the dresser drawer and hanging them on the rack at the end of the washstand, I started unpacking my things and putting them in the cabinet. I waited until after Annie returned to remove my boots and hide my money, but it took her longer than I was expecting so I stepped to the door and opened it enough to poke my head outside and see Annie halfway down the hall by the staircase talking to a gentleman, or at least I thought so at the time.

My landlady glimpsed at me and waved with her free hand. "H.H., I've got someone here to introduce you to."

I motioned her over and saw the fellow take the pitcher from her and tote it the rest of the way to my room. Swinging the door open, I stepped aside as Annie marched in, the pack mule behind her heading straight to the washstand and placing the container by the wash basin. He turned around and straightened his coat lapels, neither grinning nor frowning, and I estimated him to be about three inches shy of six feet and a hundred and eighty pounds. His thick, dark brown hair hovered over a tall forehead, matching eyebrows, and a broad mustache. Mostly I noticed his eyes, a deep gray with a serpentine look about them.

"This is the lawyer I was telling you about," Annie announced. "He's working on his biography, the one that I thought you might be able to help."

He stood stationary as a lamppost as I approached him, drawing near enough to see the evil in his eyes and smell the whiskey on his breath. Honestly, I was not surprised because I had met lawyers before, but this was to be the worst of an inferior breed of humanity.

"John Wesley Hardin," she continued, "I'd like you to meet Henry Lomax or H.H. as he prefers."

Hardin's name meant nothing to me then, so I extended my hand, hoping God would forgive me for befriending a member of such an evil profession, one that did the devil's work on earth. He hesitated, then lifted his big paw to grab mine. At first, he shook my hand like he had better things to do.

"Where you from, Henry."

"H.H." I replied.

"Never heard of it."

"No, my name, I go by H.H. I'm originally from Arkansas."

"Glad to hear you're a Southern boy, Henry," he replied, shaking my hand vigorously. "I don't tolerate Northern boys all that much."

"Wes rooms across the hallway from you, H.H. So,

64

you'll be running into him on occasion." She cleared her throat, then continued. "Him and Beulah Morose, his lady."

I could tell by the inflection in her voice that Annie thought no higher of Beulah than a grasshopper's ankles.

Hardin dropped my hand. "She's a client of mine. We have a lot of legal affairs to straighten up after the untimely death of her late husband."

Annie shook her head slightly, letting me know that he was handling more of Beulah's assets than her husband's estate.

"Mrs. Williams says you know something about getting books published. That a fact?"

"Indeed. I'm working for a man who's led an interesting life and wants to be remembered for his accomplishments."

"That's me, Henry," Hardin continued, "though my life's been hard, and a lot of lies have grown up around me. I want to publish a book that'll tell the truth, correct all the falsehoods written about me over the years."

I suspected Hardin, as a lawyer, had told more lies than had been spoken about him but I went along with him as I saw the hip bulges beneath his coat that told me he carried two sidearms. "What kind of lies, Wes?"

Sighing deeply and giving me a strong whiff of his liquored breath, Hardin grimaced, then spoke. "Lies like I killed six men for snoring. It's a damn lie. I only killed one, and he deserved it."

Reading Hardin's face and demeanor was harder than translating the scribbling of a Chinese laundryman. I couldn't tell if he was pulling my leg or yanking his own. "Sounds mighty interesting, Wes. Perhaps we can talk about it later. I just got into town today, and I'm tired and hungry from the travel. Maybe we can visit tomorrow when I'm more rested."

Hardin shrugged. "Henry, it's up to you. I'll be dropping by or seeing you in the hallway." He turned around, marched past Annie and into his room directly across the hallway.

After he closed his door, I turned to Annie. "Remind

me not to snore too loudly."

"Believe me," my landlady replied, "he'll make more noise than you at night. Truth be, he's an odd one, as mean as they come when he's sober, but not quite so bad when he's been drinking. You'd never believe he's the son of a Methodist preacher."

Scratching my chin, I agreed. "But I can sure see him as a crooked lawyer. Fact is, I never met an attorney that wasn't crooked. Tell me more about Wes Hardin."

Annie waved my request aside. "Maybe during one of our Bible readings. You're tired and hungry and need some rest. Let's talk about it later." She turned to leave.

"Before you go, tell me where I can find the *El Paso Times* office."

"Next block over at the corner of South Oregon. You planning on buying an ad?"

"I'm planning on complaining about one of their newsboys."

"Good luck with that." Annie exited the room, shutting the door behind her.

Once she left, I turned to the washstand and quickly cleaned my face, hoping to remove the train soot and scrubbed my fingers and palms, trying to erase the stain of shaking hands with a lawyer. I checked my cheeks in the mirror. They looked clean, though my hand was likely soiled forever. As it was getting near closing time, I decided to leave my money in my boots and visit the newspaper first, then find an eatery to quell the growls in my stomach. Grabbing my hat, I left my room and locked the door behind me, then moved down the hall, praying not to run into Hardin again. I scampered down the stairs and onto the street, planning to register my complaint with the owner of the paper. I turned west on Overland and strode toward the newspaper office to demand my ninety-five cents.

As I neared the newspaper office, I spotted the little scamp across the street, hawking the afternoon edition of the *Times*. I tugged my hat low over my forehead, hoping to slip up on the waif and get my ninety-five cents, maybe with a little interest.

"*Periódicos de la tarde a la venta*," he cried, as he peddled the evening paper. He had no takers, as apparently, he had previously done business with most of the passing pedestrians. I slipped up on him like I was trailing a Comanche. When he finally looked up and saw me, it was too late for him to escape. I grabbed him by the twine suspenders that held up his baggy pants.

"Now I got you," I called.

The boy dropped the papers, then swung his tiny fists at me, screaming, "*Liberame, liberame.*"

I had no intention of releasing him until I got my money. "Give me the ninety-five cents you owe me, boy."

He wailed again, drawing the attention of a handful of passersby including a matron, who shouted, "Let him go, you bully."

"Not until he pays me the money he stole!"

Just as I was about to shove my fingers in his pants pocket, I felt a strong hand grab my shoulder.

"Aren't you a bit big to be picking on one this little?"

"He robbed me," I cried.

"Let him go," said a deep voice as the man's grip bit into my flesh.

I released the kid, who scrambled to pick up his papers, then flee.

"See what you've done? He's getting away." I yanked my shoulder free and spun around to face my opponent.

First, I saw a face as serious as a sawed-off shotgun. Then I spotted a silver star encircled in a silver band. Above the star was engraved TEXAS. Beneath the star was carved RANGER.

CHAPTER SIX

I gulped, pointing at the fleeing newsboy. "You're letting him get away with my money."

The Ranger stood there, grimacing in disbelief. "That child robbed you?"

"Gave him a dollar for a nickel newspaper, and he kept my change, running off. Even worse, the paper he sold me was two days old."

"What's your name, fellow?"

"Lomax," I said.

He cocked his head, his granite gaze boring into me as he tugged at the end of his brown mustache, then bit his lip. He stroked his bronzed cheeks and finally spoke. "You any relation to J.H. Lomax, the foreman at the transfer company stables? He's out of Missouri."

"My folks are from Arkansas."

The ranger's stony demeanor cracked a tad. "Cane Hill, possibly?"

Surprised, I nodded. "Yep, that's right. How did you—?" Then it hit me. I was staring into the face of my brother, Andrew Jackson Lomax.

He grinned. "Henry Harrison Lomax, is it?"

Before I could answer, he flung his arms around me and hugged me so tight I feared passersby might take us as backers of Oscar Wilde. I wormed my way from his grip, thinking it unmanly for two fellows to be hugging on an El Paso street. "I go by H.H. now, Andy. It sounds more distinguished," I informed him.

"You'll always be Henry to me. Last I heard from folks, you were running in bad company. Nothing distinguished about that. You always were a wandering pup, getting into more mischief than the rest of your brothers combined."

I grinned. "Times were tough back during the war, not the best time to grow up."

"You should've married LouAnne Burke and settled down, made something of yourself."

My growling stomach interrupted our family reunion. "I haven't eaten in a day," I said.

"You that bad off? I can loan you a grubstake."

"I have money, just been pressed for time since I arrived this afternoon from Langtry."

"We've got a lot to catch up on, Henry, and supper's on me," he announced, throwing his arm around my shoulder, and steering me down the street toward an eatery. "Did you run into that old coot Roy Bean 'cause I have some questions for you if you did?"

"The judge tried to fleece me of every cent I had, but I boarded the train with my money and two hundred of his."

"Just as mischievous as ever, but let's catch up on family before we talk business." Andy steered me toward a nicer-looking restaurant. Once inside, he saw we were seated in a back corner where he could watch the door. As soon as the waiter took our order, we visited about our deceased parents and the two brothers we had lost during the war, John at Gettysburg, and Van at Prairie Grove. Then we discussed our surviving siblings, starting with our oldest brother Tom, who had married DeeAnne Burke and took over farming the Burke and Lomax places where we grew up. Tom had six daughters. Our baby sister, Harriet, and her husband Jason Scott managed land they had secured after the Oklahoma Land Rush and were doing fine in Oklahoma Territory with a boy and a girl. Andy on occasion ran into our brother Jim, a successful West Texas rancher around Colorado City with a wife, three sons, and a daughter. Even less frequently he saw our sister Lissa, who still toured the west with a troupe of actors and singers, having married the road manager and raising two daughters and a son. I had seen Lissa once in Utah since leaving home. Andy had lost track of our oldest sister Constance, but I informed him I had seen Connie in Deadwood, Dakota Territory, where she ran a successful business. I withheld she was a prosperous brothel madam. As for Andy, he had lost his wife and son during childbirth and never remarried. Devastated by the loss, he made the Rangers his new family. He bit his lip after he told me of his deceased family. Though he didn't acknowledge it, I think the deaths of his loved ones made him as fearless a lawman as there ever was, not caring if he died, since life had dealt him such a sorrowful hand. I saw a glistening in his eyes for a moment, then he changed the subject.

"Tell me about Langtry," he said.

I regaled him with my unfortunate gambling luck on the Southern Pacific westbound and how I had been tossed off in Langtry where the honorable Judge Roy Bean had marched me naked through town and back before marrying and divorcing me and fining me all of my cash.

"That's Roy," Andy agreed, "but how'd you get your money back and some of his?"

"After he found out I'd accompanied the writer Oscar Wilde."

"The sodomist in the London trial the papers have been writing about?"

I nodded and continued. "during part of his American tour."

Andy's eyes narrowed as he next spoke, "You didn't, I mean, do anything?"

"Hell, no, Andy. My job was to protect him, and that's what I did. Nothing more! I knew nothing about those things back then."

My brother sighed with relief as the waiter delivered our thick T-bone steaks, boiled potatoes, frijoles, and hot bread. We continued our conversation between bites.

"He was such an odd and ugly duck I wondered how anyone could find him appealing, but the women sure

70

flocked around him to hear his lectures about beauty, of all things, and nonsense like that. As for Judge Bean, he decided I was a literary figure having been around Wilde, who by the way had shaken hands with Lilly Langtry."

Andy shook his head. "He always loved Miss Langtry."

"Anyway, he's interested in finding someone to write up and publish his life for posterity. Since I had met Wilde, he thought I could be his representative in getting a book published so his story would live forever."

"Old Roy," Andy said, thumping the table with his fingers, "there's never been a judge like him. I've always debated if he was the law west of the Pecos or outlaw west of the Pecos."

"He spoke highly of you, as brave and honest a ranger as he ever encountered."

"Do you know anything about book publishing?"

"Only a little more than a tree stump, but you'd be surprised by the people that want to publish a book. There's a lawyer across the hall from me at my boarding house that's asked me to help him with a book as well."

Andy's eyes narrowed again. "Where are you staying?"

"Herndon House."

Chewing his steak with greater vigor, Andy pointed his fork at me, swallowed, then spoke. "Did this man tell you his name?"

"Hardin, Wes Hardin," as I recall.

Andy nodded. "Do you know who he is?"

"A preacher's son and a drunken lawyer."

"That's John Wesley Hardin, likely the meanest killer in the history of Texas."

Vaguely, I remember having heard the gunfighter's name, but I didn't connect it with my boarding room neighbor

"If he's so mean, and Texas is so tough, why isn't he in prison, Mr. Lawman?"

"He was until the governor pardoned him a couple years ago. He's only been here since the spring, but he's caused plenty of trouble."

"Tell me about it," I said, then took another bite of steak and potatoes.

"I will, but first I need to know something about Langtry."

"Shoot."

"There's stories circulating around El Paso the past week about some Gringo Bandito terrorizing Langtry and the surrounding country on both sides of the river. You know anything about that?"

Snickering, I shook my head. "When the judge's bear was too tired or lazy to drink a bottle of beer for the passengers off the train, Roy dressed up some poor fool in sombrero, serape, and bandoliers, put him in Bruno's cage, and promoted him as the meanest man to ravage the Rio Grande since Satan himself."

"Were you that poor old fool?"

I nodded. "But don't tell anybody. I'd hate for my landlady to find out."

Andy grinned. "Let's just keep that as our little secret as the Gringo Bandito might come in handy someday."

My brother had a good streak of the Lomax mischief in him as well. "Now tell me about John Wesley Hardin."

"Between the war's end and eighteen-seventy-eight when he went to prison for murdering two men, he is rumored to have killed over twenty others. Six of those, so they say, for snoring too loudly."

"Hardin claims only one for snoring and says he deserved it. That's why he wants to write a book, to clear his name."

"His name'll never be cleared in Texas, the governor notwithstanding. He's a vicious man you best tread softly around."

We both finished our plates and when the waiter returned to clear the table, we ordered hot slices of apple pie with cold milk for dessert.

"What's Hardin done in El Paso."

"Threatened a half-dozen men or more, stopped gambling losing streaks by robbing the pot of his losses, and, so a lot of folks think, killed a man named Martin Morose."

"Any kin to Beulah Morose?"

The waiter arrived with our pie and milk, Andy delaying his response until the server had departed.

My brother nodded. "Her late husband. Martin was a troublemaker disguised as a New Mexico rancher for years. He sold his land for ten or twelve thousand dollars, so they say, but got in trouble in El Paso and escaped to Juarez. He got in more mischief there and the Mexican lawmen arrested him, confiscating the twelve hundred dollars he carried. Beulah hired Hardin to get that money back and her husband's bank account."

I pointed my fork at Andy. "I see where this is going. Hardin wanted Beulah."

"He wanted the money more. Beulah was just a side pot for him."

"Beulah's always been a woman of stained reputation, and she stopped visiting her husband across the river. He wanted his money, but she told him she was too scared to visit him in Mexico anymore so he would have to come to her. He hesitated, knowing if he crossed into El Paso he could be arrested or worse killed, but Deputy U.S. Marshal George Scarborough convinced Morose he could slip into town at dusk last month, see his wife and work out their problems, financial and otherwise."

I realized where this was headed. "Beulah knew nothing about this, right?"

"You're right, leading some to believe Hardin put Scarborough up to it on the promise of splitting Morose's money when he got it. So, Scarborough recruited another deputy marshal, a constable, and, I'm embarrassed to say, a Texas Ranger to ambush him. At dusk, Scarborough met Morose on the railroad trestle between Juarez and El Paso and escorted him through the dump on the Texas side of the river. That's where Morose died. All but the constable have been indicted, but most people think Hardin planned it, even if he didn't pull the trigger."

I'd always known lawyers were crooks, but Hardin added murder to the profession's list of legal misdeeds. "I'll be on my guard."

"And don't snore too loudly," Andy joked.

"How'd the widow Morose take the death?"

"She attended her husband's burial with only one

other mourner."

"Her lawyer," I guessed.

"Nailed it. Hardin's jumpy, drinking, and gambling too much. He's aged, but he's still fast on the draw. I suggest you find another place to board."

"I'm paid up through a week from Friday. Besides, it's a corner room with a ceiling fan that can help me get through these hot July nights."

Andy smiled. "Temperatures will taper off next month. After a spell, you'll get used to the heat."

"Maybe so, but not thieving newsboys."

"Chalk it up to lessons learned. It's not a good sight, you picking on a young'un half your size, especially if you plan to go to his newspaper and see if he'll publish Bean's story."

Shrugging, I replied. "Maybe you're right."

"Another thing, Henry. I see you're armed. When I saw you with the newsboy, I wasn't certain I could charge you with assault, but I knew I could arrest you for carrying a weapon. The side holster's obvious, so leave it in your room. By the bulge in your coat, I think you're carrying one there and by your stride, I think you've got one in your boot as well. That can get you jailed and fined."

"Sounds like I need a cannon to defend myself. It against the law to pull a cannon around town?"

"Just be more discreet with the pocket weapons, though I'd leave the holster and sidearm in your room. If a local lawman takes a dislike to you, he'll arrest you on a gun charge."

I grinned. "Can I tell them you're my brother?"

"Unwise, Henry. Being my kin would hold sway with the honest but would annoy the shady ones. There's more crooked than straight lawmen in this town, I'm sorry to say."

"Where's your office?"

"South of here in Ysleta, but you let me find you, rather than you finding me. If you break the law wrong, I don't want you tarnishing my reputation."

I released a long, slow breath. "I never thought I'd hear my flesh and blood say something like that, Andy, though you're probably right!"

We finished our pie slices and got up to leave. I put a dollar tip on the table as Andy strode to the counter to pay up. Outside Andy told me it was great to visit after all these years and warned me to be careful in El Paso. He said he didn't make it into town more than twice a week, but he would drop in occasionally to see me. Andy pointed me toward the Herndon House, then marched off in the opposite direction.

I headed to the boarding house, deciding to check out the bathing facilities before calling it a long day. Back at my room, I shucked my coat, holster, shirt, and boots, shoving them under the bed, figuring no one would look for my money in my boots. I opened the top dresser drawer and grabbed my clean long johns, spotting the Testament Annie had given the Gringo Bandito and tossing it atop the corner table. I marched out the hall and locked the door, relieved not to run into any fellow boarders in the hall. The toilet was open, and I stepped inside, closing, and latching the door. The wall-mounted porcelain basin had a faucet and handle, which I twisted to get cold water. There was a sit-down toilet and on the back side of the small room was a lead-walled shower. I undressed and stepped in the lead-floored shower and turned on the valve. Cold water sprayed on me from the overhead nozzle, the frigid shock startling me, though in a few seconds I relished the relief the cool liquid provided from the heat. After ten minutes, I felt refreshed, even if I wasn't soap clean. I dried off, put my clean long johns and pants back on, then grabbed my dirties and headed back to my room, again fortunate not to run into any of my neighbors. I unlocked the door, then secured it behind me and took a chair, and wedged it under the doorknob.

Next, I opened the corner windows, hoping the soft breeze would augment the cool of the ceiling fan overhead. The draft was good, though the shouts of people outside, the clip clop of horses on the macadamized street, and the pianos and banjos from saloons and brothels annoyed me when I finally undressed and laid on the bed before the sun had set. I thought of Bruno and wondered if he missed me, then arose and retrieved the Testament, reading it to ease myself into slumber, but sleep gave me the runaround, even after the dying sunlight gave way to the soft glow of the electric street lamps. My room, though, was just as bright with the electric lamps. I got up to turn off the light switch by the door. As I did, I heard Hardin stomping down the hall, mumbling something to himself about being tired of all his gambling losses. He slammed his door as I headed back to bed, stopping at the water pitcher to dip my hand inside and sprinkle some water over the mattress to help cool it and ease me into sleep.

Just about the time I dozed off, I heard the shrill scream of a woman in the hall and the grumble of Hardin answering his door. I figured it was Beulah, still mourning over the loss of her husband—or perhaps his bank account—and wanting into Hardin's lair. They yelled at each other for half an hour, so much so that I covered my head with my pillow and almost smothered myself. When I lifted the cushion from my sweaty face, tranquility followed, at least briefly. Then I heard Beulah moaning and groaning, and I figured she was committing another stain on her reputation, either that or discussing the intricate legal matters of settling her late husband's estate. Finally, I fell asleep from sheer exhaustion and got a decent night's sleep.

Come morning, I put on clean clothes and the same boots where I kept my money and my dagger. I left my holster and Colt.45 hanging from the bedpost and slipped my smaller weapons into my coat pockets. Next, I adjusted my lapels, then looked in the mirror over the washstand, making sure I was presentable since I would represent the honorable Judge Roy Bean to potential publishers on this day. Then I gathered my dirty clothes into a bundle that I tucked under my arm and headed out for the day, locking the door behind me. I ambled down the hallway to the stairs, then descended and marched into the stifling morning heat, only slightly more oppressive than its afternoon brother. A half block down the street, I found a Chinese laundry and entered through a door adorned with a dozen bells that tinkled and jangled to announce my arrival. The proprietor came through a beaded doorway, lips grinning, pigtail bouncing, hands clasped over his chest.

"Washee clothesees?" he asked.

I nodded.

"Name, please."

"H.H. Lomax," I announced.

"H.H. Romax," he repeated.

I nodded as he scribbled on a piece of paper, which he handed me.

"For claim. Tomorrow." He nodded his head, grabbed my clothes, and disappeared in the back.

I jingled my way out the front door and went looking for a place for breakfast, finding a cheap eatery across the street where I ate scrambled eggs and bacon plus four buttered biscuits with a delicious cane syrup. I liked the syrup so much, I asked the cook the brand and where I might find some. He responded Wes-Tex Syrup and noted that tins were available at a grocery store facing San Antonio Street on the opposite end of the block from the Herndon House. I inquired if he made pancakes, and he admitted he did, so I told him I would see him the next morning and to have plenty of his syrup on hand.

Leaving the eatery, I walked around the block, getting the feel for El Paso, then headed back to Overland Street for the office of the *El Paso Times*, the employer of the little rascal that stole my change. The *Times* building stood on Overland at the opposite end of the block from my room. Approaching the edifice, I studied the name painted on the window and the claim to be the best, brightest, and newsiest paper in the Southwest. And, they might add, home to some of the smallest thieves in the country. Through the window, I saw a counter where a man and a woman stood discussing advertisements. Beyond them, I saw several desks with typewriters where a trio of men plunked away at the keys. Taking a deep breath and wishing myself and Judge Roy Bean good luck, I entered, trying to look as important as any literary representative ever.

A freckled fellow with a pencil on his ear and a printer's apron over his torso welcomed me. "How can we help you at the *El Paso Times*, the best, brightest, and newsiest paper in the Southwest?" he announced. It was sure the noisiest, as I could hear the clatter of the typesetting machines in the back room.

"I'm here to talk to someone about publishing a book, a biography on the greatest legal mind in Texas and perhaps in these forty-four United States," I announced.

"You're not peddling that tripe from that so-called lawyer John Wesley Hardin, are you?"

"Absolutely not. I arrived yesterday from Langtry to represent the honorable Judge Roy Bean on this matter."

Behind the clerk, I saw a man arise from his typewriter and point his index finger at me.

"Did I hear the name, Langtry?"

"You did, indeed. I'm fresh from there to handle business for Judge Roy Bean."

The fellow bolted my way, pointing to a knee-level wooden gate that allowed admission behind the counter. I met him there, and he opened the entry for me. "Please join me at my desk. I'm known to our thousands of readers as Rip Enreed."

I didn't have time to even tell him my name before he grabbed my hand, shook it with enthusiasm, then yanked me to his desk, pushing me into the seat. Rip took his chair in front of the typewriter and leaned toward me.

"So, you've just arrived from Langtry."

"That's right with a proposition from Judge Roy Bean."

"I'm not interested in him, but this new brigand causing a stir up and down the Rio Grande, all the way from where we're sitting to Brownsville on the coast. Do you know anything about him? I hear he's meaner than Billy the Kid, Doc Holliday, Wild Bill Hickok, and Susan B. Anthony combined, God rest their souls."

"Is Miss Anthony dead? I didn't know," I replied, remembering my Colorado encounter with her.

"Unfortunately not, but she should be. No, I'm interested in the Gringo Bandito. Reports say he's terrorizing every man, woman, and child, white or brown, along the

Rio Grande. Do you know anything about him?"

I hesitated, realizing the truth wouldn't sell newspapers, but my Texas Ranger brother wasn't interested in the facts coming out for the time being. "I saw the beast in Langtry, so yes I know a little about him, at least what my eyes beheld and what my ears heard."

"Describe him, would you?"

"He was caged, so I didn't see him stand to his full height, but I suspect he was a good six foot six in his bare feet. He wore a broad sombrero over a bronzed face, handsome features in a rugged way, and a pair of baggy Mexican pants. Across his bronzed chest were two bandoliers of bullets meant for anyone who offended him. Despite his handsome features, he was as cruel a man as I ever saw. I was literally shaking as I—"

Before I could finish, another man bolted across the room. "What the hell's going on, Enreed?"

The reporter looked at me. "That's my editor," he said, as he shot up from his chair. "What is it, Ax?"

"Do you know who this is? It's that fellow that bullied our newsboy yesterday, the orphan Juan. If I hadn't seen the Texas Ranger take him into custody, I planned to teach this son of a bitch a lesson."

"But he was telling me about the Gringo Bandito."

The editor shook his fist at the both of us. "I don't care. Throw him out of here, and I'll fire any man that lets him in these offices again."

Hearing his words, I jumped up from my seat, scurried through the wooden gate, and back onto the streets of El Paso. I realized it might be harder than I thought to see Bean's book published, thanks to that little brown scalawag of an orphan news peddler.

CHAPTER SEVEN

After such a rude reception at The *Times* office, I retraced my steps from the previous afternoon and returned to the Southern Pacific Depot to send a telegram to Bean, figuring I should tell him I had arrived and had started peddling his life story. The depot nested between the main track and a half-dozen sidetracks that served the city. I passed the Wells Fargo Express Company offices and went around the depot to the telegraph office that overlooked the main track. Arriving between trains, I found business at a standstill and walked inside where a telegrapher wearing a green eyeshade and sleeve garters on his white shirt greeted me. I told him I needed to send a message, and he shoved a notepad and a pencil across the counter to me, instructing me to write down the recipient's name, location, and message. After a moment's thought, I scrawled out: *Roy Bean, Langtry, Tex, No Cattle Yet, One Rancher Declined, GB*. When the clerk told me the cost, I choked that it cost more than a newspaper sold by a crooked orphan. I dug into my pocket and pulled out two-dollar bills and three nickels and gave them to the telegrapher. Sure, it was Bean's money, but it galled me to pay such a price just to update my partner. The Southern Pacific certainly valued their copper wires. I decided I could mail a letter with more information for only two cents once I bought some stationery. After taking my money, the clerk offered his thanks for the business and told me the telegram would go out within the hour. I noticed an El Paso City Directory on his desk behind the counter and asked if I could borrow it. He said he lacked authority to loan out Southern Pacific property, but that I could buy a copy for three dollars at the El Paso Steam Printing Co. on South Oregon Street. That was a steep price, but I would use Bean's money as I needed to find other publishing possibilities in El Paso since the *Times* was out of the question. Leaving the office, I walked along the platform, and at the corner of the station, I spotted a stack of *El Paso Times* topped with a red brick. Figuring the paper still owed me nineteen papers, I checked both ways to ensure no one was looking, then bent down, grabbed the day's edition, and scurried around the corner, rolling up the paper and stuffing it inside my coat.

Just as I descended the steps from the platform, I heard a wailing voice crying after me. I spotted the little Mexican waif shaking his brown fist at me and yelling something in Spanish I couldn't understand. Whatever he was saying, it wasn't here's the rest of your change back. I looked over my shoulder and cried, "You owe me eighteen more papers or my money!" The orphan ignored my justification and jabbered until I passed the Wells Fargo building and turned toward my boarding house.

As I neared home, I saw a narrow brick building squeezed between two bulkier stone edifices, advertising itself as a palace of the Kinetoscope, the most amazing invention of today with sights for the ages. Doubting anything amazing could be in a building so narrow, I sauntered inside, taking in a row of a dozen wooden contraptions lining each side wall. Three customers leaned over different machines, looking in a curved peephole viewer at the top as the machine made a clicking noise.

An attendant in coat and bow tie approached me on the worn plank floor that creaked with every step. "Welcome, sir. Have you visited our parlor before?"

"What's a Kinetoscope? Never heard of such a thing."

"It's the visual wonder of the world, my good man."

"I'm hearing your words, but I'm still wondering what this is."

"It's a machine that captures a moment for posterity. You won't believe anything I say unless you see it for yourself. For newcomers, we have a special Kinetoscope that you can see for a penny. If you like, you're welcome to view any of the others for a nickel." He leaned into me and whispered, "We have two special Kinetoscopes in the back room that the men especially like, but they will cost you a dime. All you've got to do is put your coin in the slot and watch the action."

Intrigued, I stepped to the penny machine, dropped a copper coin in the slot, and leaned over the viewing piece. To my amazement, I saw a photograph of a horse that started galloping, then raced by in the flickering light of the machine's innards. I'd seen nothing like it before, a tintype that came to life for a minute.

The attendant informed me I could watch prizefighter Gentleman Jim Corbett go six sixty-second rounds with Pete Courtney. He pointed out the half-dozen machines that showed the fight. Over the years, I'd watched plenty of saloon fights and never had to pay for a single one, much less thirty cents hunched over a bulky clacking machine for the privilege. "What's in the backroom?"

"A cultured gentleman you must be, sir. Just follow me." I trailed him through a curtained door where two men were leaning over the room's two whirring machines. When one machine went silent, the customer straightened and whistled, grabbing the attendant's hand, and shaking it like he was pumping water from a well.

"That's the most amazing thing I've ever seen. I'll be back."

"You're always welcome to the Grand Palace of Kinetoscopic Wonders," the fellow said. "Be sure and bring your friends when you return."

Deciding I needed to be amazed, I extracted a dime, dropped it in the slot, and leaned over the peephole viewer. As the machine whirred, I saw a raven-haired beauty standing beside a flower bouquet on a pedestal. She waved at me and slowly doffed her top and bared her bosom. Then she blew me a kiss, and the machine went dark and quiet. Behind me, the other customer inserted another coin and watched his beauty again.

"How about that?" the attendant asked.

"Much better than watching a prizefight."

"Stay as long as you like but tell your friends and let them know about the amazing marvels to behold at the Grand Palace of Kinetoscopic Wonders."

Nodding, I figured a man could spend a lot of money on these distractions and as for the back room, a fellow could find the real thing just two blocks from my boarding house. I thanked the proprietor and marched out the door, to the groan of the floor and the clicking of the machines.

From there I went to the El Paso Steam Printing Company and purchased a city directory, planning to return in a day or two and proposition them on publishing Bean's life story. As high sun approached, I found a Mexican eatery and ordered a bowl of goat stew. As I waited, I unrolled my copy of the *Times* and caught up on the news until the waiter brought my meal. I asked for soda crackers, but the waiter gave me corn tortillas instead. Even so, I put my money on the table for my meal, and he snapped it up. As I spooned away at the stew, I kept reading the news, learning the Corbett-Fitzsimmons prizefight was still in doubt and El Paso appeared as a possible nesting spot for sportsmen wanting to see it happen. I figured they should just fight in one of those Kinetoscopic contraptions and get it over with. Other news came from London, where Oscar Wilde had lost his second trial. He had failed to win a libel case against a nobleman who had accused him of posing as a sodomite, and in the wake of that loss, a criminal charge had been filed against him. Again, the court held against him, and he and his consort were sentenced to two years of hard labor in an English penitentiary. Having traveled with Wilde for a few months, I doubted he would survive forced work, as there wasn't much beauty in a prison cell.

Finishing lunch, I headed back to my room, spitting on the walk in front of the *Times*. As I was unlocking my door, I heard the one across the hall open and a voice from the day before.

"So there you are, Henry. I've been looking for you because I'm ready for you to find me a publisher. Come on over and meet my partner."

I turned to Wes Hardin and shrugged. "I'm busy," I said, figuring to end any affiliation with Hardin right then and there.

Evil washed across his face at that moment as sure as the devil was standing behind him. "No, you're not," he answered with a grumble that surely had its birth in hell.

A chill ran up my spine. "Maybe you're right. Just let me put my book and paper away, and I'll be right there." I entered without shutting the door, as I didn't care for him to think I had changed my mind. Next, I tossed the city directory and the paper on the bed, then removed my coat, draping it over a wall hook out of Hardin's sight. I took the derringer out of the coat pocket and slipped it in my pants pocket. Taking a deep breath and wondering if goat stew and corn tortillas were going to be my last meal on earth, I stepped back to the entry and locked the door under Hardin's hard gaze, then strode past him into his room where a woman sat in a rocking chair beside their unmade bed, reading leafs of paper. She wore a gray, high-topped blouse with a long black skirt, though her undergarments lay scattered on the floor by the bedstead.

When she glanced up at me, I nodded, figuring she was Beulah Morose, Hardin's client, mistress, and bank account. Hardin never introduced us, but as he shut the door, she winked at me. I didn't know if she was flirting or merely acknowledging Hardin's lack of manners. Beulah's dirty blonde hair was mussed, and her dark eyes were alluring, the dominant feature on an otherwise plain face. She was endowed with a mountainous bosom. No lawyer, especially one as scrupulous as my neighbor, could pass up getting his hands on those assets.

When Hardin turned around, he pulled up two chairs opposite his woman and pointed for me to sit in one. "This is the man I was telling you about. He's agreed to publish my memoirs."

As I slid into the seat, I explained publishing a book

is a hard business as I had learned firsthand at the *Times* that very morning.

"A promise is a promise, Henry." Sulfur seeped from his words. "If you've got another client, you know what you're doing."

"He's a paying client," I responded.

"I'll pay you when you get me published, and when I have the money."

Those were two possibilities I doubted would ever come true, but I didn't think Hardin cared to hear what I thought.

Beulah saved me. "This is how John Wesley begins his recollections: 'I was born in Bonham, Fannin County, Texas, on the twenty-sixth of May, eighteen fifty-three.'" She looked up at me. "Doesn't John Wesley have a way with words, Henry?"

"Very imaginative, his start," I replied. "Who would've thought to begin his life story with the place and date of his birth?"

Beulah smiled and leaned forward in her rocking chair, offering me the stack of handwritten papers. "Care to read more?"

"I've heard enough, ma'am. It's obvious your man has a talent with the pen."

"Pencil actually," Beulah corrected.

"How long until I can sell copies, Henry? Things are tight and I need the money."

"It's the end of July now," I replied, calculating when I expected to leave El Paso forever. "With a little luck, we could have it out by Christmas, and your book would be the perfect gift for everyone." Especially illiterates and idiots, I thought without saying. "You need a great book title, something that'll draw readers, something like 'It Don't Pay to Snore.' That'll catch a reader's eye for sure."

Hardin seemed impressed and touched. "Whatever happens in all of this, Beulah is my full partner in the book. I just want you to understand that. I've already signed over the agreement to her, and what she says carries as much weight as what I tell you, Henry."

"That's good to know, John Wesley. Maybe I should

take what you've done so far and read it overnight, give me a better idea about finding the right printer." I wanted to escape those two nuts.

Beulah smiled softly, reflecting a gentle side, but Hardin remained as sour as a boxcar of rotten apples.

"That's fine, Henry, but you guard those papers with your life as that's my only copy."

"They'll be as safe as if they were in a Wells Fargo strongbox."

His woman handed me the papers, and I stood up, moving as quickly as I could toward the door to escape these two sticks of dynamite. Hardin, though, grabbed my arm. "I feel like a drink and playing some cards. You care to go with me, Henry?"

"I've too much work to do, John Wesley, if I'm to get your book out by Christmas."

He released my arm, and I made for his door, then out into the hall, unlocking my room and scrambling inside, not closing the door until I had placed the papers on the table in the corner. As I returned to the entry, a gust of wind blew through the open windows, catching the door and slamming it shut. Turning around, I saw four or five sheets of paper sailing out the window onto Overland.

As they disappeared from sight, I realized I was a dead man!

I jumped for the door, then retreated to the table, picking up Annie's Testament and placing it atop the remaining pages so no more would take flight. Then I bolted for the exit, slamming it behind me and sprinting down the stairs out onto the street, drawing the stares of startled pedestrians. Spotting saw one sheet on the plank walk, I grabbed it: then another along the curb. I captured it. In the middle of the street, I spotted a third and dodged a horse and buggy to reach it, only to have a bicyclist ride by it, so fast it lifted the sheet, which fluttered atop a horse apple, just as another buggy rolled over it. When the conveyance passed, I yanked the crumpled and droppings-smeared page from the road.

Three down, two to go, I thought as I looked frantically around. A comely young woman I took to be a lady of the line waved a sheet at me. "Yoo hoo, is this what you're after?" I darted her way, grabbed it from her hand, and thanked her. "Come see me at Dollie's place," she replied, "and I can return the favor."

I scooted around her, looking everywhere along the walk and out in the street, moving with the breeze down the street to the *Times* office. I spat on the walk outside the newspaper entrance and realized I had probably lost one sheet and maybe more of Hardin's writings. Once Hardin found out I'd lost part of his epic, I figured I'd spend eternity buried in a local cemetery, though hell would be an improvement and likely cooler than El Paso.

I started back for the Herndon House, wiping the manure off one sheet when I reached the door just as Hardin emerged. Hiding the papers behind my back, I grinned.

"You sure you don't want to play cards and have a few drinks, Henry?"

"Too much work to do."

Hardin wrinkled his nose. "What's that I smell?" he said, looking down at my boots. "You either soiled your britches or stepped in horse dung, Henry! Don't go visiting any editor on my account smelling like a stockyard." He turned and marched off.

I should've pulled my derringer from my pocket and plugged him, but I let it go. Fact was, my boots didn't smell nearly as bad as his writing. I scraped on the walk the horse apple from my boot and straightened the papers, then walked in the building and up the stairs to my room, where I saw Beulah Morose knocking on my door. I cleared my throat to announce my approach, and she spun around, her hand flying to her mouth.

"Oh, you scared me, Henry. I feared you were John Wesley. With him gone, I thought we might discuss his book. How much money do you think it'll make?"

"I can't tell until I read it a couple times, get a feel for the real John Wesley Hardin."

Beulah smiled and sidled up beside me. "Would you like to get a feel of the real Beulah Morose?" She ran her hand down the front of my pants.

Now I hadn't always used sound judgment when such

an opportunity presented itself, but this was the woman of the meanest killer and worst lawyer in Texas. If he didn't shoot me, he could sue me to death.

"You're not my type."

"What's your type," she cooed, walking her fingers up and down my fly.

A choice between my life or my reputation faced me. I weighed my options, choosing to live, regardless of the implications for my semi-good name.

"What's your type?" she whispered again, while her fingers kept walking over my netherworld.

"Oscar Wilde," I finally proclaimed.

"Eeeewww," she cried, backing away from me like she'd touched a hot stove. "That's what John Wesley said prison was like."

"Can't speak for jail, but a lot of us book types are that way."

She put her hands on her hips, then licked her lips. "I don't believe you. I was getting to you. You're just scared of John Wesley."

I shrugged. "I heard what happened to your husband."

Beulah didn't seem at all moved by the memory of her deceased spouse, as I guessed she had had plenty of men during her career and saw one about the same as the next. She backed across the hallway, cocking her head and eying me. "Still don't believe you."

"I've got work to do," I said, barging into my room, locking the door behind me, and wedging a chair under the handle for extra protection from Beulah and her illicit intentions. Striding to the table, I stared at the Testament atop the Hardin papers and thought what a sacrilege it was for those two documents to touch. I removed the Good Book and slipped the recovered pages beneath the others, then placed them all in the bottom drawer of my dresser so a breeze wouldn't blow them and my future out the window.

Grabbing the city directory from the bed, I sat in the rocking chair thumbing through it for printer possibilities for Bean and, unfortunately, Hardin. Then I napped a bit before Hardin and Beulah resumed their nightly arguing or rutting. About supper time, I left my room quietly, so I wouldn't attract Beulah's attention and affections, then stepped easily downstairs and out into the scorching street. I found an eatery down Overland and had a bowl of chili with soda crackers.

As I was leaving the place, I remembered my clothes to be cleaned and jogged over to the Chinese laundry just as the proprietor was closing up. I waved my hand at him and held my claim ticket up against the glass for him to see. He smiled and unlocked the door, letting me slip past. He returned with my bundled clothes and handed me a receipt with the price. I dug the change out of my pocket and paid him for his work, then started back down Overland to the Herndon House.

When I neared the boarding house, I spotted midway down the block the reporter that had been so interested in learning about the Gringo Bandito until his hatchet of an editor kicked me out of the office. He saw me, but he stopped and pulled a pocket watch from his vest to check the time. Reaching the Herndon House, I turned inside and climbed the stairs. Walking down the hallway to my room, I thought I heard the soft tread of someone on the stairway. Reaching my door, I inserted the key, unlocked it, swung it open, then closed it, remaining in the hall, and staring at the stairway. Shortly, the reporter's head poked gingerly up enough to scan the hall. Seeing him, I waved, but he ducked his head. Then I heard the tramp of his retreating boots as he raced down the steps and slammed the front door as he emerged onto the street. With a full stomach and clean clothes, I thought little about it other than the natural curiosity of a stupid newspaperman.

Figuring another shower would cool me off and help me sleep better, I prepared myself, hiding my boots and money, then taking my key and towel to the end of the hall, where I found the facility empty. I slipped inside, latched the door, and started the shower, enjoying the brisk water as a cure for the hot oven that was El Paso. I relished the moment until I heard a pounding on the door.

"Who is it?" I yelled.

Receiving no answer, I kept bathing, but the pounding grew stronger.

Leaving the water going, I stepped from the lead-bottomed shower and unlatched the door with my shoulder wedged against it until I determined the problem. I feared it might be John Wesley Hardin come to kill me, but it wasn't him. No, it was much worse. It was Beulah Morose. As soon as I cracked the door, she shoved herself against it and cooed at me.

"Let me shower with you, Henry. I can cure you."

In a miracle of Biblical proportions, I fought off her bosomous avalanche against the door and latched the thing long enough to finish my shower. As soon as I dried and dressed, I unlatched the door, flung it open, and darted down the hallway to avoid Beulah, wherever she might be hiding. I was lucky and reached my room without spotting her. Unlocking my door, I jumped in, half expecting her to be waiting for me or climbing in through one of the open windows.

Fortunately, her ardor had dwindled, and I went about my business. I studied the city directory by window light until dusk then turned on the electric light. As I did, a rap came on my door.

"Henry, might we visit?" came a familiar voice.

"Sure," I replied, opening the room to see my landlady standing there, a book in her hand.

"Might I come in?" Annie asked. "You'd talked about reading the scriptures together, and I decided we should tonight because I know you had trouble with Wes and Beulah today."

I stepped aside and let her in, shutting the door.

"Leave it open," she said. "It prevents gossip."

"What about Beulah?"

"She won't bother you as long as I'm in here. She's a woman of lusty appetites. I've tried to convert her, but her heart's too hardened."

I motioned toward the rocking chair. As she seated herself there, I grabbed my Testament and pulled a chair from the table to sit opposite her. She gave a funny glance at the book I was holding.

"That looks like the Testament I left with the Gringo Bandito."

"It is," I acknowledged. "After he escaped, I bought it from Judge Roy Bean."

She smiled. "I'm glad it's wound up in the hands of a decent man."

"Thank you," I replied, figuring God was toying with my mind.

We read some scriptures together, Annie reading me her favorite and me just finding random passages. A few made sense and a few didn't, but Annie was pleased to have a man recite scriptures with her. After that, I asked her about Hardin and Beulah and told her how noisy they had been the previous night. She said since her husband's death, Beulah had fought Hardin daily, their encounters made worse by Hardin's drinking.

"It's odd," she said, "but she stays with him even though he's threatened to kill her, even forced her to write out a suicide note he kept for himself so if he killed her, he could make it look like she did it. She keeps a gun hidden in her dress to fend for herself. You remember that."

"I will."

"Another odd thing, I find him more dangerous when he's sober than when he's been drinking. He's more mannerly to me when he's drunk than when he's not. There's just a mean streak in him from one side to the other."

We told a few more stories, then Annie announced her bedtime. I saw her to the door, latched it behind her, and went to bed. If Beulah and Hardin argued that night, I never heard it. I slept soundly, waking up around nine o'clock in the morning, not on my own, but from a pounding on the door. That Beulah was going to be the death of me yet. I arose and walked in my long johns to the door, opening it and preparing to punch her in the nose.

Instead of Beulah Morose, I saw two men wearing badges.

"Fellow," said the one leaning on a cane in his left hand, "you're under arrest."

"What?" I asked.
"You're under arrest," repeated the younger one.
"What for?" I demanded.
"Robbery," the older officer announced.

CHAPTER EIGHT

I stood there as dumbfounded as a yearling at steering time. "You've got the wrong man. What did I rob?"

"The Southern Pacific Depot."

"What?" I shouted. "You two have been chewing on loco weed. Who are you?"

The one leaning on the cane introduced himself. "I'm Constable John Selman."

His younger partner said, "I'm John Selman with the El Paso Police Department."

"I'm hearing and seeing double," I said, "and I haven't been drinking."

The policeman replied, "I'm Junior, his son."

"You robbed the orphan newsboy at gunpoint yesterday, stealing a newspaper, an *El Paso Times* to be exact. The editor filed a complaint after one of his men trailed you to your room last evening." The constable tapped his cane on the floor.

I stood there as perplexed as a mule that had just been swatted on the jaw with a two-by-four. For a moment, I stared at the pair, seeing the family resemblance. Old Selman was a frail fellow with an enlarged nose over a brown mustache and a set of brown teeth. The larceny in his eyes beneath his felt hat suggested he was not a man you wanted to cross. Junior shared the same enormous nose but lacked the mustache and vindictiveness. Heftier than his old man, he looked healthier and less sinister than his pa, but more mannerly, as he held his hat in his hand.

"Put some clothes on so we can haul your ass over to the jail. There's a robbery charge and carrying a prohibited weapon charge you'll be facing," Old Selman informed me.

I crossed my arms over my chest and shouted, "You're not taking me to jail. I didn't rob anybody. That scamp robbed me of ninety-five cents when he didn't give me change for a paper. When I saw the newspapers on the platform, I took one." I stomped my foot on the floor and assessed the situation. "Way I see it; you should arrest the kid for stealing from me."

Old Selman grew impatient, his eyes and lips narrowing. He banged his cane against the floor. "Get dressed or we'll take you in naked," he screamed.

That threat held no sway with me, not after I had paraded twice through Langtry in my altogether. "I'm not gonna do it," I cried.

The constable lifted his cane like he intended to swat me with it until the three of us heard a clatter from across the room.

"What the hell's going on?" cried John Wesley Hardin, as he barged into the hallway, holding a revolver in his right hand, and rubbing his red eyes with his left.

"We're arresting this man, whoever he is, for robbing the Southern Pacific Depot," Old Selman announced.

"I took a newspaper I was owed from an unattended stack. That's all," I explained.

"Not according to the *Times* editor," interjected Junior.

Hardin scowled. "I've had enough lies written about me in newspapers to know you can't trust a newspaperman any more than you can a rattlesnake."

"Stay out of this, Wes. It's a legal matter."

My neighbor shook his head and his gun in Selman's direction. "If it's a legal situation, I'm his lawyer. Did you say you didn't know who he was?"

"Just his room number," Old Selman admitted.

"That's not good enough in the eyes of the law."

"We'll take care of that at the jail," Junior acknowledged.

"His name is Henry Lomax, and he does legal work for me on my book. I suggest the two of you leave him alone."

"The editor won't like it if we don't bring him in," Old Selman said. "He'll write bad things that could damage my reelection."

Hardin cocked his revolver. "He'll be writing your obituary if you do." Next, he waved his gun at me. "Fetch a dime, Henry, and the constable can pay him double what was taken."

I scurried to my pants and dug in my pocket, but I had spent all my change on supper and laundry last evening. Taking a dollar bill, I returned to the door and gave the greenback to Junior just as Beulah Morose walked out in the hall, still in her nightgown.

Old Selman reached for his sidearm at the noise, but seeing Hardin's consort, he removed his hat. "Good morning, Miss Beulah," he greeted her, ogling her gown, which clung to her like snow on mountain peaks.

"Good day, gentlemen," Beulah answered, then curtsied to the old lawman. "Wes," she said, "hurry up. I've got the urge."

"Get back to bed, Beulah. I'll be there shortly once these fine gentlemen depart."

"I don't like this, Wes, just like I don't like the way you—" Selman halted until Beulah retreated in the room. "—you know, not splitting the money after the incident at the trestle."

"And I resent you interrupting my sleep, John. Now go on about your other business. This issue is settled."

Now I was indebted to John Wesley Hardin for unscrambling my eggs. I watched the two Selman's retreat to the stairs, as did Hardin. After they disappeared down the steps, and we heard the front door slam shut, Hardin turned to his room without so much as a glance at me. The way I figured it, I was still out ninety cents from my first transaction with the orphan and another whole dollar from my second. Here I was in the meanest surviving town in the west with more gunmen per head than even the penitentiary, and I was being swindled by a little motherless waif. As I closed my door, I heard the squeaking of bedsprings from across the hall and Beulah's morning moans.

I dressed. As my carrying cash had dwindled to a couple bucks, I pulled another twenty-dollar bill from my stash in my boots before I slipped them on and headed back outside, vowing to run the other direction if I ran into that orphan newsboy again. I found the breakfast eatery I enjoyed and had a full stack of pancakes slathered in a gallon of the Wes-Tex Syrup I so enjoyed. The cook reminded me of the grocer who carried the brand, so I headed there after breakfast and bought a tin and a loaf of bread I could keep in my room to eat when I didn't care to go out. I returned the food to my room. On my next errand, I located a stationery store to buy some paper and envelopes to keep Roy Bean apprised of my valiant efforts to find an author and a publisher for his story. After lunch, I remained in my room and out of sight, as there was no telling when I might run into the newsboy again. I feared him more than the Selman's, though not as much as I feared Beulah.

In my room I wrote Roy Bean a long letter, explaining my lack of progress, especially with the *El Paso Times*, but a half dozen other printers worked in El Paso and even a couple in Juarez where I might have a chance if I could overcome the language. Additionally, I sent Bean regards from my Texas Ranger brother and how he spoke fondly of his dealings with the judge. The next morning, I dropped off my letter at the Post Office. I bought an *El Paso Times* inside my breakfast eatery. As I awaited my plate, I found a story devoted to my encounter with the Selman's. The article was headlined: THE LAW AT ITS WORST. As I sipped my coffee, I read and grinned at the story:

What good is the law in El Paso if it is not enforced? The editor of the Times *earlier this week notified the constable of an unfortunate incident of a newly arrived scoundrel who assaulted a* Times *newsboy in broad daylight on an El Paso street before a Texas Ranger came to the young orphan's aid. The next day, this very same man robbed at gunpoint our innocent young paper peddler and stole all his earnings. Thanks to the intrepid work of Times newspaperman Rip Enreed, who risked his life to find the location of the bully, the Times was able to provide Constable Selman with the address of the accosting tyrant. Constable Selman, accompanied by an El Paso policeman, found the accused in his boarding house and instead of arresting him merely accepted a few pennies which he delivered to the Times office and said the matter was closed. Why does the constable not do his job? What (or who?) does Constable Selman fear? Until those enforcing the laws of our community do it squarely for everyone, including those as helpless as an orphan, El Paso will continue to suffer from the lawless reputation that hinders our growth and prosperity.*

Less than a week in El Paso and I was already making the news, though fortunately not by name. I wondered how Old Selman and Junior were handling the story. When my pancakes arrived, I asked for extra syrup and enjoyed my meal, chuckling occasionally at the newspaper story and wondering if Hardin would be equally amused. That afternoon, I visited the El Paso Steam Printing Company and talked to the manager about publishing Judge Roy Bean's recollections. He agreed to consider it, provided we found someone willing to write the biography, suggesting I check with the *Times*, especially Rip Enreed, who relished those types of stories. I told him I had already done so, but Enreed had declined to listen to the proposal, though I didn't tell him why.

The manager, a barrel-bellied giant in a printer's apron, nodded. "I'm not surprised, not with grown men around town robbing innocent newsboys. That's bound to be the paper's focus until those thugs are captured and castrated." He spat on the sawdust-covered floor.

"There's two sides to every story," I responded.

"Not in the newspaper business," he answered.

I thanked him for the information, promising to return if I found a writer.

As the calendar turned to August, it was the same with every place I visited over the next two weeks. The *Daily*

Herald put out an evening paper and did job publishing, but the editor there said Bean was an old fool whose life story wasn't worth a bucket of warm spit. At the *Democrat*, another evening paper that did publishing work, the manager told me to bring a finished manuscript when Bean finished it, and he would publish it at cost plus a ten percent return on the sales price. It was much the same at the *Evening Tribune*, lukewarm interest in the subject but willing to work out a deal if someone wrote the book.

To keep Bean optimistic, I wrote to him the *Democrat* would publish it at cost if we could find someone to write it and that was my next task. I wondered if Hardin or even Beulah might take up the task as they were the only ones I knew in El Paso involved in writing a biography.

Wanting to stay on my landlady's good side, I paid her my weekly rent a day early on Thursdays. Two or three evenings a week, we would read scriptures in my room or her office, always leaving the door open for propriety. One night as I exited her office, I saw my brother climbing the stairs.

Andy nodded. "Got time for a visit, Henry?"

"I'll make time for my brother. You want me to take you some place to eat?"

He wagged his head. "Let's visit in your room so we won't be overheard."

We shook hands as he reached the top of the stairway, then marched wordlessly down the hall. I unlocked the door and let us in, punching the button to turn on the electric lights. Andy shut the door and headed to the corner table. As I sat down, I placed the Testament on the table.

"Taken up religion, have you, Henry?"

"I read the scriptures some with my landlady."

My brother grimaced. "That's probably a good thing because the Selman's are carrying a grudge for you after that newspaper article."

Snickering, I nodded. "I saw it."

"The Selman's are looking for any reason they can find to arrest you. Once they get you in jail and out of sight, no telling what they'll do to you."

"What do you suggest?"

"Stay on your best behavior and quit carrying any weapons."

Cocking my head, I stared at my brother in disbelief. "These two are after me, and you tell me I can't carry a weapon for self-defense."

Andy grimaced. "That's about the size of it. If they find you with a gun or a knife, they'll arrest you for carrying an unlawful weapon. They'll throw you in jail and work you over. Don't carry a weapon on you, even in your boot. They'll look there first."

"That's where I keep my money."

"Then hide it elsewhere and only carry what you need. Selman's a so-called lawman now, but in his younger days, he murdered men and scavenged on the outskirts of the Lincoln County War. He works both sides of the law, whatever serves him and his boy best."

Andy quickly convinced me leaving my weapons behind was the safest course. We visited on other matters for an hour, him and me tearing chunks of bread from my loaf and dipping them in the tin of syrup for supper. My brother inquired about Hardin and Beulah.

"Lately, they've been fighting more than rutting from what I hear across the room. You know Hardin stopped the Selman's from arresting me for stealing a newspaper at the depot."

"So that's what that note was about in the *Times*, was it?"

"The *Times* has it in for me, thinking I'm bullying the newsboy when it's the other way around."

"I'll have a talk with the editor, tell him to leave you alone."

"And Rip Enreed, too. He told the Selman's where to find me."

"What I tell to the editor will apply to them all. And right now, they need the rangers."

"How's that?"

"Have you read anything about this Corbett-Fitzsimmons fight?"

"I've seen a few things in the paper and heard some

talk."

"There's talk of this fistic carnival in Dallas. The governor has vowed to stop the fight, even telling the Dallas sheriff to shoot the prizefighters if that's the only way to prevent it."

I whistled. "What does Dallas have to do with El Paso and the *Times*?"

"Rumor says the promoter may move his operation here to stage the fight in town or across the river in Juarez. The governor's vowed to stop it in Texas."

"But how does that affect me and the *Times*?"

"They'll want information from the law if this comes to pass. They know not to alienate me or any of the rangers in our company."

"I always knew there were advantages to having a big brother."

Andy grinned. "As long as you stay out of trouble. If you break the law in my jurisdiction, I'll arrest you like any other crook. Just don't embarrass me once more folks find out you're my kid brother." He grinned. "I'm still picking up rumors Langtry way of the Gringo Bandito and all his depredations."

We both laughed.

"Just make sure," Andy chided me, "that only the Gringo Bandito is breaking the law." He arose and shook my hand, saying he needed to get back to Ysleta and attend to ranger paperwork before he called it a day.

I told him I'd accompany him to the stairs, and we walked down the hallway, nearing the banister just as John Wesley Hardin reached the second-floor landing. The moment the two men saw each other, they froze.

"Andy," Hardin acknowledged.

"Wes," Andy answered, then passed Hardin and descended the stairs.

As both Hardin and I heard the front door close, he looked at me. "Do you know who that was? That was Andrew Lomax. He's one Texas Ranger you shouldn't mess with, Henry."

"He's my brother," I confessed.

Hardin paled for a moment, like he'd see a ghost, then

grimaced and clenched his jaw until his face reddened. "Are you spying on me for the law, Henry?"

"Hell, no!" I answered. "Ask Andy, if you don't believe me."

The gunman backed off. "I believe you. I don't want to tangle with Andy Lomax. He's tough but worse than that, he's as honest as any lawman I ever met. I've never had good luck against honest lawmen."

"That's my brother." I could tell Hardin was shaken.

Hardin pushed past me and strode to his room. I didn't envy Beulah when he got there. He barged in, slammed the door, and immediately started yelling at his mistress. Meek gal that she was, Beulah screamed her reply and threw something at him that shattered against the floor. I raced back to my room and locked myself in before the fireworks moved into the hall. I figured this wasn't the best time to return Hardin's manuscript, which had remained untouched in my bottom dresser drawer since I had retrieved the fugitive pages from the street.

Hardin's profane outbursts grew more frequent and louder. Beulah returned his verbal compliments with lewd rejoinders of her own. After about three nights of this, Annie Williams came to my room and asked if I could tell them to keep quiet as other boarders were threatening to move out if the nightly commotions didn't stop. I declined at first, then Annie offered me my next week at the Herndon House for free. Her desperate offer shamed me so much, I told her I would do it at no charge, even as Hardin and Beulah screamed at each other across the hall.

I hoisted up my britches, strapped on my gun belt for the first time in a while, and strode across the hall, knocking firmly on the door. "It's Henry," I called, "can I come in?"

"It's unlocked," Hardin replied.

Turning the doorknob, I eased inside and saw Hardin, standing against the opposite wall and holding his revolver aimed at my chest. Something told me I couldn't outdraw him, so I smiled, and he slowly lowered the gun.

"The landlady asked that you two keep the noise

down," I said.

"She's told me that before," Hardin answered.

"Yeah," echoed Beulah, finding something they could agree on for the first time in days.

"I'm not just asking for Annie," I continued. "I'm asking for myself and for my brother. Andy's coming over in a few minutes, and he gets a little jumpy when he hears yelling and screaming. It reminds him of the war, and sometimes he just goes a little berserk, like he's fighting Yankees."

Hardin grimaced as he pointed his gun at Beulah. "I'll behave, but I can't guarantee about her."

Beulah nodded without looking at me, her gaze focusing on the gun barrel. "I'll shut up."

"How long is Andy planning on visiting?" Hardin wanted to know.

Shrugging, I answered in a way that I hoped would give us all a peaceful night's rest. "Can't say for certain. He may stay the night with me."

Hardin nodded. "We can be quiet."

"Just behave yourselves, and our lovely landlady and my Texas Ranger brother will thank you." I slowly pulled the door shut and returned to my room, where Annie threw her arms around my shoulders and planted a kiss on my cheek.

"Thanks so much," she said, then left the room.

I went to bed an hour later and slept as well as I had in a week, until about seven o'clock the next morning, when Hardin and Beulah started at it again, yelling and screaming, this time carrying their dispute out into the hallway. Jumping up from my bed, I strapped my holster back on over my long johns and flung open the door.

Both saw me and instantly fell quiet.

Hardin apologized. "I hope we didn't wake your brother."

"He's already left," I replied.

"I'm leaving, too," Hardin said, lifting a valise for me to see. "I've had enough of Beulah's insults."

She heard him and responded. "And I'm tired of your drinking and gambling. I'm fed up with you holding out on my money."

"You wouldn't have any money except for me," he shot back and stomped down the hall to the stairs, quickly disappearing. We both heard him slam the front door.

"I'll show him," she said to me. "He thinks he can go to New Mexico Territory and improve his luck at gambling and women. He can't do either." She looked at me. "I'm sorry you're an Oscar Wilde or I'd show him right now."

I spun around and retreated to my room, locking the door, and wedging a chair under the knob for my safety. The next three days were as quiet as I remembered since arriving in El Paso. With my options narrowing for finding a writer for Bean's biography, I wrote him a letter, informing him that it didn't look good. I told him he could write me in care of the Herndon House, 207 East Overland, El Paso, Texas. The next day I mailed the letter and walked the streets of El Paso to whittle away the time. As my brother recommended, I went unarmed and only with a few dollars in my pocket, the rest stashed in various places around my room. Occasionally, I saw Old Selman or Junior eyeing me from afar, but they never approached me, likely having learned that Andy Lomax was my brother.

One day as I was returning from supper, I saw Old Selman visiting with Beulah beneath an awning of a building between the boarding house and the *Times* office. The moment the constable saw me, he lifted his hand to screen his face and turned away from me. I thought little about it at the time as long as he left me alone. I returned to my room, read the updates on the prizefight in the newspaper, then retired.

In an hour I heard the bed springs creaking across the hall and the rising moans that Beulah emitted while practicing her craft. I realized Hardin must have come back from New Mexico Territory. As long as they didn't yell, I didn't care. I went to sleep to the sound of them rutting and woke up the next morning to the same noise. Beulah must have had another of her morning urges, and Hardin, like any man, was certainly glad to oblige. I would've envied him had it been any woman other than

Beulah.

I arose to the call of nature and decided I'd run down the hall to the facilities in my long johns. Hardin must have had the same idea because just as I swung my door open, the one across the hallway parted.

"Morning, neighb..." I started, expecting to see John Wesley Hardin, then halted as quick as if I'd run into a brick wall.

Across from me, also in his long johns, stood Old Selman himself.

I saw him but for an instant, as he violently slammed the door when he spotted me, but I knew this would lead to nothing but trouble for me and for El Paso.

CHAPTER NINE

I stayed in my room most of the day, figuring it safer inside than out on the street. I debated whether to carry a gun to defend myself against the Selman's the next time I ventured out or to go defenseless and protect myself from a weapons charge. Just walking to the toilet could be dangerous if I encountered Old Selman or his son in the hallway. Fortunately, I had half of my loaf of bread to eat and plenty of syrup to dip it in for food plus the pitcher of water to drink. I expected I would have a solitary time, but El Paso was never predictable, and I had more visitors than ever.

Just before noon, I heard a banging on the door and knew it had to be Beulah Morose. Only she knocked like discharging a cannon. "Henry," she screamed. "Let's visit."

"I'm not here," I answered, trying to confuse her. She had more smarts than I thought and saw through my guise. "We must visit."

"I didn't see anything."

"That's not what you know who said."

"You know what? I have no idea who you're talking about."

"I feel an urge coming on. Care to tickle my urge?"

"Not on your life. That's what's caused all your troubles, and mine, to begin with."

She might have pestered me for the rest of the day, but another visitor arrived, my landlady, and shooed Beulah to her room.

A gentle rap on my door followed the sound of Beulah's closing across the hall. "H.H., it's Annie. Can we talk?"

I cracked the door to confirm it was Annie and her alone, then realized I was still in my long joins only. "Wait until I put on some britches." I scrambled to the bed and tugged my trousers on, then opened the entry for Annie.

"May I come in?" she asked, running her fingers through her auburn hair. Before I could answer, she continued. "I wanted to thank you for the quiet the last few days."

I moved aside and let her in, closing up behind her.

"Shouldn't we leave the door open, so people won't talk?" she asked.

"No, I'm making more enemies, just by going to the bathroom."

Annie looked at me bewildered. "All the paying boarders asked me to thank you for getting Hardin and Beulah to behave."

"I fear she hasn't been a good girl in Hardin's absence." Then I told Annie about believing Hardin had returned until I saw Old Selman emerging from her room in his long johns. He'd been urging Beulah on so much so late night and early morning, I figured Hardin was back.

"A tarnished woman leaves a stain on every man she touches," Annie observed.

While I'd tried to keep my distance from Beulah, I worried she had set me up for bloodstains, though I had never touched her. "This'll lead to no good."

Annie patted my shoulder. "I'm buying a police whistle."

"What good'll that do?"

"Over in the reservation, all the madams carry one. If trouble breaks out, they whistle until the officers arrive."

"I doubt that'll help, as I've more enemies among the lawmen than the scofflaws." I shrugged.

"They're often one and the same here in El Paso," she admitted.

"That's why I'm sticking to my room today."

"You need anything?"

"If you're going out, bring me a loaf of fresh bread, a tin cup to drink water from the pitcher, and a newspaper to keep me occupied or soak up the blood after a Selman shoots me."

Annie took both my hands and squeezed them. "I'll pray for you, Lomax. Maybe we can read scriptures tonight. Perhaps that will ease your worries."

I thanked her and sent her on her errands, glad to have at least one ally in El Paso besides my brother. Shutting the door, I locked it and wedged a chair beneath the knob. After I finished dressing, I went to the table by the Overland window. As I watched the pedestrians and traffic along the street, I dipped the remnants of my bread in the syrup tin for lunch.

About an hour after Annie left my room, I heard a slight rap on my door and went to thank her for running my errands, but when I opened up, I discovered the one that had started most of my El Paso problems, the orphan newsboy! Despite his smile, I moved to slam the door before the waif got me in more trouble, but the newspaperman, intrigued about the Gringo Bandito, stepped beside his fellow *Times* gang member. He held up his hand.

"Hold on, friend," said Rip Enreed. "Juan's come to apologize." He swatted the kid's mop of coal-black hair, and the little fellow rattled out words so quickly I could never have understood them, even if I spoke Spanish.

"*Lo siento. Aqui esta tu dinero,*" he started, then blabber, blabber, blabber as he reached in his pants pocket.

"He said he's sorry about taking your change," Enreed informed me.

The boy lifted his hand, palm up. I saw three quarters and two dimes.

"Is this a trick, Enreed, something where you can accuse me of stealing from a *Times* newsboy and slander me in ink once again, soil my good name?"

Enreed rocked his head. "Oh, no, if we had known you were brother to Andy Lomax, we would never have attacked you."

Once I took the money from the lad's hand, Enreed swatted him on the head again and cried "*Vamos, Juan.*" The barefooted scamp darted away and down the stairs. I hoped never to see him again. The reporter reached into his pocket and handed me a dime. "That's to make good what you sent by the constable."

Taking the dime, I frowned. "I gave him a dollar to give you."

Enreed shrugged. "He only presented us two nickels."

"Somebody's lying," I observed.

The newspaperman raised his arms, licking his lips, and I could've sworn I saw a forked tongue before it disappeared back in his mouth. "You are indeed a cynical man if you can't accept the word of Rip Enreed, the preeminent purveyor of the journalistic truth in all of El Paso, Mr. Lomax. Perhaps we can visit, pick up our conversation about the Gringo Bandito."

Crossing my arms over my chest, I scowled and shook my head. "I'll take my story to one of your competitors, Enreed, before I tell it to you unless—"

"Unless what?"

"—unless you write Judge Roy Bean's story and help get the book published."

"I'd have to check with Ax, my editor first."

"Then good day, Enreed, as our business is concluded." I slammed the door in his face, feeling ninety-five cents richer and a little better about El Paso affairs.

A few minutes later, Annie returned with my bread, my tin cup, a *Times,* and a fresh pitcher of water to replace the one on my washstand. I thanked her and spent the rest of the afternoon reading the paper. The big prizefight news was that Gentlemen Jim Corbett and Australian Bob Fitzsimmons had encountered each other by accident in the bar of Philadelphia's Green Hotel, getting into a scuffle that required two dozen police officers to break up. I found nothing on Oscar Wilde in the day's news, so I figured he was finally in prison for his two-year term. I doubted he would find any daffodils in the penitentiary, though a lot of pansies.

After supper, I heard a light rap on the door. Arising from my table where I had watched the streets, I opened up, expecting my landlady to read scriptures. Instead, I faced Old Selman, leaning on his cane with his left hand, his right hand tapping the butt of his revolver.

"We need to visit," he announced, then stepped past me before I could stop him. "Close the door."

I hesitated.

"I'm just here to talk. If your name wasn't Lomax, you'd be right to be worried, but I don't want to fool with your brother."

Though I wasn't sure I could trust him, I eased the door shut.

Selman lifted his hand from his revolver and scratched his big nose. "I hear you got stumbling drunk last night and woke up this morning seeing things, hallucinating is what I've heard it called."

Shaking my head, I denied his accusation. "I haven't had a drink of liquor since I've been in El Paso."

The constable's hand dropped back down to his pistol, which he tapped with his trigger finger. "No, I hear you were so drunk you were imagining things."

"Like you coming out of Beulah's room?" I asked.

Selman tightened his lips and cocked his head, tapping his revolver harder. "You must've been drunk because I haven't been in this place since my boy, and I first visited you."

"Our recollections are different, Constable."

"Be that as it may, Lomax, John Wesley Hardin owes me a couple thousand dollars for some work we did together—"

"Killing Beulah's husband?"

He grabbed the butt of his revolver and pulled it out, then hesitated, letting it slide back into the well-worn leather. "I despise Hardin, and I don't care for you, either," he growled. "That aside, nothing can happen to him until he pays me what I'm owed. After that, I don't give a damn about him. What I'm telling you, Lomax, is I don't want you squealing to Hardin about what you may or may not have seen coming out of his room this morning and giving him a reason not to pony up with what he owes me." He paused and squinted. "I don't care if your brother is a ranger because I already killed one, and another won't matter."

"I'll make sure Andy hears of your threat."

My response softened the anger in his eyes. I could tell the constable didn't relish facing Andy, at least in a fair fight, so I pointed my trigger finger at his enormous nose. "I'm not interested in what you or Hardin do as long as it doesn't harm me or my brother. If you understand that, then get out of here. I don't want you or your boy harassing me. You don't stop me outside; you don't check me for carrying a weapon, and you don't crowd me on the street. If you understand that, then I didn't hear anything last night or see anything this morning. If you harass me or Andy, I'll tell Hardin you were banging Beulah's drum until the band was exhausted."

Old Selman scowled but finally nodded. "I'll tell my boy. You won't have any trouble as long as you keep your mouth shut."

"It's shut tighter than Beulah's thighs, I assure you."

The Constable marched past me, swinging the door open and letting it bang against the wall as he stepped across the hall and entered Hardin's room, no longer caring what I saw. Within minutes, I heard Old Selman banging on Beulah's drum. In my game of chance, I didn't know who held the better hand, me, or the constable. It likely would've been a draw, except that Junior muddled up everything a few days later.

That evening, though, I went down the hall to Annie's office carrying my Testament and opting to escape the noise of the drum beating across the hall. That was the last time I overheard Selman's and Beulah's rutting, as the constable must have feared Hardin would return soon to El Paso. Annie welcomed me that night and offered me a seat across from her rocking chair.

"You appear a tad nervous," she noted.

"Constable Selman came by today to threaten me if I told Hardin about him and Beulah. If my brother weren't a ranger, I figure I'd already be dead. Hardin owes him money, so Selman said, and he doesn't want Wes using Beulah as an excuse to renege on the debt."

"I'm sure it's ill-gotten money if it involves those two."

"Tell me something, Annie. Has Selman killed a Texas Ranger?"

She nodded. "Sort of. April a year ago Selman shot a disgraced, onetime ranger named Bass Outlaw. Odd, isn't it, a lawman carrying the name Outlaw? Bass got drunk and was tearing up Tillie Howard's place when she started blowing her whistle to summon police. Selman and another Texas Ranger arrived and chased Outlaw behind Tillie's place where they shot it out. Outlaw killed the ranger and hit Selman with a couple of bullets in the leg, that's why the constable uses a cane, before he returned a fatal shot to Outlaw's chest. No doubt Selman is fearless, but he's not guiltless in anything he's ever been involved in."

"He and Hardin fear Andy."

Annie smiled as she opened her Bible. "They don't fear him as much as what he stands for, the law and what's right."

A surge of family pride coursed through my body. I wondered if people would ever think such honorable things about me, considering all the mischief I created over the course of my life.

We reviewed scriptures for half an hour, then I retired for the night after an exhausting and troubling day with too many visitors, too many problems, and not enough answers. After that troublesome day, I took to carrying my dagger in my boot, my derringer in my pants pocket, and my five-shot revolver in my coat as I walked the streets of El Paso. I stopped a couple times over the next two days at the *El Paso Times* office, hoping to find Enreed and convince him to write Bean's life story so it could get published, but he was never in, always out chasing lies to immortalize in ink. I visited the usual places for my meals and took a load of laundry to the Chinaman down the street. After two silent nights across the hall, I returned from supper the next evening after and saw Beulah coming out of her room, all dolled up with a nice blue dress that exposed a little ankle and carrying a matching blue parasol, which struck me as odd since the sun was going down and rain hadn't fallen in El Paso since Noah's time. I tipped my hat at her and said, "Ma'am."

"Well, if it isn't Henry. You got the urge?"

I had the urge to plant a fist in her nose but figured that would only complicate my affairs with John Wesley Hardin and John Selman the elder. "No, Miss Beulah, I intend to retire and read my newspaper." Lifting the rolled paper in my hand, I shook it at that nose I would've loved to plaster with my fist.

"I'm planning to have some drinks and a good time with the right fellow, Henry, not some eunuch like you."

"What you got against uncles?" I asked, hacking her off.

Rolling her eyes, she twirled her parasol like a sword and then pranced past me. I feared she'd return drunk with some guy and make enough noise to wake me and the others. But I was wrong about her on this night. She was quiet as a mouse, or at least her room was as she spent the evening in jail.

The best I pieced it together from gossip and the story in the *Times*, Beulah had gotten drunk, then flirted with John Selman Jr., who refused her urgent needs, infuriating her. Then she responded if she was good enough for his father, she was damn sure good enough for him. Taken by surprise at his father's poor taste in women, discounting his own mother, of course, Junior informed her that she was under arrest. She declined his offer of a free jail cell and threatened to shoot him with a pistol she carried in her parasol. Junior disarmed her, and she blessed him with such words, as the newspaper put it, that the paint scaled off the neighboring wall. Beulah did indeed rest a night in the crowbar hotel. The next afternoon in court, she paid a fifty-dollar fine for carrying a gun and disturbing the peace. Word was, she even apologized to young Selman for the unseemly confrontation. She returned meekly to the Herndon House that evening, still wearing the same blue dress from the previous night, though it was as mussed as her hair was disheveled.

Her room might have remained quiet except for one thing: John Wesley Hardin returned from New Mexico that evening. As I was heading out to buy some supper, I encountered him on the stairs. "Evening, Henry," he said, even tossing me a smile, which was unusual for him.

"You're looking rested and calm," I observed.

"Not a problem in the world that Beulah can't solve on the sheets," he winked as he passed me on the staircase.

After a decent supper, I headed back to the boarding house. Even outside the Herndon House, I heard both of them arguing and screaming. Evidently, Hardin had more problems than even Beulah could manage. I darted up the stairs and into my room, wondering if I'd get any sleep at all. From the snatches of the argument I could decipher, Hardin had exploded over Junior arresting his woman. I wondered if Beulah would reveal how attentive Old Selman was to her in Hardin's absence. They argued in language that would've made the devil blush, though I suspect he was too scared ever to set foot in El Paso.

I sat at my table, trying to read the latest newspaper when Annie knocked. "Henry, Henry," she cried. "We've got to do something."

Jumping up, I put on my holster, checked the load in my revolver, and started for the door, unlocking it, and moving past her toward Hardin's room. I burst in, with Annie behind me. Hardin stood on the far side by the window, his brow dark and brooding. Then I saw the reason why. Standing by me was Beulah, holding a .32 caliber pistol pointed at Hardin's heart.

"Don't," cried Annie, leaping in front of me and grabbing Beulah's wrist, aiming the gun at the floor. "I don't want any killings in my place."

As I saw Hardin move for his gun on the bed, I yanked mine free and pointed it at him. "Don't do it, Wes," I shouted. "If you do, you'll never see your book again."

Though smaller, Annie wrestled the gun away from Beulah, then dashed to the open window. She stuck her head outside and started blowing her police whistle like a maniac. Hardin had been in enough El Paso brothels to know what that meant. He grabbed his gun belt and hat and sprinted out of the room and down the stairs.

"He's gone," I called, but Annie kept blowing on the whistle like Gabriel on his horn.

Within three minutes, I heard a lawman charging up the stairs and down the hall toward us. Two officers, one tall and the other pudgy burst inside, guns drawn.

"It's over, fellows," I said. "Hardin ran out."

Relief washed over their faces. Beulah was sobbing with abandon, her responses to their questions unintelligible. Annie explained all the problems the two had been having and how we had entered to find her holding a gun on Hardin.

"Wish she'd pulled the trigger," mumbled the tall policeman.

After ten minutes, Beulah calmed enough to tell the lawmen he had threatened to kill her, and she had drawn her pistol in self-defense. Annie confirmed she had heard Hardin terrorize her in the past.

"He's taken my dead husband's money," Beulah continued, "and won't let me have it. He's my lawyer. Lawyers shouldn't steal from you, should they?"

The policemen shook their heads. "She don't know lawyers," said the pudgy one. They discussed the situation and decided they should arrest him once they got reinforcements.

"Any idea where he went?" the tall one asked.

"Someplace to drink," Beulah replied. "He prefers the Gem, the Wigwam, or the Acme."

"We know," the officers said in unison. They were torn between their safety and their duty. Either way, they needed help and left, promising to arrest John Wesley Hardin if it took every policeman in El Paso.

As the lawmen scampered down the hall, Beulah turned and hugged me, then twisted about to Annie. "Thank you, thank you, both," she said, tears running down her cheeks.

For the first time in our acquaintance, I felt sorry for the woman. Lewd and profane as she was, she didn't deserve this treatment.

"I'm leaving," she said. "The money's not as important as my life. I've got a little boy, you know, with kin in Arizona. I'll find him, and we'll make do." She pulled a suitcase from under the bed and started gathering her belongings, tossing them in the bag.

"Do you need any money for a train ticket?" Annie asked.

"Count on me for a few dollars if you need it," I offered.

"All the money I need, Wes has. I've been begging him for it. It's mine, but he won't give it to me. When he gave half his book to me, I signed papers on my money. He says my signature gave him the right to do whatever he wanted with *my* money. Can you believe that?"

"He's a lawyer," I replied. "I believe anything about them vermin, but do you need money for train fare?"

Beulah stopped throwing her things in the suitcase long enough to answer me. "In my line of work, you always squirrel away enough to move to the next town and to eat for a few days. I've got enough to reach my son in Arizona. After that, I'll have to see."

Turning around, I called over my shoulder. "I'll be back." I strode into my room and went to the dresser, pulling out the bottom drawer. There were the pages Hardin had written about his sordid life, his excuses for all the wrongs he had committed in his terrible career. I scooped up the papers and carried them across the hall, where I piled them in Beulah's suitcase. "There's his book. A page or two may be missing, and another is dung-smeared, but take it with you. Maybe you can sell it for something or start a fire with it."

"Would you care to stay in my room tonight?" Annie offered.

She shook her head vigorously. "I want to get out of town as fast as I can, so I don't run into him again. Ever!"

I didn't blame her because I didn't care to run into him again or Old Selman or Junior or just about anybody else in El Paso, save for Annie Williams or Andy Lomax. After she piled her suitcase with clothes, a tintype of her son, and her hairbrush and mirror, Beulah closed it up and pulled out a valise from under the bed to carry the rest of her belongings. Then she went around the room, opening every drawer that held Hardin's things, dumping them on the floor. Among his possessions, she found a roll of bills that looked to be a hundred dollars or more and stuck it down her dress.

Annie walked over and returned her revolver. "You may need this," she said.

Beulah shoved it in the valise and snapped it shut. "I'm done with you, John Wesley Hardin. You may take away my money, but you won't take my life." She spat on Hardin's clothes on the floor, grabbed her bags, and started for the door, struggling to carry the luggage.

I slipped my hand under the suitcase handle and took the bag for her. "I'll carry it to the station for you."

Beulah smiled. "You're a decent man, Henry. And between the two of us, I know you're not a eunuch or an Oscar man."

We walked down the stairs and out of the building as streetlights were coming on. Passing the Acme Saloon, one of Hardin's favorites, Beulah spat at the thought of him. We said little the rest of the way to the depot, where she bought a ticket and sat on a wooden bench to await her train. Three others with forlorn expressions waited, too. I wished her well and left her.

Returning to the route I had taken; I reached the Acme Saloon where a great commotion spilled into the street. As I watched, a dozen policemen barged out of the building, pushing a crook.

Their prisoner carried the name, John Wesley Hardin.

CHAPTER TEN

Whatever he had done with Beulah Morose's money, John Wesley Hardin lacked both the funds to post his bail and any friends that would provide it for him, so he stayed in jail for two days. Some folks speculated he had drank all of Beulah's funds, while others thought he had stashed them in some bank in New Mexico Territory during his recent trip. Perhaps, believed a few, he simply played cagey to appear as if he was broke. The other Herndon House boarders and I let them worry about the missing funds, as we enjoyed two nights of restful sleep thanks to his incarceration.

On the second night of his imprisonment, I celebrated by going out for a drink once it got dark, something I'd denied myself since arriving in El Paso. Not that I had taken up the cry of the prohibitionists, but just to avoid the temptation to gamble away Bean's money or mine. As a precaution, I took only ten dollars in bills and what change I had on me, leaving the rest of the money stowed away in different hiding spots in my room. To quench my craving for a shot of whiskey, I headed out into the darkness to visit the Acme Saloon, the next block over north of the boarding house. While I left my Colt.45 holstered in my gun belt hanging from my bedpost, I carried my dagger in my boot, my derringer in my coat pocket, and my little Smith & Wesson in my pants pocket. Emerging into the stale El Paso air, I turned left on Overland, then left onto Utah, passing the grocery store where I bought my Wes-Tex Syrup. As I strode down the plank walk, I saw the Acme Saloon on the opposite corner of San Antonio, fetid yellow light seeping in shafts out the dirty windows. The closer I approached the establishment, the louder came the baritone noises of men at play. The one-story Acme anchored the end of a triangular block, where San Antonio and Utah streets intersected and stood beneath a domed roof sign emblazoned in bold white letters against a blood-red background, tinted pink in the streetlight. On either side of the sign stood a stuffed stag and atop the rounded marker a stuffed coyote, its head forever lifted in a silent howl.

I opened the twin doors and marched in, everyone oblivious to my entry because they were still talking about Hardin's arrest the night before or arguing if the Corbett-Fitzsimmons fight would ever come to pass. Every face carried a smile, either from the whiskey, the conversation, or the knowledge that Hardin was behind bars for a spell. The room was odd-shaped, the bar barely a dozen feet from the door along the wall to the left and a half-dozen tables scattered between the counter and the opposite wall, which angled toward another door opening onto Utah Street. On the wall opposite my entrance was the door into a windowless gambling room where men could play faro or poker without drawing the stares of do-gooders trying to stifle their fun. After closing the door, I studied the patrons, making sure neither the Selman's nor anyone else I took to be a threat were inside. Then I stepped to the bar and watched the bartender shake a rattling tin cup, then dump six clattering dice onto the counter in front of three customers more interested in the game of chance than the drinks in front of them.

Spotting me, the slender, bespectacled bartender nodded. "I'll be with you in a second." Once the three patrons exchanged money with each other and the bartender, the barkeep stepped over to me. "What'll it be?"

"Whiskey," I answered.

"Twelve cents a glass," he informed me.

I extracted all the change from my pocket and plopped

118

on the bar the coins that totaled a dollar and a dime. When the proprietor confirmed I could afford what I ordered, he introduced himself. "I'm Frank Patterson. This your first time here?"

"I'm new to town; H.H. Lomax is my name."

"Any relation to the Lomax over at the stables or the Texas Ranger?"

"Andy's my brother."

"He's a good man," Patterson said as he turned around, picked up a shot glass and whiskey bottle from the back-bar where a key-wind clock kept time. He slid the glass in front of me and filled it to the brim, then placed the bottle in front of me and counted out twelve cents from my cache.

"Pour your own and keep up with your total," he said.

"Not all bartenders are so generous and trusting," I answered, picking up the glass and taking a sip.

"Everybody's more trusting with John Wesley Hardin in jail. Besides," he said, pointing to the three men next to me, "these boys are in a tight game of counter Klondike. Care to play?"

Pointing to my drink, I said, "I'll let this settle first, then decide." I didn't tell him I was unfamiliar with the dice game. When he stepped back to the sports, I threw back my next drink and noticed the clock said seven-thirty-five. I vowed to take no more than two drinks an hour as I watched the game down the counter.

Studying them, I discovered that the bartender rolled the six dice, then identified the best poker hand to beat: a pair, two pairs, three of a kind, four of a kind, and five of a kind. Straights didn't count, nor did flushes because with dice every roll would be a flush. If the players beat the banker's hand, they won. If they lost or tied, the house won. A simple game that could be played atop the bar, Klondike allowed the players to gamble, yet quickly hide their bets and dice if some do-gooder or letter-of-the-law policeman entered, intent on denying grown men their fun.

I drank slowly and quietly, filling my shot glass every thirty minutes to the cry of "Two pair to beat" or "three of a kind to win" or "dammit, my luck's clabbered." I watched silently, though the later it got, the more the rattle and rumble of the dice in the tin cup or on the wooden countertop annoyed me.

Just after ten-thirty and my fifth glass of whiskey, the door swung open, and a man entered. I didn't pay attention except everything went quiet for an instant. Then the bar patrons applauded and cheered. Turning from my whiskey, I saw John Selman Jr. doff his hat, relishing the acclaim.

"What's that about?" I asked Patterson. "Did he learn to cut his own steak?"

"Junior there arrested Hardin, hadn't you heard?"

From what I had seen, it was Junior and a dozen other officers. I took an unscheduled drink, then two more, gulping them down and hoping Selman missed me. He didn't.

The policeman sauntered over like he'd just won an election. "Well, if it isn't Henry Lomax," he called so everyone would hear. "Is it true you've been bedding Hardin's woman?" He paused and turned to the bar customers. "This here's the reason Hardin went on his rampage. While Hardin was in the territory, Lomax was sleeping with the Morose woman."

I ignored him, pouring myself another drink, and using the last of my counter change.

"You can't trust a man who would do such a thing to a friend," Junior called.

"Like your father," I grumbled, sliding my right hand off the bar and into my pants pocket, fingering the five-shot revolver.

Junior's face reddened as he shook his fist at my nose. "Don't defame my father, or I'll run you to the calaboose."

"I was minding my own business until you came in, Junior. Insulting your father's no crime for jail. Now if I'd called your mother a whore, that might be reason for arrest."

Selman reached for my arm as I slid the gun out of my pocket, then he hesitated. "I got a better idea for you, Lomax." With that, he turned around, strode to the doors, flung them open, and marched outside into the night.

Awash in surprised silence, the barroom reflected the blank stares of everyone trying to make sense out of what had just transpired until a customer with a beer mug in his hand closed the doors. Then the noise resumed.

"Must be some bad blood between you and the Selman's," Patterson observed.

"I caught them stump-breaking a ginny one time out at the stables," I lied.

The bartender shook his head. "Wouldn't surprise me," he offered, then returned to his game of Klondike.

I looked at my remaining change, fourteen cents, and knew I had enough for one more drink. Filling my glass a final time, I shoved the balance and the whiskey bottle down the counter to the barkeep, tipping my hat to him. Then I lifted my last jigger of liquor to my lips and gulped it down. Around eleven o'clock, I pushed myself away from the bar and headed for the doors, a little unsteady on my feet.

Reaching the exit, I poked my head out to study the passersby. When no one paid me any attention, I pulled the doors ajar, slipped outside, and shut them. Taking one, two, three steps, I managed okay until I hit the edge of the plank walk. I misjudged my step, just as I caught a cry from across the street.

"That's him!"

I tumbled forward, stumbling just as I heard two gunshots from the opposite sidewalk. I collapsed on the macadamized street.

"You got him! You got him!" cried a voice that sounded vaguely like Junior talking in a barrel. The pistol retorts had un-muddled my mind. The next sound I heard was an odd noise, step-thump, step-thump, step-thump. I remained motionless as spectators gathered around me.

"Call an undertaker," one fellow shouted, until I got up, dusted myself off, and walked away, leaving people behind me thinking I was either invincible or a ghost.

Once I crossed San Antonio Street and slipped into the darkness away from those still huddled outside the Acme, I raced to the Herndon House, up the stairs, and into my room, quickly locking the door and wedging a chair under the knob. I slept fretfully, knowing the Selman's planned to kill me. After sunup, a rapping on the door exploded in my brain. I sat up suddenly in my bed, my head throbbing, and my eyes blurry. "What do you want?"

"It's Annie," answered my landlady. "I heard you were shot last night and wanted to check on you."

"No blood on your sheets, if that's what you're worried about."

"It's you I'm worried about, H.H."

"Just a minute," I answered. Grimacing, I fought my way out of bed and tugged on trousers over my long johns, and stumbled to the entry, shoving the chair aside and unlocking the door. As I opened it, I swayed on my feet, trying to focus on Annie as she stepped inside.

"You look like death warmed over," she said. "You must've been drinking last night."

Like a schoolboy caught stealing biscuits, I shrugged my guilt away.

"Nothing good ever comes from drinking," my landlady informed me.

"It saved my life," I replied.

"You can tell me later. Get in bed and sleep off your liquor. I'm taking your key, and I'll return in an hour and a half with coffee and breakfast. Right now, just rest."

Annie received no protest from me. I limped to my mattress as she shut the door and locked it. I fell into bed, not bothering to remove my pants, and slipped into a trance until I heard gentle sounds in the room and felt a cool cloth on my cheeks and forehead. Gradually, I returned to reality, the journey made smoother by Annie's cooing sounds as she stroked my face. When I opened my eyes and focused on her features, she smiled.

"I brought you coffee and breakfast, even bought you a newspaper. I doubted you'd feel up to getting out this morning."

Letting out a long sigh, I whiffed the lingering aroma of liquor on my breath. Annie smelled it, too.

"You should be embarrassed, being out drinking."

"Whiskey saved my life," I said, but she doubted me. "Somebody tried to ambush me last night and might've killed me, except I stumbled from the liquor and fell as they fired."

"If you hadn't been in a sinful saloon, it wouldn't have happened to begin with." She clucked her tongue, then grabbed my shoulder and gently eased me into a sitting position. Annie helped me stand, then guided me to the table where she had placed a pot of coffee and a tin plate with four fried eggs, a half dozen slices of bacon, four biscuits, and a dollop of apricot preserves.

I slid into the chair, picked up the fork, and started eating as she poured coffee into my tin cup. The food tasted as good as the cool draft felt wafting in through the window, though the street noise jangled at my brain. Gradually, the grub and the breeze restored my senses enough to converse with Annie.

"You should know, people are gossiping about you and Beulah Morose, say you was seeing her behind Hardin's back and sending her to Arizona so ya'll could get married."

"It's gossip and nothing more, you know that."

"I do, but people saw you escorting her to the Southern Pacific Depot, and the Selman's are spreading such lies around town. I fear they're laying tracks that'll lead Hardin to kill you when he gets out of jail."

"They're also covering Old Selman's tracks. He was cavorting with Beulah while Hardin was in New Mexico Territory. I think you know that."

She nodded. "You told me."

"Old Selman thinks Hardin owes him considerable money, so he doesn't want Wes harmed until he's got his cut."

"I suspect it's related to her husband's murder and money."

"Likely," I said, "but just as Beulah chose her life over the money, you must be careful once Hardin gets out of jail. He'll come back here meaner than a prohibitionist in a brewery."

Annie placed her hand upon mine and squeezed it.

"What about you?"

"Over the years, I've learned to survive against men as bad as him, though I don't remember one nastier."

After my meal and Annie's departure, I stayed in my room the rest of the day and wrote a letter to Judge Roy Bean, informing him I might have found a man to write his story if I ever caught Rip Enreed to discuss the project. Then I advised Bean to keep the tales of the Gringo Bandito alive as the reporter seemed hooked on learning more about the bad man, who, real or not, might just be the angle to get the *Times* newspaperman to take on Bean's project. Next, I admitted I had encountered some troubles with some very evil men, and if he didn't hear from me for a spell, I was either on the run or dead. Toward dusk, Annie delivered me a supper of two fried chicken drumsticks, a healthy serving of mashed potatoes, and some boiled prunes plus an evening paper. After she had returned the dishes to her room, she brought her Bible back, and we read scriptures with the door open, of course.

As my book of scriptures only provided the New Testament, Annie wanted to read from the Old Testament. She read several verses and then turned to one in Deuteronomy. As she named the verse and chapter, I saw John Wesley Hardin stop outside his door. As he turned to look at me, Annie, oblivious to his arrival, read the passage, her gentle voice soothing my nerves as the meanest man in Texas glared at me with eyes of fire.

"The Lord shall cause thine enemies that rise up against thee to be smitten before thy face; they shall come out against thee one way and flee before thee seven ways." When she completed the scripture, she looked up and gasped as Hardin strode into our room.

He pointed his finger at me. "Henry, we need to talk about some mean gossip concerning you and Beulah."

"None of it's true."

"How do you know? I haven't even told you what it is?

"The Selman's have been spreading the rumors to cover their tracks with Beulah."

"That witch of a woman."

Annie stood up from her chair and shook her Bible at Hardin's face. "You'll not talk about Beulah that way. If it's true your father was a Methodist preacher, you sure didn't listen to his sermons."

Hardin's lips quivered, and his hand shook when he pointed at Annie. "Dammit to hell, preacher lady." He spun around and retreated to his room, unlocked it, then cursed when he saw the mess Beulah had left as a going away gift. "Bitch," he shouted this time, then slammed the door behind him.

I stood up and approached Annie. "You've got grit in your craw; I'll tell you that."

She trembled like leaves in a stiff breeze. "The strength came from a power greater than me." She sighed, then whispered the verse she had just read, "The Lord shall cause thine enemies that rise up against thee to be smitten before thy face; they shall come out against thee one way and flee before thee seven ways."

"I'll see you to your room, Annie, before the evil returns."

She threw her arms around my shoulders and hugged me. "Thank you, and you be careful," she whispered.

I retreated to the bedpost where my holster rested and pulled my Colt.45 free, then took her hand and led Annie to her room. "I never wanted a killing in my boarding house, but I don't care now, as long as it's him and not you, H.H."

Returning to my place, I eyed Hardin's door every step of the way, ready to plug him if he accosted me. His door never twitched, and I got inside my corner safely, quickly locking the door and wedging a chair under it. Not trusting my neighbor and knowing he knew my bed faced the door, I tucked my revolver back in its holster and scooted the bed out from the wall, and swapped places with the dresser. Hardin's anger reverberated through the walls as he was mad and likely drinking. I slept with my .45 under my pillow.

The night passed without incident, but mid-morning Hardin started pounding on my door and grumbling, "Henry, we need to talk."

"Give me a minute, Wes." I arose, buckled my gun belt around my long johns, slid my revolver back in the holster, and hid the derringer in my left hand. I eased to the entry, treading softly so he could not guess my location, and shoot through the door. "Back away, Wes."

Hearing his footfall retreating, I slipped to the side of the entry, inserted the key, unlocked it, then flung the door open while the wall screened me. I poked my head into the opening until I saw him, standing in the hallway, his revolver holstered.

As I stepped in the open doorway, he studied me, as if preparing to draw on me. I had the derringer for my defense, as I knew I would never outdraw him.

"You look like you're expecting trouble, Henry."

"I'm prepared for it if it comes."

"I need to borrow some money. Can you loan me some?"

"Nope."

"You haven't sold my book, dammit. Give me money until you do, then repay yourself from the earnings."

"I haven't sold the other book, either."

"Then give me my writings so I can sell them."

"Not possible, Wes."

"Why not?"

"Beulah took them when she left."

"Witch," he screamed.

"You said the papers were half hers."

"I made a mistake."

"I can't do anything about it now."

Hardin softened a bit. "I've made some mistakes, Henry, I admit. I'm running out of friends. Can't even get someone to go drinking or gambling with me. How about us burying our hard feelings and having a drink tonight at the Acme? I want to show everybody I'm out of jail and fear no one."

"Afraid not, Wes."

He cocked his head at me and stared with fiery eyes. "Yes, you will, Henry," he growled.

By the tone of his voice, I knew he would kill me if I didn't accept the invitation. "Okay, Wes, for a while, but

I'm not drinking. A few nights ago, I had a hangover that wouldn't stop."

Hardin smiled. "That's okay, as long as you're there. We'll play some Klondike at the bar. It's easy enough to follow, even for a pea brain like you."

"I'm looking forward to it," I lied. He was up to something, but I didn't know what.

"Bring your money when we go."

He returned to his room, and I shut my door, fretting the afternoon away, though Hardin was in and out of his place three or four times for a half hour or more. Mid-afternoon, I detected his return accompanied by someone with an odd footfall. It came as a step-thump, step-thump, step-thump, the same noise, though less hurried, I had heard when I was ambushed outside the Acme. After an hour, I caught the noise again, retreating down the hall. I slipped to the door, cracked it, and saw Old Selman easing down the hall, his boots making the step sound and his cane the thumping noise. He disappeared and left me wondering what the two had been discussing.

Later Annie brought me supper and prayed for my deliverance for whatever was about to happen. She stayed with me; the door open until Hardin emerged from his room.

"Ready to head to the Acme, *friend?*" he asked, the emphasis on the last word so evil it could only come from a man with murder on his mind. I arose from my chair slowly so Hardin could see I was wearing my holster and Colt.45. I carried my five-shooter in my pants pocket and when I put on my coat, I slipped the derringer in my left hand and planned on keeping it there all night. As I grabbed my hat with my free hand, Annie came over and hugged me. She whispered into my ear, "The Lord shall cause thine enemies that rise up against thee to be smitten before thy face; they shall come out against thee one way and flee before thee seven ways."

I hugged her and whispered, "There's a couple hundred dollars hidden beneath the syrup tin. Keep what's left over after my funeral expenses."

Hardin smiled as best an evil man can. "Got your money, Henry?"

"All fifty bucks," I said, though I only carried twenty.

We left the room, went down the stairs, out on the street, and down to the Acme. We exchanged nary a word, for what do you say to a man you loathe, and you suspect plans to kill you?

At the Acme, Wes planted himself at end of the bar closest to the door and told Frank Patterson he wanted to play counter Klondike. I walked around Hardin, where I could watch him and the door, in case I needed to dash to safety. Hardin demanded drinks for himself and me. I waved away the offer. Patterson obliged, but Wes shook his head. "You'll both do what I say if you know what's best for you."

Patterson poured us both drinks, then brought out the dice and tin can for counter Klondike. As he rolled the gambling cubes or Hardin looked away, I dumped each shot glass of liquor on the floor or in the closest spittoon and squeezed my fingers around the derringer in my left hand, just waiting for him to make his play. We played for a twenty-five cents a roll from arrival to nine-thirty, then ten-thirty, few patrons approaching the bar because they feared interrupting Hardin's game. The grocer from across the street where I bought my Wes-Tex Syrup accepted Hardin's invitation to join us a few minutes before eleven o'clock, standing between me and my adversary and introducing himself as Henry Brown. With every roll, Hardin cried "two pair to beat" or a "full house to top." I held my own and maybe was slightly ahead when the key-wind clock on the backbar showed it was closing in on eleven o'clock. On the next roll, Hardin cried, "Four sixes to beat."

The moment he said that the doors flung open and Old Selman burst inside, gun drawn and pointed at me. "Now you die, Lomax!" he screamed, as Hardin spun around to get out of the way. I lifted my derringer hand toward Selman, just as Brown dove to the floor, knocking the weapon from my grip.

The sons of bitches had set me up to die!

CHAPTER ELEVEN

Staring death in the single eye of Old Selman's Colt, I clambered atop the bar, scattering dice and wagers, as I screened myself behind Hardin until I could roll off the opposite side of the counter where the barkeep had thrown himself on the floor. Just as I scrambled around Hardin, Selman fired, the gunshot reverberating around the room while patrons dove for cover, knocking over tables and chairs. Through the fog of gunpowder, I glimpsed Hardin toppling over in front of the counter toward the door as I rolled off the back side, landing on the bartender, who grunted. My left palm throbbed from a fiery pain as I shoved myself from the barkeep and yanked my Colt to defend myself.

I scurried on my hands and knees toward the opposite end of the bar where I might return fire, but every time my left hand hit the sawdust floor it sent an electric jolt of pain up my arm and left a bloody palm print on the wooden planks.

Another gunshot exploded in the room, though I was uncertain who fired it. More gun smoke clouded the air. A third and a fourth pistol retort echoed across the saloon, sending more of death's acrid fog over the counter. I pushed myself to my knees and prepared to stand and return fire at Selman, but in the brief moment of silence, as I took a deep breath of acrid smoke and courage, I heard the saloon doors slam open and bang against the walls, the clop of boots on the sawdust floor, then a winded but familiar voice.

"Don't shoot anymore," cried Junior. "He's already dead."

At the sound of retreating boots on the wooden floor, I pushed myself to my feet, ready to fire at my attackers, but I saw their retreating backs only for an instant until the outside darkness enveloped them.

The haze in the room distorted my view as men arose and dusted their clothes. Confirming that none of the men were Hardin, I shoved my revolver back in its holster as Frank Patterson got up at the other end of the bar. He boosted himself up enough to lean over the counter and inspect the floor across from him. The bartender shook his head and slid back down to his feet.

"Hardin's dead," Patterson announced, drawing both gasps and cheers from the Acme patrons, most of them too cowardly to approach him when he played Klondike but now gloating over his corpse sprawled on the floor, the sawdust soaking up the blood of the meanest man and the worst lawyer ever to set foot in Texas.

Patterson turned to me. "Did Selman say he aimed to kill you, Lomax?"

"Can't say for sure." I shrugged, though I knew he had.

"Your hand," the bartender said, pointing at my left side.

The excitement of the shooting had dulled my senses until Patterson reminded me of my injury. I lifted my wounded limb, sticky with a trickle of blood. At first, I thought I had been hit, by a bullet, but I twisted my bloody palm, held it against the light, and looked for a hole. Finding none, I inspected it for a graze and spotted shards of glass embedded in my flesh. When I had climbed atop the counter to screen myself behind Hardin, I had crushed a shot glass beneath my palm. I counted five shards of glass poking from my hand. Using my right fingers, I plucked all the glass I spotted, then Patterson brought over a wet towel to wash my wound. When it was clean, the bartender gave me a rag to wrap my hand.

Next, I stepped around the bar and wedged my way through the spectators, so I could see for myself that

Hardin was dead. The scowl etched in his face showed a contempt for humanity, nothing different in his demeanor other than the bullet hole between his left eyebrow and eye. Best I could tell, he had also been plugged in the chest and the left arm. The tip of his left little finger had been clipped as well.

I'd seen enough of the corpse, so I turned to look for my derringer on the floor, but I couldn't find it among the men standing around the late John Wesley Hardin. As lawmen arrived, I decided to return to my room as I was in no mood to answer questions. I checked the bar top for the few dollars I had in the game, but like my derringer, they were gone, either scattered about the room or taken by someone during the excitement.

I worked my way through the crowd growing in number and noise as the murmuring picked up and the lawmen began shouting for witnesses to come forward. The policemen called for them to identify themselves. Frank Patterson admitted he'd seen most of the action, then climbed on the bar and stood up, identifying other onlookers he knew, including me as I neared the side door on Utah Street.

"There's H.H. Lomax," the bartender called, pointing at me. "He was playing Klondike with Hardin when he was shot, just like Henry Brown."

Immediately, a policeman stepped to me and grabbed my arm. "Where are you going?" he demanded.

"To my doctor," I replied, raising my left hand so the lawman could see my bloody bandage.

"You'll need to testify at the inquiry. Where can we find you?"

"Room Number One, Herndon House."

The officer nodded and let me go. "We'll be in touch with you."

Just trying to get out of the Acme, I was going upstream as more curious fellows and even a couple of boys pushed their way inside to see the circus. When I squeezed outside, men were still running toward the saloon, some shouting, "Wes Hardin's been shot" or "Hardin's dead." I scurried to the boarding house and climbed the stairs, finding my landlady's office door wide open. She sat in her rocker, sewing on a dress until she looked up. Annie flung the cloth to the floor and jumped up, running to my side, and throwing her arms around me.

"You're safe," she cried. "My prayers have been answered." She pushed herself away and smiled until she spotted the red-stained bandage on my hand. "You're hurt."

"A broken glass cut me, that's all."

Annie pointed me down the hall. "Go to your room. I'll come tend your wound. There's been a lot of commotion on the street for the last half hour, more than I ever recall."

"Hardin's dead," I told her.

Her hand flew to her mouth, then fell away as a smile worked its way across her lips. "My prayers really have been answered." Annie laughed. "Now, we can all sleep at night."

I turned and marched from her doorway down the hall to my room. After taking off my weapons, I returned the bed and the dresser to their original locations, pulled off my boots, and fell on my mattress, wondering how Hardin's killing would turn out in court. Annie knocked shortly and entered the unlocked door, leaving it open as usual. She carried a box of rolled cotton, some safety pins, a pair of tweezers, a clean towel, and a bottle of whiskey, which shocked me.

"Taking up drinking, have you?" I nodded at the amber bottle.

"It was my former husband's. It's good for cleaning wounds."

"And forgetting them," I replied.

Annie pointed to the table. "My doctoring will work better over there." After putting her supplies on the tabletop, she pulled out a chair for me. I got up and joined her, taking my place at the table to her right. She sat down beside me, took my hand, and turned it palm up, then removed the rag bandage. My hand seeped blood.

"Did you remove all the glass?"

"I don't know. It's still throbbing."

132

Annie tore tufts of fiber from the roll, doused them with whiskey, then gently rubbed the cotton balls over my sticky red palm. On her third swipe, pain shot through my hand and arm like I had been branded with a red-hot poker. I screamed and caught a profanity on my tongue before it slipped into the open and embarrassed me and her.

"No, you didn't get it all." Annie dropped the cotton, picked up her tweezers, lifted my hand closer to her face, and looked for the glass fragment. "Tell me what happened. It'll keep your mind off this."

I told the story as I recalled it with Old Selman coming in, calling my name, and firing. Scrambling over the bar behind Hardin had cut my hand but likely saved my life. "I came out better than Hardin did, but don't you repeat any of this to anyone. When I testify at the inquiry, I intend to say whatever'll serve me best." I grimaced as Annie extracted another sliver of glass.

"Maybe Selman intended to kill Hardin all along. Wasn't there bad blood between them after Junior arrested Beulah?"

"Could've been, but Selman visited Hardin in his room this afternoon. I suspect they planned it to ambush me, but Old Selman hit Hardin by accident when I jumped behind him."

"At least you won't have to worry about Hardin anymore."

"Yeah, but the Selman's remain, and they both wear badges."

Annie nodded. "I'll bring you meals and newspapers, so you can remain in your room until everything sorts itself out." She patiently tended my wound, finding three more pieces of glass before dousing my palm with whiskey, which burned like lava. Then she layered clean cotton over my wound and tied the towel around it. "You'll survive, but you'll stay hidden in your room until I say different."

"Yes, ma'am, but in the morning don't wake me up before noon," I replied as she gathered her supplies to leave. I accompanied her to the door, locked it behind her, then yanked off my clothes and collapsed in bed. My last thought before sinking into a deep sleep was that I had survived this day while Wes Hardin had not. However, the Selman's endured, though my slumber did not.

While I had planned to sleep until noon, a pounding on the door awakened me.

"Go away," I cried, grabbing a pillow, and covering my head.

"It's Andy, we need to talk."

Why couldn't my brother wait until later or another day so I could catch up on the sleep I'd missed rooming across the hall from Hardin and Beulah? Then I realized it had to be important for the Texas Ranger to call. "Just a minute," I grumbled, throwing my pillow aside and pushing myself up from the soft mattress. I stumbled across the room, unlocked the door, and let my brother enter.

"You're okay, aren't you, Henry?" He strode in and shut the entrance, his jaw tight and lips drawn as he studied me.

I lifted my bandaged hand. "Cut my palm, but nothing more serious than that."

Andy strode to the table, grabbed a chair, turned the back to face me, straddled it, and placed his arms on the back rest, studying me closely. "What do you know about the Hardin killing at the Acme?"

Retreating to the bed, I sat on the mattress and faced my brother. "I was there last night."

The tension in Andy's face softened. "What happened?"

I leveled with my brother, telling him what I remembered.

"You know they'll call you to testify at the inquiry, don't you?"

I nodded.

"There's rumors among the bad breed that Selman intended to kill you, not Hardin."

"A definite possibility," I admitted, then explained how Selman wanted me dead so I wouldn't reveal his relations with Beulah and jeopardize money the constable said Hardin owed him. "Hardin had a manuscript of his life that he insisted I read, but I gave it to Beulah, which angered him. Besides that, Hardin suspected I had some money. With me out of the way, I figure he would've ransacked my room looking for the cash."

"You're still in danger, Henry. What I hear is the constable has put out to the police that you are to be arrested as soon as they can find an excuse. They'll try to get you on a weapons charge, put you in jail and beat you up."

"My landlady's agreed to provide me meals in my room until all this blows over."

"The only way it'll blow over in their minds is with you dead and buried. Don't talk to anybody about what you saw until the inquiry is over." Andy laughed. "If he intended to kill you, Henry, I suspect the story will change when the inquiry starts. Imagine him saying he intended to shoot you but hit Hardin instead. He'd be a laughing-stock from one end of the Rio Grande to the other. The way I figure it, Selman will claim Hardin threatened him or his son and he had to kill him in self-defense, though Hardin never pulled a gun in the encounter. That aside, Henry, you can't leave here, especially if you're carrying a weapon. They'll probably watch your building until you come out. Then they'll arrest you."

"How am I going to get around this and defend myself?"

"I've got to work out something so you can legally carry a gun. Leave that up to me, Henry." Andy stood up and replaced the chair, then laughed. "You remember our friend the Gringo Bandito? Well, Rip Enreed of the *Times* came a calling at Ysleta, wanting to know what I knew about him."

"What did you tell him?"

"Just that he was elusive, almost ghost-like, and Judge Bean was the only lawman to ever best him. Rip's eyes widened like washtubs when I told him that."

We both laughed as Andy let himself out.

"Thanks, Andy."

"Stay off the streets, Henry, and keep an eye out for trouble."

Over the following days, Annie became my link with the outside, feeding me and providing me all the local newspapers and whatever gossip came her way. I learned they left Hardin's body on the Acme floor for over four hours that Monday night into Tuesday. Early on Tuesday the fellows at Starr Undertakers claimed the body, did an autopsy, embalmed him, and put him out for display. Hundreds passed by his coffin and nary a one shed a tear. The *Times* reported one lawman as saying, "When I read this morning that Hardin was dead, I drew a deep breath of relief. Every day I feared I would be called into some saloon to arrest Hardin and run the risk of being killed. I never felt better when I saw him dead, and I do not think Hardin ever looked better." In describing the journey of Hardin's hearse to Concordia Cemetery, the *Herald* observed that Constable Selman, "whose six-shooter balanced Hardin's accounts, stood calmly on the street corner and watched the procession file by." Methodist minister C.J. Oxley conducted the graveside service for the wayward son of a Methodist minister. Like many others, I believed Hardin's grave was the first step on his way to hell. The *Times* summed up Hardin's brief stay in Hell Paso, noting "Hardin met the same fate as all bad men who come to El Paso looking for a fight." I disagreed. The Selman's, among other scofflaws, still roamed the city at will.

The day of Hardin's burial, the courts resolved their jurisdiction issues and began the inquiry that Thursday, the same day the court sent men to Hardin's room to catalog the deceased's possessions. Annie watched the process to make certain no boarding house items were included and made a list, which she shared with me. In addition to the two guns and the $94.85 in cash they found on him at the Acme, he had three law books, a dictionary, a copy of *The Rise and Fall of the Confederacy*: a dozen tintypes, two gold rings, an Elgin watch with gold chain, a trunk, a leather valise, clothing, two additional revolvers and, oddly, a pair of opera glasses. Since Hardin had made it known he was writing his life story, the officials sought the manuscript. Annie brought them to me, and I told them the 165 pages were in Beulah Morose's possession, as Hardin had told me she had half interest in the papers for all the work she had put in. As for Beulah, she was in Phoenix when she heard the news, and she telegraphed El Paso authorities that she hoped to return to El Paso and settle his affairs.

Before the court officials left the boarding house, they served me with a subpoena to appear before the hearing the next day. I told them I wasn't sure I could make it as I had been warned my life was in danger. They replied either show up or go to jail, which I thought would play into the hands of the Selman's. I would have to attend after all.

Things turned worse after the court staff left when Rip Enreed arrived at my door, insisting that he needed to interview me about the events behind Hardin's killing. I told him to attend the hearing if he wanted to know what I had to say.

"Just don't talk to any other newspaper or I'll skewer you in print," he warned. After the threat, he asked me if he could interview Annie Williams.

"Ask her," I told him.

"I did, but she said I should get your permission first."

"See me after the hearing," I replied, "but it'll be unlikely if you don't agree to take on Judge Roy Bean's biography."

"A garrulous old fool," he said.

"An old fool that holds the key to you ever getting information from me or Annie. Now get out of my room."

Enreed skulked away in disbelief that I had turned down an offer to be quoted in El Paso's premier newspaper, or as the rag itself proclaimed "the best, brightest and newsiest paper in the Southwest."

When I wasn't fending off officials, newspapermen, and the curious wanting to know my take on the late John Wesley Hardin, I spent my time sitting at the table by the window, watching the foot, horse, wagon, and bicycle traffic pass by. Like Andy had predicted, there always seemed to be a policeman across the street watching my building, likely waiting for me to leave. I fretted about making the trip to the courthouse the next day, but that night, Andy sent a note that he would accompany me to the hearing. After getting his message, I felt like I might somehow survive because I doubted any sane man wanted to cross my Texas Ranger brother. Of course, there were still a lot of loco men in El Paso.

Sure enough, Andy Lomax knocked on my door at eight-thirty the next morning after Annie had brought me breakfast and a newspaper. Besides his sidearm, Andy carried a Winchester. After I showed him I was unarmed from head to toe, we left the room and building, me walking in the open air for the first time since I had returned from the Acme shooting. The policeman on the opposite side of the street saw me and tailed us all the way to the courthouse. While several folks looked and pointed at me, gossiping that I had something to do with Hardin's death, what stuck in my mind the most about that walk was the seven cats, four dogs, and two pig carcasses that littered the streets. Between the wagons, horses, and careening bicycles, the little creatures didn't stand a chance.

"Henry, the safest thing for you to say is that you witnessed nothing."

"That's the truth," I nodded. "I never saw a shot fired, just heard them all and the commotion all around me."

"Say that and nothing else. The less you say, the better."

Reaching the courthouse, Andy led me up the stairs to a second-floor courtroom filled with lawyers, witnesses, newspapermen, spectators, a few women of questionable repute, and several lawmen with even more doubtful reputations, including the Selman's. Precisely at nine o'clock, the judge gaveled the courtroom to order, and everyone settled in for the show. I was the second witness called, forty minutes after the session began.

The prosecutor was a lanky man with a full gray beard and a habit of tugging on his lapels when he thought he was making a point in favor of charging the constable with murder. His counterpart wore reading glasses, peering over the wire rims whenever he questioned my predecessor. Once I was sworn in, I sat down in the witness chair and awaited the assault.

After getting the preliminaries like my name and address out of the way, the prosecutor started grilling me about the night four days ago when John Wesley Hardin died. I explained I had been playing counter Klondike with Hardin for more than three hours when Constable John Selman came in, gun drawn.

"Did he say anything?"

"He made a threat, but as soon as I spotted him, I tried to get out of the way."

"What happened then?"

"I climbed atop the bar and scrambled over to the other side."

"Did you see Constable Selman fire his guns?"

"All I saw was the sawdust floor and the bartender who broke my fall."

"But you know Constable Selman must've fired the shots."

I glanced from the prosecutor to Selman, sitting by his lawyer across from me. He wore a curious snarl as if worried about what I might say.

"I only know what I saw, and I didn't see any shots fired, just heard four of five."

"Did you see anyone else with a pistol?"

"I wasn't looking," I said, although I remembered pulling my own sidearm.

The prosecutor tried but extracted nothing of value from me. Then the defense attorney stood up and asked if I knew the deceased and the accused.

"Knew them both, cared for neither," I replied, drawing a laugh from the crowd that mostly shared my sentiment.

"Then you can't confirm who shot John Wesley Hardin."

"That's correct."

Selman's lawyer turned to the judge. "Your Honor, I have no further questions as I have proven my point," he said, staring over his wire-rim glasses at the judge.

"You may step down, Mr. Lomax," the judge said.

Just like that, my testimony ended. I moved from the

witness chair to Andy, who stood up and made certain everyone saw the Winchester he was carrying. Wordlessly, we both walked out of the courtroom, down the stairs, and onto the street.

"You handled it fine, Henry. I don't think you created any new problems. Besides that, I'm glad folks saw us together. That should let them know you're not to be messed with."

"Can I walk the streets again?"

"Nope. Look behind you."

I twisted about and noted the same policeman that had tailed me from the boarding house following us down the street.

"Until they call in the hounds or you can carry a gun, you're still not safe."

"This could go on for a long spell."

"Give me until Monday, Henry. I'm working on something."

"What's that?"

"I can't say for certain right now, but have you ever thought of wearing a badge, enforcing the rules, and cleaning up the streets of El Paso?"

"No," I admitted.

"Give me until Monday afternoon. By then I may be able to work something out."

Like a schoolboy before Christmas, I just couldn't wait. I had an inkling how Andy would favor me. I was destined to become a Texas Ranger.

CHAPTER TWELVE

Anxious as I was for Monday to arrive, time dragged by, and Rip Enreed returned late that afternoon to pester me for an interview. "I said in the hearing everything I intend to say," I advised him at my door.

"What about talking with Annie Williams about being Hardin's landlady?"

"Not until you agree to visit Judge Roy Bean."

Enreed shuffled his feet and looked down at his scuffed shoes, then lifted his head and nodded. "I'll interview him, but only on the Gringo Bandito. If we get along, I'll consider writing the book."

That was the best I could hope for at the moment, so I agreed, then escorted him down to Annie's office, rapping on the door and telling her I was fine with her talking to the reporter. She invited him inside, leaving the entry open as usual. I rushed to my room, found my stationery and pencil, then wrote out a quick note to Bean, advising him Rip Enreed would contact him for an interview on the Gringo Bandito. If the reporter got along with Bean, he might consider writing the judge's life story. I suggested Bean make the imaginary outlaw into the most dangerous white man he had ever seen in Texas and think up some exploits worthy of a dime novel character. Next, I advised the judge that his money was holding out as I had limited expenses on his behalf. I told him to give Bruno my regards and Sam my disdain. Finishing the letter, I sealed it up and sat by the window, watching the traffic pass by on Overland until Annie came to my room to report on the Enreed interview.

"He was cordial," she said, "and it went well as it should when you tell the truth."

"Wait until you see it in print," I advised her, "then decide how it went."

She nodded, telling me the meeting had delayed her getting my supper, but that she would head right out and buy me a meal and the afternoon papers.

I handed her the Bean letter. "Would you post this for me while you're out? And this is rent day, so let me pay you and reimburse you for all the meals you've brought me."

"It was worth it to get rid of Hardin. Now that they've removed his belongings, I can clean up his room and lease it out."

Tipping the syrup tin on the table, I slipped my hand beneath it and extracted the stack of bills I had hidden there. I extracted two tens and a five and handed them to her. "The five covers my weekly charge with a little extra. One ten is to cover the meals you've been buying or cooking and the other is to treat yourself."

Annie took the five but hesitated to accept the other two bills. I took her hand and pressed the remaining money in her palm. She smiled. "Thank you, though you didn't have to do that."

"And you didn't have to do all you've done for me this past week, cooking or fetching my meals, buying me newspapers, even talking to Rip Enreed."

"I just wanna see you get out of this mess, so you can live a normal life."

After looking at the open door to make sure no one was eavesdropping, I said, "I think that's about to happen, Annie. I'll let you in on a secret. I suspect Andy is working on getting me an appointment as a Texas Ranger. He talked today about securing me a badge."

Annie's lips smiled, but her eyes did not. "That could be even more dangerous."

"At least I could carry a gun to defend myself."

"And you might have to, even more than now."

"Everything carries a cost."

Wanting to change the subject, she looked at my left hand. "I see you've removed the bandage. How's your palm?"

"Still a little tender but getting better."

This time Annie smiled with her lips and her eyes. She tucked the money in her pocket and lifted my letter to Bean. "It's late. I best run to the post office before it closes and then purchase your supper."

"Buy a fine meal for us both. We can sit by the window here and watch the street."

Annie scurried away on her errands while I sat back down at my table, observing the traffic and the policeman stationed on the corner to spy on me. When he looked my way, I stuck my hand out and waved. The lawman, obviously bored, responded with an obscene gesture. I refrained from returning the signal as I figured El Paso had some ordinance prohibiting such displays of friendship and affection, or at least forbidding the regular citizen from doing it, as the law officers and their elected bosses got away with anything.

An hour later, Annie returned smiling like she'd found a twenty-dollar gold piece and carrying a large market basket in her right hand and my afternoon newspapers under the left. She dropped the newspapers on the bed and came to the table. "Got to the post office before it closed, so your letter's on the way. And I splurged and got me a basket for seventy-five cents and two fiber lunch boxes, it's the latest thing for fifty-two cents apiece. It'll make bringing you meals much easier." She opened her basket and pulled out two brown fiber containers, placing one by me and the other in front of the empty chair. I lifted the lid on mine and pulled out a tin of ham hocks, boiled cabbage, and turnips as she lifted a large square of cornbread wrapped in a towel, then placed it between our meals. Annie took my tin cup from the table and another one from her basket and filled them from the pitcher on the washstand. Once she sat the drinks down, she took her seat. After she blessed the meal, we started eating. Not a fan of turnips, I ate them anyway so not to offend

143

the woman who had been so nice to me. As much as the food, save for the turnips, we enjoyed the tranquility of a hallway without Hardin and the distractions that followed him. The meal was filling, and I saved a slab of my cornbread so I could smother it in syrup for breakfast. Annie surprised me by pulling out two more cloth-covered dishes and revealing a slice of cherry pie for each of us. The sweetness was intoxicating, as Annie seldom brought dessert. When we finished, we visited a spell, then Annie cleared the table and went to her room, while I reclined on the bed and read the afternoon papers.

Rip Enreed's *El Paso Times* account of the hearing infuriated me, saying "a blind man would have seen more of the shooting than Henry Lomax, who claimed to have been standing at the bar with the deceased, but vaulted behind the counter at the first sign of trouble and cowered out of sight with the difficulties ongoing." The *Herald, Democrat,* and *Tribune* each offered a more accurate description of my testimony. All said a decision whether to have Constable Selman stand for trial would come early the next week.

Those papers and the weekend editions that Annie brought sustained me through an anxious time, not fearing for my future but expecting my appointment as a Texas Ranger and maybe even throwing my loop around the Selmans and jailing them. Annie's interview with Enreed appeared in the paper on Saturday. "It's not exactly right, but it's not exactly wrong, either," she assessed after reading the piece three times.

"You came out better than I and most others do that deal with newspapermen. Count your blessings," I said.

"I want nothing more to do with him," she replied.

"Neither do I, but I must convince him to write Judge Bean's life story so I can get it published."

"Do you owe the judge a book? Why are you working so hard for him?"

I'd never really thought about it. I could've left Langtry with his money, and he'd never caught up with me. "I saw a lot of me in him."

"Did he save you from the Gringo Bandito?"

"The meanest living man in Texas, now that Hardin's passed."

"So, I'm talking to the meanest man alive in Texas right now, right?"

I cocked my head at her and gave her as blank an expression as I could. "What? What are you talking about?"

"You're the Gringo Bandito."

"How'd you find out?"

"I knew all along. Your story didn't make sense. That and the Testament. Too much of a coincidence for a Gringo lookalike to wind up with it."

"Why didn't you tell me before now or turn me into the law?"

"I thought if you were, you might keep John Wesley Hardin at bay. If you weren't, it was fun to see how you weaseled your way around things."

"I have to admit, you've caught the Gringo Bandito, something no living man besides Judge Roy Bean has ever done or ever will, except perhaps Rip Enreed. He believes the Bandito exists. If you get a chance and can stand it, tell Enreed you saw the Gringo Bandito caged in Langtry, and he was the meanest man you ever laid eyes on, sending shudders down your spine at the mere glimpse of him. That may help Enreed interview the judge and Bean get his biography published."

Annie clucked her tongue. "You are a devious one, H.H. Lomax."

"Does that mean you won't play along?"

She laughed, then played coy. "We'll see!" She left me to my newspapers and returned to her office.

For most of the weekend, I read the papers, everything front to back, including all the ads and the personal notices. The big story in Texas and likely the rest of the nation remained the Corbett-Fitzsimmons prizefight and if they would ever get in the ring together. Promoter Dan Stuart had set the last day of October as the date of the encounter. He selected Dallas as the site of the fisticuffs, sending the state into a tizzy. The businessmen and the sporting crowd of Dallas welcomed the match for the money it would bring into the community. The

Baptists and other fine citizens in north Texas opposed it for the vice it would import to town. Stuart, though, envisioned more than a single fight, proposing a "Fistic Carnival," as he called it, with a week of activities and lesser fights culminating in the championship heavy-weight bout. More money and fun for everyone argued the proponents. More vice and misery for all countered the opponents.

The Texas attorney general, a fellow named Martin Crane, informed Dallas that the state's anti-riot laws could stop the title match. Under the law, Crane told the press that state and local authorities could use force—including killing—to suppress the fight, which was basically an unlawful riot by another name. Governor Culberson echoed Crane, leaving me to scratch my head at how politicians thought. Here the government was willing to murder people to stop two grown men on their own volition from punching each other with gloves on their fists, but that was Texans for you, long on bravado but short on brains. This was the same state where the Selmans—two so-called Texas lawmen—were trying to destroy me, while the governor and all the preachers in the state were worried about two outsiders, one a foreigner, simply wanting to punch each other around. When were the preachers, the governor, or the attorney general coming to my aid? If I hadn't had a Texas Ranger for a brother, I'd likely have been killed already and buried in Concordia Cemetery, where I would have roomed near Hardin for eternity. Thanks to Andy, though, once I got my badge I would have the cover of the law on my side as well, and perhaps the opportunity to plug a few troublemakers for free if they asked me to put down a riot. I was looking forward to Monday when I could throw my weight around behind the power of a Texas Ranger badge.

When the day finally came, I fretted the morning away, visiting with Annie at lunch, but mostly watching the traffic on Overland and spotting the officer that was spying on me for the Selmans. To amuse myself, I counted passing horsemen and wagons, then pedestrians

146

and even bicyclists, some rolling by on those big-wheeled ones, but most on those newer models with wheels equal in size. I also spotted two dead dogs in the road and counted how many bicyclists ran over the carcasses. Of the thirty-seven bicycles I counted, eleven ran over one of the dead dogs, three tumbling to the street, three more barely staying astride their conveyance and the other five riding off as if they ran over animal carcasses every day.

Toward four o'clock, I saw Andy striding down the far side of Overland toward the Herndon House. He had an easy, confident gait. Perhaps that swagger came from wearing a Texas Ranger badge on his chest. I figured I would soon know the feeling once he pinned a silver star on my chest. Standing up from the table, I shoved my shirttail in my pants so I would look the part of Texas's newest ranger with a gleaming new badge pinned to my shirt.

I checked out the window and saw my brother confronting the policeman assigned to watch my boarding house. Andy pulled something out of his pants pocket and showed it to the lawman, who shook his head, then shrugged and walked away. When my brother slipped the item back in his pocket, I caught the glint of metal and knew it was the Texas Ranger badge that would soon glisten on my chest.

Andy turned from the corner, and as he crossed Overland, the bicycles, wagons, and horsemen moved aside to let him pass so much was the aura of the legendary Texas Rangers. With a ranger badge on my chest, I figured even the Rio Grande would part to let me pass. Maybe Andy and I would be the first brothers sworn in as Rangers. As he disappeared beneath the wooden awning over my walk, I stepped to the washstand, looked at myself in the mirror, cocked my head, and stuck out my chin to prove that I had the look of a lawman who could handle anything. I swelled with so much pride that I thought I might pop the buttons on my shirt. For an instant, I considered opening the door to await my destiny but decided I shouldn't appear too eager to assume the awesome responsibilities that would soon be placed upon

147

my shoulders. It amazed me to think that the fellow who only weeks earlier had been the Gringo Bandito was about to become a Texas Ranger.

Hearing the footfall of Andy's boots in the hallway, I checked my lawman gaze in the mirror a final time and turned to greet and accept my destiny. My brother rapped on the door. "Henry, it's Andy."

I counted to ten and then walked across the floor, opening the door, and greeting my brother warmly. "Glad to see you, Andy. I've been looking forward to your company and getting out of this room."

Andy took off his hat and stepped in. "That shouldn't be a problem much longer," he answered as I closed the door. He pointed to the table. "How about us taking a seat?"

I'd rather have stood to accept my Ranger appointment as that seemed more formal, but maybe the Rangers had their own procedure for swearing in new lawmen. As I sat down, Andy reached into his pocket and pulled out a badge, placing it face down on the table by my tin of Wes-Tex Syrup. Shaped like a shield rather than that silver ring surrounding a five-pointed star I was expecting, the badge exuded authority and power. Perhaps, I thought, Andy had been promoted to a higher rank and once he donned that badge, I would receive his Ranger medallion, starting a family tradition. Perhaps one day we would even have dime novels written about us.

"Before we get to the business at hand, Henry, you should know that the inquiry into Hardin's death should end tomorrow. It's certain that Selman will stand trial, likely in the spring, for the killing."

"Old Selman killed him. The whole town knows that."

Andy nodded. "That's true. Near everybody was afraid of Hardin, so most were glad to see him die, even if it was murder."

"So, he won't be convicted. Is that what you're saying, Andy?"

"Maybe, maybe not. Selman won't leave things to chance. Since you were one of the witnesses, even if you didn't see anything, he might think it safer to have someone ambush you before your testimony that might send him to prison."

Knowing I had to adopt the attitude of a Texas Ranger, I shook my head. "That doesn't scare me. I've faced tougher men with bigger reputations than this crippled old constable," I answered as the names of Billy the Kid, Wyatt Earp, Jesse, and Frank James, Wild Bill Hickok, Doc Holliday, Johnny Ringo, Bat Masterson, Calamity Jane, and even Susan B. Anthony flashed through my mind, but I didn't share those experiences with Andy, as I didn't want to come off as bragging. After all, a Texas Ranger let his actions, not his words, talk for him. My brave words failed to impress my brother.

"As we've discussed," Andy continued, "there are state laws and local ordinances in Texas prohibiting the carrying of weapons. I needed to find a way so you could legally carry a weapon to defend yourself."

Here it came, I thought, my appointment to the Texas Rangers. "I'm obliged to you, Andy. I never dreamed of wearing a badge."

"Any time you wear a badge, you are swearing to do your job and protect the greater good. Do you feel up to that responsibility?"

"Definitely, Andy. I will do everything in my power to uphold the law and further the reputation of the Texas Rangers."

Andy flinched, then stared at me with cocked head and mouth agape. "Texas Rangers?"

I pointed to the badge.

He shook his head from side to side. "You're not Texas Ranger material, Henry."

"But what about the badge?" I poked my finger at it again.

Andy picked it up and dropped it facedown, in my still tender left palm. I grabbed it and turned it over, quickly seeing that it was an El Paso city badge with the town's name emblazoned across the center of the medallion. Looking more closely at the embossed bronze letters, I read OFFICE OF SCAVENGER & IMPOUND-KEEPER atop the city name and OFFICER beneath the hell hole's name. "What's a scavenger office, Andy?"

"It controls dogs and other animals—"

"What?" I cried.

"—impounding loose dogs, killing mean and rabid ones, and collecting dead animals from the streets and disposing of them."

"Are you telling me I'm a dogcatcher?"

Grimacing, Andy nodded. "That's about the size of it. If you want to leave this room with a chance of defending yourself and surviving in El Paso, you better take the job. Otherwise, you best get out of town quick."

Mulling over my options, I tossed the badge from hand to hand. Visions of dime novels evaporated in my mind as quickly as cool on a typical El Paso day. They didn't write dime novels about dogcatchers.

"It was the best I could do for you, Henry. You need to let me know *now*. The scavenger officer is staying late at the impound so I can bring you by and complete the arrangement."

"But why?"

"He owed me a favor. Besides that, you haven't worked since you've been in town. One day you'll run out of money. A job'll bring in cash. Main thing, though, is you can carry all the weapons you need, and the law can't stop you."

Still, I hesitated to accept the appointment. Perhaps it was best if I just left El Paso for good, but I felt a strange allegiance to Judge Roy Bean and seeing about getting his life story in print. Too, I'd taken a liking to my landlady, the first decent woman I'd spent much time with since a forlorn experience with another Texas woman prior to my first cattle drive to Abilene in the years following the war. Finally, I nodded. "Okay, Andy, if that's what you think best."

"Leaving El Paso's the safest, but this is your second-best option. Let's go meet your new boss." Andy arose from his chair.

I stood up and slid the badge into my pants pocket, then grabbed my hat.

"Take a gun as well," Andy said.

Grabbing the five-shot Smith & Wesson, I followed him into the hall and down the stairs and out the front door, running into Annie Williams as we exited.

I held the door for her as she carried her new market basket on her arm. When she passed, she whispered, "Did you get a badge?"

Not having time to explain, I nodded.

Annie smiled. "I'm so happy."

My brother and I went west on Overland, walked to the end of the block, and turned south on Utah, then walked twelve blocks toward the Rio Grande, where the impound was situated a block from the city dump. As we neared the river, I saw a railroad trestle and then a pair of wooden bridges on either side of the railway structure for horse and pedestrian traffic. Andy pointed to the rail bridge. "That's where Martin Morose crossed into El Paso." He aimed his finger at the adjacent mounds of refuse. "Morose was murdered near the dump."

"Poor Beulah," I replied.

Andy nodded. "Word is she's returning to El Paso from Arizona to handle Hardin's affairs."

"How much grief can one woman take?"

After a moment of strained silence, we both snickered.

Approaching the impound, I saw a modest weather-beaten office, its sign faded by the scorching El Paso sun. On one side of the building stood one communal and two dozen individual chicken wire cages where mutts of all colors, sizes, and parentage protested their incarceration with barks and wails. On the opposite side of the building was a corral holding four mules and beyond the pen rested a pair of freight wagons.

Reaching the office, Andy knocked, then led me inside, where a slender fellow with a mustache looked up from his desk and greeted my brother.

"So, he accepted the job, did he?"

"Henry," said my brother, "meet Aaron Schloss, El Paso city scavenger and your new boss."

Schloss stood up and grabbed my hand across his desk and pumped it until I figured it might drop off. "Glad to have you joining me, Henry. This isn't glamorous work, but it's gotta be done, removing carcasses from the street."

"Sure thing, Aaron," I replied, "but I figure I can handle dog, cat, goat, and pig carcasses—"

"Don't forget birds," he interjected.

"—but what about mules and horses, big animals?"

"I'll be there to help you, Henry. You can count on it."

Throughout our thirty-minute conversation, Schloss remained enthusiastic, explaining how they fed the animals, disposed of carcasses, and kept the streets clean of animals.

"Does that include scat?"

"No," he replied. "The street office handles that." My new boss then gave me a copy of the city ordinance establishing the office and delineating its duties. "Read that tonight and report here in the morning, say seven o'clock, and we'll work out a schedule." Next, he gave me a gray frock coat with double buttons up the front. He pointed to the holes in the fabric where I could pin my badge. "Always wear your coat and badge on duty." He ended our meeting by giving me and Andy a tour of his empire. Once he finished, Andy thanked him for taking me on, and we went our separate ways, Schloss back to his desk, Andy to the street car that would take him back to Ysleta, and me back to the Herndon House.

I hoped to slip by Annie's office, but she had left the door open to catch me. She came out and threw her arms around me.

"First time I ever hugged a Texas Ranger," she said.

"I'm not a ranger."

"No?"

"A dogcatcher," I replied.

CHAPTER THIRTEEN

After reading the ordinance that night, I learned that the city scavenger's duties not only included disposing of dead animals *and* street droppings but also removing privy waste when requested by a resident or business owner. My new boss had lied to me. The city permitted privy work only between nine o'clock in the evening and sunrise the next day with the filth to be removed in closed containers or closely covered wagons. Schloss had said nothing about night work, but I feared I'd be up to my knees in slop every evening and needing a full bath before Annie would let me back in the Herndon House. The city earned fifteen cents for every cubic foot of slop removed from privy vaults and cesspools. I thanked providence that I had learned to swim in Arkansas because I might need the skill in the course of my new job. Hauling away dead dogs at twenty-five cents apiece, cats at twelve-and-a-half cents each, and dead birds a nickel a fowl seemed plush compared to dealing with muck and droppings. Considering the new job my brother had lined up for me, I questioned if Andy was truly my friend.

Despite the stinking work ahead of me, I reported for duty the next morning at seven o'clock, wearing my badge and gray frock coat over my holster and Colt.45. I didn't figure I'd need my revolver against the Selmans because once they saw me in my uniform they would die laughing. I felt like the circus band director without musicians, or worse yet, the trained monkey with an organ grinder. But at least I wore a badge and could carry a gun within the law as established by the great state of Texas and adapted by the awful city of El Paso. As I approached the impound afoot, I saw Schloss already hitching up the mule team.

The dogs alerted my boss of my approach with their barks, growls, and howls. I greeted my new boss with all the enthusiasm of a politician meeting a voter too poor to offer a bribe.

Schloss laughed. "Your frown tells me you read the ordinance."

Nodding, I crossed my arms over my frock coat and badge, then admitted, "I didn't know I'd be wallowing around in the muck of every outhouse in town."

"Don't jump to conclusions, Henry. You're lucky to have a Texas Ranger for a brother, especially one that I owe a favor."

"How's that?"

"He shot an irate dog owner before he could shoot me. Long story, but your brother saved my life."

"What's the favor?"

"Andy asked me to hire you for street duty, not privy work. I obliged. Now I did fib to you yesterday. I will require you to shovel up droppings, but I figured that wouldn't be so revolting once you read the ordinance and realized what you could be doing."

"What about nightwork?"

Schloss nodded. "At times dogs rove in packs around town, a danger to citizens. When we get such reports, we stay out late to kill them. Don't want them biting people and giving them hydrophobia. Rabies is a death sentence and a horrible way to die."

"That's fine as long as there's no muck work."

My boss smiled. "Not for you."

Andy had looked out for me after all. I grinned for the first time since finding out I'd be a dogcatcher rather than a Texas Ranger.

"Feel better about your job?"

"Yes, sir," I answered, looking around the impound. "Where's the equipment for the privy duty?"

Schloss pointed toward the city dump. "We keep the honey wagons on the other side of the dump grounds, so the perfume is sweetened by the mingling aromas of the garbage."

"Is that where you empty the honey pots?"

"On no," Schloss answered. "We dump the muck in waste beds about five miles out of town, so the aroma doesn't diminish El Paso's reputation as the paradise city of the Southwest." Schloss winked. "Eventually the slop dries out and some folks gather it to fertilize their gardens."

"That's why I never cared to farm. Too much manure."

"Same reason, I suppose, you never got into politics."

"Never have, never will. Can't remember the last time I cast a vote. Seems to me nothing changes for the better, no matter who's elected."

"I have to run for election every other year. Eventually, you hack off enough folks that you get voted out, but that's my problem, not yours. What do you say we get to work? I'll show you how it's done."

Schloss told me to inspect the wagon while he finished hitching up the team. About ten feet long, not counting the tongue, the equipment was a flare-sided harvest wagon with a four-foot-wide box and thirty-inch wheels with steel rim and wooden spokes. Wooden partitions separated the box into two lengthwise compartments, the narrow foot-wide one for droppings and the wider one for carcasses. Two cages sat in the broader compartment to haul live animals. The sturdy iron axles were mounted springless to the wagon bed, though the seat rested on twin-leaf springs, providing some comfort to the workers. A grain scoop and hoe were secured to the left sideboard, and a spade and rake clung to the opposite side. I spotted a six-foot pole with a wire loop at the end leaning against the seat and a twenty-foot lariat in the floorboard beneath it.

After he finished hitching the mules, he told me to follow him into the office where he swore me in as an official enforcement officer for the city of El Paso scavenger office. "Now you're official," he said, then motioned for me to take a seat. He explained in more detail my job, collecting dead animals from streets, gutters, and alleys as the priority, then scooping droppings from the principal streets. Any dog that was a threat was to be shot, and any loose dog that was tagged was to be captured, caged and delivered to the impound. Schloss opened his desk and pulled out a small .22-caliber revolver and two boxes of ammunition, explaining I was to use this gun to kill dogs and other little animals, including skunks and cats, that appeared to have gone mad. That was the simple part. Next, he explained the importance of documenting my actions on a log sheet that listed the date, time, and place of every carcass retrieved, animal shot, or step taken in fulfilling my sworn duties.

"What about the scat? Do I log every dropping?"

Grinning, Schloss shook his head. "Not for now, but who knows what the city council or attorney might decide in the future. You know how politicians are. That aside, it's time we start our rounds."

I led Schloss outside, and once he locked the door, we climbed into the wagon, and I started my job with a badge on my chest. We made the rounds of the blocks downtown and those streets leading from the five train depots to the center of El Paso. "We want to keep up appearances as a civilized city," my boss said, "even though we aren't."

"Nowhere near it," I answered.

Whenever we spotted a dead animal, Schloss stopped the wagon, and I jumped out, taking the scoop, and collecting the carcass.

"Always approach it upwind," Schloss suggested.

I would scrape the carcass from the road and toss it in the back of the wagon, then we would move along.

"As for the horse apples and street dumplings, it's an unending fight. I pay special attention around city hall, the courthouse, and the jail. After that, I get what I can. Folks are more accustomed to the droppings than rotting flesh."

Working our way around town and through the traffic of bicycles, horses, and wagons, we headed up San

Antonio Street. As we approached the 400 block of the avenue, Schloss tensed. "I always have trouble on San Antonio. There's a butcher that operates a shop there, the busiest in town, and he hates my guts."

"For taking your business elsewhere?"

"No, for shooting his dog. I believed it rabid. He disagreed and sued me in court. I won, but that didn't settle it. Every day when I or one of my hires drives by he and an employee or two come out and dump four or five buckets of offal in the street for me to remove. The council won't pass an ordinance making that illegal, I suspect because he pays them off. He's got a vindictive streak as wide as a brisket and plenty of money from selling briskets to spend on antagonizing me."

Midway down the block, I saw a butcher shop with customers lined outside the door. Someone must have told them of our approach because shortly four men marched outside, each hauling a pail in both hands. They quickly dumped the offal in a street already stained from past loads of entrails and other inedible remnants of his business. Three of the men traipsed back into the shop, the last one in the door taking the two pails from the fourth, who stood akimbo in his blood-splattered white apron. He was a burly man with a thick mustache, round eyes that matched his gut, and a sneer across puffy lips and cheeks. "What's his name?"

"The butcher? Charlie Barnett, but most people just call him Butch." Schloss angled his wagon across our half of the street to block traffic so a horse, wagon, or bicycle wouldn't run us over while we cleaned up the mess. "I'll help you with this load," Schloss said as he tugged on the reins, set the brake, and tied the lines.

Grabbing his arm, I told him to stay where he was. "Let me handle this." For a moment, I studied Barnett, rocking on his heels with a leer on his face beneath the sign which advertised beef, buffalo, pork, rabbit, fowl, and other fine meats. I jumped from the wagon and marched to make acquaintance. Stepping up on the plank walk, I extended my hand.

"Let me introduce myself, Mr. Barnett. I'm the new

157

scavenger officer for the city of El Paso and thought we should meet."

Barnett didn't know what to say when I stuck my hand within two inches of his gut. Reluctantly, he lifted his, and I grabbed it, shaking it firmly but despising the stickiness of his grip and releasing his puffy fingers as quickly as I could without being rude, of course.

"I'm H.H. Lomax, Mr. Barnett. I just wanted to let you know that I'll be covering this route regularly now, and I would appreciate it if you and your men would refrain from soiling the beautiful streets of El Paso."

"Go to hell," Barnett replied.

"I would, good sir, because it would be cooler there than here, but I am employed to clean up the streets of El Paso, and I would appreciate your cooperation in this worthwhile civic endeavor."

"It's your job to clean it up, Lomax."

"Well, sir, I'm no lawyer, but if I read the El Paso City Ordinance Number Eleven correctly, material such as this should be dumped in a privy vault or cesspool, which upon request will be cleaned by the city scavenger office for fifteen cents for a cubic foot."

Barnett snickered. "I don't have to pay nothing to dispose of it like this. And if you don't clean it up, I complain to the mayor and council members. I suspect they'll see it my way as much as I contribute to their campaigns."

"Now that's a shame, Mr. Barnett. I was hoping we could settle this in a gentlemanly manner."

"Schloss shot my dog."

"You should've seen the loss of your dog as a business opportunity."

Barnett yanked his hands from his hips and shrugged. "What?"

"You're a butcher. Your dog was meat. Surely there's a market for it in El Paso, surely among the Chinamen."

"You're an animal, Lomax, not deserving of the funeral we gave Bailey."

"Okay, Butch, if that's the way you want to play it—"

"Only my friends call me Butch."

"—but this will change, or it will cost you business,

158

Butch."

Barnett scoffed at me. "Give a guy a badge, and he thinks he runs the town."

Shrugging, I said, "You'll be sorry, *Butch.*" I strode back to the wagon, picked up the scoop and rake, and spent ten minutes cleaning up the mess as Barnett glared the entire time at me and my boss.

As I finished and put my tools in place, the butcher called, "You missed a spot, Dumax," or at least that was what I thought he said.

I spun around and grinned. "You're cleverer than you look, *Butch.*"

He pointed to a wad of entrails I had overlooked. After scooping them up, I tossed the load in the back, tipped my hat, put up my tools, and climbed into the wagon. Then Schloss started us on down the street. "I don't know how," I scowled to Schloss, "but I'll make him stop or run him out of business."

My boss shrugged. "Nothing I've come up with works."

"Is it true he gave his dog a funeral?"

Schloss nodded. "You would've thought Queen Victoria had died."

We went on about our task, weaving in and out of the traffic to pick up carcasses. I loaded them, and Schloss logged them on the forms on his clipboard. Later we passed the courthouse just as the Selmans emerged. Junior spotted me and pointed me out to his father, who squinted, then both men took to laughing at me. Unfortunately, they did not drop dead as I had predicted. Maybe I didn't appear as goofy as I thought. Or maybe it was just nervous laughter, as they feared me now that I wore a badge and carried a gun.

Once we finished our rounds, we headed to the dump where we discarded our cargo. A couple of Mexicans met us each day at the dump with buckets. As we unloaded the dogs, cats, and birds, the Mexicans took their knives and skinned and carved up some dead animals, though always saving the fresher ones for themselves, and carried the meat to the pound for the other dogs to eat. "It's not to my taste," Schloss admitted, "but it saves the city money."

That night back in my room after supper with Annie, I wrote Judge Roy Bean and informed him I was now wearing a badge and cleaning up the streets of El Paso. I also reminded him I expected Rip Enreed to be contacting him shortly about an interview on the Gringo Bandito, who would be referred to as BM—for Bad Man—if I had to send a coded telegram on the situation. Enreed's code word would be EPT for *El Paso Times*. I explained that playing along with the newspaperman on the Gringo Bandito might convince him to write Bean's life story. With my new job, I told him mine and his money were holding out well and I planned to stay in El Paso until I got his book published or made him famous. When I finished my letter, I picked up the afternoon papers Annie had delivered and learned that Constable Selman would be tried in the spring for the murder of John Wesley Hardin. That outcome was good news for me because it meant Old Selman and his son would have to be on their best behavior until the trial date. While not guaranteeing they wouldn't ambush me on some dark night with no one else about, it did mean they had to be careful around me in public.

During my rounds the next day, I posted the letter. That day and the following one were like the first, Schloss accompanying me and acquainting me with my responsibilities, me dodging bicycles and riders while removing carcasses and both of us cursing Charlie Barnett for making our jobs more difficult. It became so routine, our dispute with the butcher, that I wondered if the people lined up outside his shop were there to purchase his meats or to watch him and his battalion of assistants dirty the street. On the third day, Schloss had me log in the carcasses and stops. Convinced I could handle all the tasks with the job, he sent me out on my own the fourth day. Two things bothered me about the job. First, I resented Butch and his buddies mocking me each day when I cleaned up the street mess in front of his shop. Second, I never got used to killing the dogs and cats. Over the first two weeks on the job, I shot eleven dogs and three cats with my city-issued.22 revolver and captured five or six dogs a week for the impound.

August ended with me in my new job and September continued with me developing a consistent routine. About once a week, Schloss would accompany me on my rounds, and we talked about a lot of things, but mostly the pending prizefight between Corbett and Fitzsimmons. Promoter Dan Stuart throughout September promised a fight would take place, even shipping in lumber and materials to build a special arena in Dallas for the October 31st showdown and Kinetoscopic equipment to document the bout. He announced special days leading up to the match, starting with Republican Day, followed by Educational and Drummer Day; Colored People's Day; Comic Opera Day; Populist Day; Free Silver Day, featuring a speech by William Jennings Bryan himself; Chrysanthemum and Woman's Day; and National Passengers and Ticket Agents Day to promote rail traffic to the event. The more Stuart discussed his dreams, the madder state officials got, especially after Stuart won a state court case that sided with him that state laws did not prohibit a refereed pugilistic encounter.

If the papers and the gossip were to be believed, Governor Culberson vowed to work with the attorney general to stop the bout by any available means, then threatened to call a special session of the Texas Legislature to pass an emergency measure prohibiting in the future what they had failed to prohibit in the past. Then rumors spread that Corbett wearied of the whole racket and considered retiring. At that point, the wise boosters of El Paso decided they should enter the prizefight sweepstakes and created a carnival committee to visit Dallas and sweet talk promoter Stuart, in case the prizefight fell through there.

No sooner than the El Paso delegation arrived in Dallas, the local ministerial association took to claiming the number of fallen women had mushroomed in the previous two days. The pastors also noted that in the days before and after a recent fight in New Orleans, street robberies had averaged fifty-seven a night, which

161

was a reduction from El Paso's daily count.

"You think the fight will ever come off?" Schloss asked me during a round together, as he pointed to a dead rabbit in the gutter.

"There's more than one way to skin a cat," I said, hopping from the wagon seat onto the ground. As I grabbed the scoop to retrieve the rabbit, it struck me like a locomotive how I would get even with Charlie Barnett for his ongoing vendetta against Aaron Schloss and H.H. Lomax.

I retrieved the rabbit, tossed him in the back, secured the scoop, and jumped back up in the wagon, grinning like I had just been crowned heavyweight champion of the world.

"Why are you so happy?"

I laughed. "I just figured out how to get even with Charlie Barnett."

"No, kidding? What?"

"Can't tell you. I wouldn't want anyone to think you had anything to do with this."

Schloss's eyes widened. "This must be good."

"What's the busiest time of day for the butcher shop?"

"Likely mid-afternoon or later when folks are picking up something to cook for supper."

"Do you ever eat rabbit?"

"Now and then, like most folks. It's cheaper than beef or chicken. Why?"

"Just curious, that's all."

"And I'm intrigued what you've got up your sleeve."

"In good time, my friend, in good time," I replied, "but I will need you to let me off early one day and have the skinners at the dump a couple hours ahead of schedule that day."

Schloss remained both perplexed and curious, asking me each morning if this was the day. Two days before September ended, I told him the next day was the one he had been waiting for. "I can't promise you I'll drive him out of business, my friend, but I guarantee you that his sales will sink like a rock in water."

"Do you want me to accompany you on your round

tomorrow?"

"No, just have the skinners here by two o'clock at the dump, and I'll let you know what to do."

Good though my scheme was, it didn't top the news in the next morning's papers. Heavyweight contender Bob Fitzsimmons had arrived in Texas for the big fight, disembarking from the train in Houston along with his entourage and his pet African lion, to the thunderous applause of supporters. Governor Culberson, however, was not among the throng cheering this Australian pugilist. Culberson remained in Austin, calling a special session for the first week in October to cut off the head of the prizefighting viper in Texas once and for all.

I started my rounds a half hour earlier that day, heading out into the streets of El Paso and ignoring the droppings, even around city hall, the courthouse, and jail, and bypassed a few dead dogs because I was looking for cat carcasses in good shape and untrampled by street traffic. In front of Barnett's butcher shop, I made a big production, annoying the owner by telling him business must be souring because it didn't seem like the guts and innards were as thick as usual. I scooped up the offal, all the time whistling *Dixie* and acting as if I enjoyed this more than plucking a soiled dove. As I finished cleaning the street, I tipped my hat at Barnett. "I'll be back later with your order, *Butch*," I cried for all his customers to hear.

Every time I called him Butch, he called me Dumax, amusing the crowd. I waved to everyone, then climbed in my scavenger wagon and continued my duties.

By noon I had found my quarry of four dead but unmaimed cats, though I continued my rounds for another hour so I would reach the dump as scheduled. When I arrived, Schloss and the skinners were waiting, my boss as excited as a bull at heifer time. I jumped from my wagon and yanked out the four dead cats by their tails, instructing Schloss to have the Mexicans gut and skin the carcasses, except to leave the tails and heads unskinned. The Mexicans listened to his instructions, then questioned him. He nodded that they had heard right. They shrugged and went about their business as I raked out the carcasses from the back of the wagon.

When it was empty, I told Schloss to take a seat and once the skinners finished, we would go over to the office as I needed a tow sack. After another five minutes, the hands had dressed the cats to my specifications and placed them back in the wagon. Then I drove my boss back to the office. He found a burlap bag for me to carry my quarry in and held the mouth open so I could lower the cats headfirst into the sack.

When he climbed in the wagon, I handed him the reins and told him to take us into town. With time to kill, we drove around, even stopping four times for me to collect a dog carcass. As four o'clock neared, I instructed Schloss to park the scavenger wagon a couple blocks away from the butcher shop. I removed my frock coat and badge, leaving them in the floorboard, then asked Schloss to walk along the opposite walk where he could watch. I gave him a half-a-block lead, then started down the plank walk to visit Butch. As I crossed the street onto Butch's block, I saw about twenty women and a few men lined up outside his shop. Weaving among them, I stepped to the door and started in.

A woman screamed. "Get to the back of the line like the rest of us."

Lifting the tow sack, I answered, "I'm making a delivery."

Though they grumbled, I stepped inside where another eight customers waited for their turn at the counter.

Butch weighed a slab of red meat on a scale until he saw me. He pointed his finger at me. "Get out of here, Dumax."

I waved the tow sack at him. "I couldn't wait until dark to make today's delivery."

"What delivery?" he cried, as other butchers stopped their tasks.

"The rabbits you wanted."

"What are you talking about?"

Loosening my grip on the mouth of the bag with my left hand, I grabbed with my right the tails, yanked the four dead cats out of the burlap, and draped them across the counter in front of all the customers. "Four more *rabbits* just like you always order, *Butch*."

A brief silence ensued as everyone stared at the meat, then three women screamed, and everyone stampeded out the door.

"He's been selling cat meat to us," cried one man, then others took up the call, spreading the news up and down San Antonio Street.

The customers departed, leaving me with three infuriated butchers grabbing for carving knives and meat cleavers.

CHAPTER FOURTEEN

"You son of a bitch," Charlie Barnett cried as he raised his cleaver and started around the counter for me, his knife-wielding assistants following.

I pulled my Colt revolver from its holster and cocked the hammer, gripping it in my right hand and the tow sack in my left. "Why don't you dump them on the street tomorrow when the scavenger wagon comes by?"

"What are you trying to do, Dumax, ruin my business?"

"It's Lomax, *Butch*, officer Lomax. That's my name. What I'm doing is cleaning the streets of El Paso of your innards and filth. You've had your laugh at Schloss's and my expense. No more. If you or your gang dump another bucket of entrails in the street, I'll come back with more cats, dogs, snakes, and even buzzards."

"I've sold nothing but beef, pork, rabbit, and fowl. Everybody in town knows that."

"Not anymore, *Butch*. Once rumors begin, they hogtie the truth and strangle it. Dump one more bucket in the street, and I'll start leaving cat skins and dog hides at your back door. People will start asking questions about your offerings, wondering if they're eating what you say they are."

"I'll go to the mayor and council."

"No, you won't," I answered. "You might cost me my job, but I'll keep dropping dead animal skins in your alley so your reputation will be as rotten as the meat folks think you are selling them. Now lower your blades and get behind the counter."

Butch grumbled, then retreated, motioning for his two assistants to do the same. Once they dropped their weapons, I nodded. "Have a good day, boys," I called, as I released the hammer on my Colt and slid it in my holster. I exited the store and jogged across the street to where Schloss stood, eager to know what had happened. "Here's your tow sack, less the cats." I gave him the burlap bag.

"A minute after you entered," Schloss said, "customers started spilling out like red ants from an anthill."

As we walked back to the scavenger wagon, I detailed my exchange with Charlie Barnett, until this day, the most prosperous butcher in town. At the cart, Schloss climbed aboard, tossed the burlap bag in the floorboard, and took the reins.

"I have to hand it to you, Lomax. You may have solved my problem with Butch Barnett. In fact, I'm gonna drop you off at the Herndon House, so you don't have to walk back."

"A devious mind helps," I replied. "Don't know that my God-fearing ma would approve, but my pa would sure get tickled. God rest their souls."

My boss stopped the wagon in front of my boarding house, and I grabbed my gray frock coat as I stepped down onto the walk.

Schloss grinned. "I think'll ride with you tomorrow on your rounds so I'll know if Butch learned his lesson."

"See you then," I replied as he shook the reins and started back for the pound.

Annie brought me supper and said Rip Enreed had dropped by to visit with me on Judge Roy Bean and the Gringo Bandito. "When I told the newspaperman that Gringo was the meanest white man I'd ever laid eyes on, it pricked his interest."

"If he returns tomorrow, tell him to see me after six o'clock when I'm done with work."

Annie stared at me. "You seem in a jolly mood this evening."

"Just a good day on the job," I replied, "though I'm tired

and will retire early."

The next morning, I grabbed a copy of the *Times* and saw they had run a story on Barnett's Butcher Shop selling cats for meat. I could swear I heard the retching of the fine people all over El Paso as they read the paper with their eggs and bacon. Or was it cat meat?

Schloss and I began our route and worked double to make up for anything I had missed the previous day, but we still arrived outside the butcher shop at the regular time. The usual line of customers had disappeared like a handkerchief at a magic show as folks throughout El Paso were questioning if Charlie Barnett himself were a magician, turning cat meat into beef or pork or sausage. Neither Barnett nor any of his helpers appeared outside with their customary load of offal for the scavenger office to remove. As long as they refrained from dirtying the street, I kept my vow not to leave dead animals at their alley door.

That evening, Enreed came to see me, asking what I knew about the butcher scandal. I advised him on the promise that he wouldn't use my name or position. I explained Barnett and his men had been tossing entrails in the street daily for the scavenger to clean up, likely because they were hiding in plain sight the evidence of their wicked ways. Then Enreed said he would travel to Langtry to interview Judge Bean on the Gringo Bandito. After that meeting, he would decide whether to take on the book project. Once the reporter departed, I put on my hat, removed the badge from my frock coat, and pinned it to my shirt, then strapped my Colt around my waist and headed to the Southern Pacific Depot to send a telegram to Bean.

In the telegraph office, I wrote out a simple message to Judge Bean: EPT TO VISIT RE BM CATTLE MAYBE and sent it, grimacing at the high price the railroad charged for its telegraphic services.

The next day the calendar turned to October, and two days after that Legislators, at least those sober enough to walk, met in the Texas Capitol to vote on prohibiting prizefighting within the bounds of the great state of Texas. The evening papers reported that a state that prided itself on its toughness had sided with the sissies in approving the prohibition. Not only that, the legislators passed the law in just a hundred and eighty minutes. Reading between the lines, I gathered that was too short a time for the state's elected representatives to even read the bill, which was one of the shortest in history. Even so, they likely couldn't read the thing, though I suspect the lawmakers celebrated with a bottle of whiskey each, then staggered back to their homes and families, proud that they had saved Texas from such iniquity. Preachers of all persuasions rejoiced once Governor Culberson signed the bill, making Texas pure and respectable forevermore.

By the following evening's newspapers, the fight scheduled for Dallas before the do-gooders got involved was headed for Hot Springs, Arkansas, my home state. I figured Arkansas had always been tougher than Texas, but Texans had always mocked us, trying to hide the fact of our superior ruggedness and intellect. But Arkansas Governor James Paul Clarke had wailed about the brutality of prizefighting and the attraction it had for the lowest class of citizens. As there was no lower class of citizens below Texans—except for their elected representatives, of course— I could see his point. On the other hand, the papers reported that Clarke, who opposed prizefighting as barbaric just six months earlier, had gotten into a hotel fistfight with an Arkansas state representative who had questioned his politics and his integrity. As the governor was getting some sense beaten into him, he reached for his revolver and planned to shoot his opponent until two other state officials grabbed him and stopped a certain killing. I'd never heard of a prizefight where the combatants brought pistols, but Governor Clarke was definitely a ringside innovator, making my state proud.

Even so, the governor sent a snooty telegram to the promoter Dan Stuart, decrying plans for the match in Hot Springs. "Such an act will be a palpable violation of our law and will be resented as an insult to our State pride. It is not only my duty but my pleasure to place at the disposal of the sheriff of Garland County all necessary

169

means of enforcing his orders. Your contemplated fight will, therefore, not take place and you will best promote the satisfaction of all if you will abandon at once your efforts to bring it about." After reading a telegram that long, I realized Arkansas's governor had likely busted the state budget if the Little Rock telegraph office charged as much as El Paso's Southern Pacific Telegraph did.

Not satisfied just to notify the promoter of Arkansas's piety, the governor, according to the newspaper reports, sent telegrams to Gentleman Jim Corbett and Australian Bob Fitzsimmons informing them they were not welcome in Arkansas and should not consider crossing the borders of the fair state. A few days later, a deputy leaked to newspapers that the fighters would be shot if they dared set foot upon the precious and virtuous soil of Arkansas. What the deputy failed to announce was whether the governor himself would shoot them. Even so, Dan Stuart announced the fight would indeed take place on the last day of October in Hot Springs.

As big a mess as the bout was causing in Texas and then Arkansas, the El Paso carnival committee decided they had more smarts than all the folks of Arkansas and the Texas governor and legislature combined. My boss knew several of the members of the committee and kept me posted on their thinking, believing they could play a fistic shell game with the authorities and pull the match off either around El Paso, in New Mexico Territory, or across the Rio Grande in Mexico. Their interest in the fight was as pure as the estimated half a million dollars in business the bout would draw to El Paso and themselves.

"Do you think it'll ever come off?" I asked Schloss one day before I started my rounds.

"It's a long shot," he admitted. "The territorial governor of New Mexico is against it, though there's no law to stop it—yet. Too, the president of Mexico and the gov-ernor of Chihuahua are stiffening their backs, opposed to it as well."

Following the progress of the ill-fated prizefight was the most excitement in El Paso since John Wesley Hardin's death in August and the subsequent squabble over whether Charlie Barnett was selling cat meat to his customers. That debate died down, but so did Butch's business, as folks no longer lined up outside his door to make purchases. Since he and his men quit dumping offal on the street, my work evolved into a routine of removing dead cats and dogs, shooting dangerous critters, and scooping up horse dung from the fine streets of El Paso. Occasionally, I ran into one of the Selman's, but they were skittish and would remain so until Old Selman faced a jury over Hardin's demise.

Through it all, the newspapers reported that promoter Dan Stuart kept promising the match would come off in Hot Springs, rather than Dallas, on the last day of October. He shipped the baggage, circus tent, lumber, and ring to Hot Springs to be ready when the courts vindicated his plan. Corbett even arrived in Hot Springs in the middle of October to prepare for the match, though Fitzsimmons remained in Texas to train until the situation clarified itself. Gentlemen Jim's arrival drew dozens of Arkansas ministers to the town to protest his arrival. Governor Clarke showed up as well, though the papers failed to say if he brought his pistol for shooting the pugilist. Shortly after Clarke reached Hot Springs, he had the sheriff arrest Corbett and put him in jail, where he stayed three days before a judge released him. Seeing the serious nature of Arkansas's opposition, Corbett decided his torso could stop an iron fist easier than a leaden slug and abandoned Arkansas, but not before calling Fitzsimmons a cur who was too yellow to even show his face in Hot Springs. The insults and tension between the two men were fanning the flames of interest in a fight to finally settle their differences on the canvas, though Corbett kept hinting he had demonstrated in the ring all he needed to prove to anyone, and he just might retire. He actually did it once, then reconsidered two days later. The situation was confusing and amusing, assuming I could believe the newspaper accounts.

While this was going on, Rip Enreed finally made his trip to Langtry and spent a couple days with Roy Bean, taking notes on the judge's life, but spending most of his listening to Bean inflate the legend of the Gringo Bandito. When Enreed returned, he came to visit me in my room and said Bean was a fascinating old fool, so we had a deal. Once he published the story on the Gringo Bandito, he would turn his spare time to fleshing out his notes on Bean and corresponding with him for more details.

"As mean as the Gringo Bandito has been over the last decade," Enreed informed me, "I'm surprised I haven't heard more about him until now."

I shrugged. "I can't vouch for these stories, but I'm told he threatened men, women, and children, never to mention his name. If they did, they would suffer dire consequences."

"Like what?" Enreed asked.

"One old man said to have mentioned Gringo's name was shortly found with his tongue cut out from his mouth and tacked to a cactus thorn as a warning to others."

Enreed whistled as he took notes. "Bean says he's a loner. Is that true?"

"Mostly from what I heard." I paused as I thought of some outlandish fact to share. "I can't vouch for this either, but I heard he once had two partners. He killed both when he thought they betrayed him. He staked one out naked atop an ant bed under the broiling July sun. What the ants didn't eat, the sun roasted."

"What about the other one?"

"Again I can't say with certainty this happened, but what I heard was the Gringo Bandito saw this partner kissing his girl. Enraged at the betrayal, Gringo roped him and took him to the banks of the Rio Grande, which was rising from floodwaters. There he hung him over the water by his ankles from the limb of a giant cottonwood tree and with the rope slowly lowered and raised his betrayer's head in and out of the river. When he tired of that, he secured the rope with his partner's hair just touching the water. As the waters rose, his onetime friend slowly drowned."

Enreed caught his breath and then let out a long sigh. "Were these Mexicans or American gang members?"

"One of each," I informed him. "The tragic thing was his *señorita* loved his partner more than him, and when she saw he had killed her lover, she threw herself into the flooding river and died amid the raging waters. The embittered Gringo took out his rage on the people on both sides of the river."

"Terrible," Enreed said, shaking his head. "I can't believe we haven't heard more of him."

"Would you want your tongue cut out and stuck to a cactus thorn?"

Enreed shuddered. "I see your point." He paused, then said, "Bean said to tell you Bruno misses you."

"He's the only beer-drinking bear I ever met."

"Bruno wasn't well during my visit, wasn't eating."

"Too much beer."

"I've got to admit Judge Roy Bean is a colorful old coot."

"The only honest judge I ever met, though he possesses an awkward manner of getting to the truth and resolving a matter."

Enreed laughed. "Maybe we need him to get that Corbett-Fitzsimmons match scheduled and over with. All this controversy is prolonging the inevitable and getting more people interested in seeing the fight."

"Any chance this carnival committee will bring it to El Paso?"

"They're more dreamers than doers, but where else in this country is the promoter going to turn?" Enreed arose from his chair. "Between you, Bean, and Mrs. Williams, I've got plenty of material on Gringo Bandito. Once I break this story, it wouldn't surprise me if I didn't get calls from the papers in Denver or St. Louis or even San Francisco to work for them."

I grinned. "Perhaps after you finish the book on Bean, you can find Gringo and interview him, though you'd need to watch your tongue, or you might actually see it on a cactus thorn."

"As I put together my story on Gringo or later Bean, I may want to contact you again to clarify some points."

"I'm here for you, Rip, at least when I'm not on the

scavenger wagon. All I'm interested in is seeing the truth in print." I smiled.

"Maybe you ought to go into the newspaper business."

"No, I'm interested in seeing the truth, not writing it. Besides, I don't have that good of an imagination."

"You don't need imagination, just the facts."

"Which you newspapermen distort all you want."

"We're only as good as our sources!" Enreed laughed and wished me a good evening as he headed out the door. As for me, I looked forward to reading the upcoming story on the legendary Gringo Bandito.

October drained away, me making my regular rounds through El Paso, collecting animal carcasses and droppings, shooting strays when I had to, occasionally running into Old Selman, and wishing he was a stray. I always tipped my hat at the cane-toting lawman and pointed to my chest, reminding him we were brothers of the badge, stepbrothers more accurately, and I carried weapons. After I had emptied my wagon at the dump and turned the carcasses over to the Mexicans for skinning, I would return to the impound, unhitch, and tend the mules, and visit with Schloss whenever he was around. We talked about the day's haul, local gossip, and the ambitions of the local carnival committee to host a fight that looked less likely to ever happen.

Still, the prizefight made the papers, dividing the nation into two warring camps, the do-gooders, and the rest of us. As October turned into November, shocking news came from New York City, where Corbett decided he would retire, after all, this time for good. That was the end of the Corbett-Fitzsimmons match, but not the end of the controversy. In announcing he was taking off his gloves for good and relinquishing the heavyweight championship, Corbett designated Irish boxer Peter Maher the new champion and gave him the coveted title belt. This snub of Fitzsimmons, the leading heavyweight contender, infuriated the Australian, who demanded at once a shot at the phony champion. With Corbett out of the match, the interest and intrigue only grew, the do-gooders demanding the sport be abolished forever and everybody else curious to see if the promoter would shift his attention to a Maher-Fitzsimmons title bout, even though Fitzsimmons had demolished Maher three years earlier in a New Orleans prizefight that left the "Dublin Terror," as Maher was called, bloodied like a slaughter pen. That Corbett would name a fighter the Aussie had beaten handily as his successor champion infuriated Fitzsimmons, who insisted there be a fight to confirm the real champion, him. But with no place to hold a bout, it looked about as likely as Judge Roy Bean ever meeting Lilly Langtry in the flesh instead of just in his dreams. Even so, Schloss thought the carnival committee might just attract the fistic circus, and its spending, to El Paso. The last day of October passed with no fighters and no match in El Paso or anywhere else. Fitzsimmons looked foolish coming out the first day of November telling the papers there would be no fight on a day that had already passed. The longer this debacle continued, the more foolish the principals looked.

One evening in early November, as I was walking back to the Herndon House after a tiring day, I noticed a rider approaching on a bay horse, his hat brim turned down to hide his face. An imposing man with a chiseled jaw and a Texas Ranger badge on his chest, he angled in beside me before I recognized my brother.

"Howdy, Andy," I called.

"Keep walking, Henry, and don't look at me," he said, his voice as serious as a Sunday sermon. "The state of Texas needs your help."

I sputtered, then coughed. "How's that? You need another Texas Ranger?"

"The governor fears the prizefight is coming to El Paso."

"So?"

"I've got to put a stop to it."

"And you want this dogcatcher to do it? Maybe if you'd seen I was a Texas Ranger rather than a badged scavenger, I could help."

"You're good where you are, in the employ of Aaron Schloss. He's friends with most of the members on the

175

local carnival committee. I need you to pump him for information you can feed me so we can stop this thing."

I stopped and shrugged.

"Keep walking," Andy commanded.

"I don't care if it's stopped or not."

"Same with me from a personal standpoint, but I'm charged with enforcing the law and orders that come from the top. This has come from the very top."

"You mean Judge Roy Bean?" I joked.

Andy saw no humor in my jest.

"If I spy on Schloss for you, does this mean I'll get sworn in as a Texas Ranger since I'm attending the governor's business?"

"You're a dogcatcher, Henry. Be glad of that and don't make this any harder on yourself or me."

"Fine, Andy. I'll do what I can."

"I or someone else will check in with you every other day at the least. So, you'll know they're acting on my behalf, they'll identify with either the name of 'Cane Hill' or one of our brothers and sisters."

Before I could answer, Andy angled his bay away from me, making it look as if this had been nothing but a chance encounter. I figured my brother had been eating loco weed and little would ever transpire, just like nothing had come of the championship match despite months of palaver and barrels full of printer's ink being spilled on the topic. Every chat I had with Schloss I asked what the latest was on the carnival committee, and he told me the members remained optimistic, though no one had figured out a way of bringing the fight off, unless they held it in Juarez, something that might be a possibility, assuming the Mexican authorities looked the other way. As Schloss explained it, they couldn't have the fighters just show up one day and box because they needed a ring for the fight and bleachers for the spectators, but those facilities required time to set up and build and once they started building them, they would tip their hand.

I figured this was all big talk, but I passed on the information to whatever Ranger or courier Andy sent my way. But the details remained skimpy and even the newspapers carried fewer stories on the prizefighting spectacle. Since bigger cities than this had failed to pull off the fistic match, I doubted Hell Paso's leaders and boosters with their sun-addled brains could manage it either. Probably my efforts wasted my time and Andy's, but he was still my brother and he had looked out for me, so I played along.

Each day I worked my rounds, then dined with Annie, who had been as faithful in providing me meals as I had been in paying her on time. Our biggest surprise came on the eighth of November when Rip Enreed printed the first of his two-part story on Gringo Bandito, "the unknown bad man of the Rio Grande," as he called him. Annie and I hooted at all the tall tales Enreed had fallen for, making Gringo out to be meaner than the devil himself. Bean even said Gringo was so tough, he chewed through the iron bars in the bear cage to manage his escape. Annie and I laughed till tears ran down our cheeks as we read the account three times. I sent Annie out to get four more copies of the paper so I could tear out the article and mail it to the judge. We couldn't wait for the next day and the second installment of the Gringo Bandito.

However, the second part of the story did not appear in print that day or any other. What did arrive in El Paso that morning on the train was Dan Stuart, promoter of fistic carnivals.

CHAPTER FIFTEEN

El Paso fluttered with excitement at the news of Stuart's arrival and anticipation of Rip Enreed's next installment on the Gringo Bandito. Perhaps the city's carnival committee members had known what they were doing after all, even if Enreed hadn't. The local group had actually persuaded the promoter to bring his sinful display of the manly arts to El Paso, so the locals could pick the pockets of the visitors who would follow.

A pounding on the door awakened me before dawn the following day. "Henry, it's Andy. We need to visit."

I grumbled and stumbled out of bed, uncertain what could be so important. As soon as I unlocked the room, my brother barged in, quickly closing the door behind him.

"What do you know?"

"I know the sun hasn't risen, and you ruined the best night of rest I've had in weeks."

Andy punched the button, and the electric light came on, blinding me for an instant. "Do you know anything about the fight? The governor's furious Dan Stuart's in El Paso, promising to hold the prizefight in this vicinity."

Wiping my eyes, I rattled my head to shake some sense into it. "Schloss said nothing about it. I don't know what he knows."

"You need to find out and report to me what you learn."

"I'll do what I can."

"And one other thing. Rip Enreed visited me after yesterday morning's paper came out, demanding to know why the Rangers had done nothing about the Gringo Bandito. I told him I hadn't heard of him nor any of his exploits, like cutting off a fellow's tongue and sticking it on a cactus thorn."

I grinned. "He's a mean one, that Gringo Bandito."

Andy shook his head. "Enreed told me I should investigate threats like him rather than trying to stop a boxing match. I informed him that the Gringo Bandito was a mirage of someone who had gotten too much sun. Thought you should know. What I need from you is anything you can find out about the prizefight as soon as possible so I can wire Austin. I'll have one of my men stop you on your rounds today for whatever you find out."

Before I could answer, he spun around and strode out the door and into the darkened hall, leaving me standing there in my long johns. Knowing I could never get back to sleep, I dressed, dipped a couple chunks of bread in my syrup tin for breakfast, and started out earlier than normal for the impound to begin my daily rounds. I beat my boss to the building, the dogs howling and growling as I approached. I hitched up my team and was killing time when my boss rode up, dismounted, and greeted me.

"You're early this morning," Schloss said, as he secured his horse to the hitching post.

"Couldn't sleep with all the excitement of Dan Stuart arriving in town for the prizefight."

A sly smile crept across his face. "Yep, the carnival committee is delighted as well, and the Texas Rangers are worried. Stuart plans to scout locations around El Paso and into New Mexico Territory, even across the Rio Grande into Mexico. He's looking not only for a place to hold the bout but for Fitzsimmons and Maher to set up their training camps. Stuart may pull this off yet, even if the entire world is against him. Now let me ask you this, what do you know about this Gringo Bandito? From what I read in the paper, he's a mean hombre. Caught my eye when I saw your name mentioned, yours and your landlady's."

I laughed. "As a public official, you understand you can't believe everything you read in the newspaper, especially if Rip Enreed wrote it."

"That's true, but as a servant of the people, I also understand you don't want to get in a peeing match with a skunk that buys printer's ink by the barrel. Being city scavenger isn't like being mayor or a councilman, but the newspapers can make my life miserable when I'm just trying to do my job."

"And I'm aiming to help you, so I'll start my rounds a little early this morning. My route's a lot easier, now that Charlie Barnett's quit dumping entrails in the street."

Schloss snickered. "I gotta hand it to you, Lomax, you stopped him cold. Rumor has it if business doesn't pick up, he may close his shop. He's already let go three of his four assistants."

"He shouldn't be selling cat meat," I said as I climbed aboard the scavenger wagon and started for downtown. Halfway there, a serious fellow wearing a Ranger badge and a stern expression rode up beside me.

"You're from Cane Hill, aren't you?"

I nodded, knowing my hometown was a code word from my brother to pass information along to whoever used it. "Dan Stuart's scouting locations for the fight, looking for places around El Paso, in New Mexico Territory, or even across the border into Mexico. Nothing certain yet."

The Ranger tipped his hat. "Obliged," he said, then turned his black gelding about and rode away to inform my brother and, likely, the governor himself.

Midmorning when I was scooping up a dead dog near the courthouse, my favorite newspaperman accosted me. "You son of a bitch," cried Rip Enreed, pointing his index finger at my nose, "you made me a laughingstock, you and your stories about the Gringo Bandito." Enreed spat at my feet. "There's no such animal."

I turned toward my newspaper friend and lifted my load in his direction. He got a whiff of the decaying canine and backed away. "Gringo is as close to an animal as any man I've ever heard of. I told you I couldn't verify things."

"You and Roy Bean and even your landlady made this all up. You may think this is funny, but I'm not doing anything else with Bean. If he lied to me about this, he'll lie to me on anything so find another sucker to write his biography. I'm done with you, Lomax. You're nothing but a lowly scavenger."

"This is honest work, unlike yours. I may collect droppings, but I don't go spreading them around town in printer's ink."

"Journalism is a noble profession," he defended his trade.

"Just whoring by another name."

He stammered, then stomped his boot on the street. "You have a way of making enemies, Lomax. There's me and Charlie Barnett and Constable Selman and his son and who knows how many others."

I dumped the carcass in the back of the wagon. "You best be careful, Rip, because you may need me one day."

Enreed scoffed. "Me? In a profession as noble as the newspaper business? Not on your life." The newspaperman spun around and marched off.

"Have a good day," I called, hoping he'd get hit by a freight train the next time he crossed the railroad tracks or by a passing bicycle, especially one with a bloomer-clad woman at the handlebars. I wrote Judge Roy Bean that night telling him Enreed had figured out the truth about Gringo and had pulled out of the book project, damaging chances for publication until I could find some other possibilities.

November passed as a daily game of prizefight hide-and-seek, with Stuart looking for sites to accommodate his vision and with Rangers tailing his every move. The longer the promoter chased his dream, the louder the opposition grew. Governor Culberson ranted so loudly Texas would never allow such an iniquity that New Mexico Territorial Governor William Thornton took up the same cry. Stuart, though, responded that no federal law prohibited a pugilistic performance in the nation's territories. As soon as he pointed that out, congressmen began drafting a bill to prohibit such dastardly displays in all lands under territorial governance. President Grover Cleveland indicated he would sign such legislation when it passed. The cry on the American side of the Rio Grande was so great that politicians in Mexico echoed their opposition. Mayor Tito Arriola of Juarez decried the sport, and General Miguel Ahumada, who also was the governor of Chihuahua, vowed to bring troops to Juarez to stop the barbaric exhibition. Even Porfirio Diaz, president of Mexico, railed against the fight. Though all three men had no qualms about bullfights in arenas under their jurisdiction, they certainly would not allow a boxing match to defile their bullfighting rings. The more opposition grew to the bout, the greater the newspapers conjectured about its location. The papers speculated that places as far away as London and Melbourne across two oceans or as near as California, Oshkosh, St. Joseph, Ardmore, or Guthrie were interested in hosting the bout, if no one was looking. Problem was, everyone was watching. Short of El Paso, the best option appeared to be in Indian Territory on the lands governed by the Choctaw, Chickasaw, Cherokee, Creek, and Seminole tribes. One scheme proposed that Fitzsimmons and Maher become honorary Indians so they could fight unchallenged on tribal lands. The commissioner of the Indian Office nixed this idea, saying he would bring in U.S. marshals and troops to prevent the fight. How much of this was true and how much was false trails offered by the promoter to keep the Rangers guessing, I could never sort out. If newspapers printed it, I learned to discount the news as more speculation than fact.

As this went on, Corbett, who had given up his title, was still insulting the Australian as a man unworthy of the crown of heavyweight champion and promising to wager $10,000 on Peter Maher to win the bout if it ever came to pass. Fitzsimmons kept training on the Texas coast, and nobody knew where Maher was training or if he ever intended to fight the Australian.

My routine stayed the same, collecting animal carcasses, scooping up horse dropping, and shooting stray or dangerous dogs. Every day I would pump Schloss for information and then pass it on to the rangers. I wondered if any of them were passing on their plans to Stuart's men. From the day of his arrival, Dan Stuart made the Gem Saloon his headquarters, a couple blocks west of the Herndon House on El Paso Street. There he plotted his options for all to hear and, I suspect, to throw the rangers off his actual planning, which I figured he did in the privacy of his room at the Vendome Hotel, the classiest lodge in El Paso, rooms going for four dollars a day and board for seven dollars a week or fifty cents a meal. Both the Gem and the Vendome were pricey for my budget, and neither offered the pleasant company of Annie Williams.

Late in November, I finished my daily round outside the county jail, scooping up a dead cat crushed by a dozen iron-rimmed wagon wheels, tromped on by a hundred horseshoes, and even rolled across by a couple bicycles. As I tossed the carcass in the back of the scavenger cart, I turned about and saw Constable John Selman glaring at me.

"I ought to kill you, Lomax."

Tossing the shovel in the back of the wagon, I unbuttoned my uniform coat to reach the Colt on my hip. "You tried once and killed Hardin instead. If you try again, you might hit some bloomer gal on a bicycle. Then you'd be up for a second murder trial."

"Once my trial is over this spring, I intend to settle our differences."

"You're forgetting I now wear a badge as well."

"Damn dogcatcher!"

"It's honest work, though not as profitable as a constable job, what with the bribes you collect not to hassle the brothels and their gals."

By the red flush of his face, I knew I had pegged him correctly. As I watched him simmer, I saw my brother spot us from across the street and angle up behind Selman just as he raised his cane to swat me. As he lifted the walking stick over his head, I stepped back and put my hand on my revolver.

Andy darted toward us, grabbing the uplifted cane, and yanking Old Selman around. His eyes narrowing, my brother yanked the pistol from Selman's holster before the unbalanced constable could grab it. "Mind your manners, Selman," Andy growled.

Selman's rage turned from me to my brother. He jerked his cane from Andy's grip, stumbling backward into me when the walking stick came free. I grabbed both his arms.

"You won't always be around to protect your little brother," Selman cried, wriggling free from my grasp.

"Maybe not, Constable, but I'll come looking for *you* if something happens to Henry, no matter who's at fault."

A slow learner, Old Selman twisted about to face me and raised his cane again. Before he could strike me with his walking stick, Andy conked him on the head with the butt of the constable's revolver. Selman melted like grease in a hot skillet, his knees buckling and him tumbling to the ground. Curious pedestrians stopped to watch until Andy turned around and motioned for them to go about their business. They obliged as Andy stared them on their way, then unloaded Selman's revolver before bending over and sticking it back in his holster.

"We ought to leave him in the street, and I can collect him tomorrow," I offered.

"Shouldn't do that," Andy said. "Let's load him in your wagon, then we should talk."

Grabbing an arm and a leg apiece, we hoisted Selman up and threw him in the wagon on the manure side, tossing his cane and hat atop him. When he came to, the constable wouldn't be smelling roses nor smelling like one.

"If he bothers you again, Henry, let me know. I suspect there's some outstanding warrants we can find on him if we need to get him off the streets."

"I'll dump him between here and the river. Now, what is it you need from me?"

"The governor's worried he'll look like a fool if this fight goes through and fears it'll damage his re-election chances."

"That's no grit in my eggs."

"But it is in mine. I need you to visit the Gem Saloon after work each day. See what kind of information you can drag up on their plans for the bout. The promoter's been sending telegrams to the Kinetoscope Exhibition Company on making moving photos of the fight. You know about Kinetoscope parlors, don't you?"

"Saw one down the street after I arrived here."

"If Dan Stuart is paying the Kinetoscope folks to come here, the bout must be soon and close by. Stuart thinks he'll make a fortune filming the fight and charging men across the country to watch."

"Maybe so." I shrugged, then remembered the two Kinetoscope players in the arcade's back room. "Likely so."

"I want you to frequent the saloon and pick up what you can."

"More and more people know we're brothers. Don't you think they'll suspect I'm spying on them?"

"You've always been able to talk your way out of a jam. You remember the time Pa sent you out to fetch a watermelon for us, and you dropped it coming to the house. He stood there watching you drop it and then pick it up and piece it together, juice streaming down your arms. When you got to the house, he asked what happened. You told him you were just walking along and it broke."

"I remember stories of it."

"Pa asked if you were sure that's what happened, and you told him you weren't certain, but it could've happened that way. That made Pa laugh. Once you made Pa laugh, you got away with your mischief without a whipping for lying."

"Perhaps it *did* happen that way," I noted, drawing a laugh from my brother.

"Will this make me a Texas Ranger?"

Andy shook his head. "No, but it may keep me a ranger. And, it may keep you alive."

I decided that was a good enough return on the deal. "Okay, but if I'm cornered, I need some ranger information to bargain with. Something that might not be common knowledge but won't hurt your efforts for it to be revealed."

Andy scratched his chin. "Within the week, we'll have a dozen more rangers joining us from across the state. We intend to put a stop to this."

We might have talked a spell longer, but Selman groaned in the back of the wagon, so I climbed aboard and told my brother I had to skedaddle and drop Selman off before he regained his senses. Andy motioned me on. I shook the reins, starting through town toward the impound and the Rio Grande. Near the city dump, I stopped, hopped out, and yanked the stirring Selman by his legs from the wagon bed. His head hit the hard-packed trail ruts and knocked him out again. I tossed his hat and cane by his side and left him to figure out how he had wound up near the river and smelling like an outhouse.

I dumped the rest of my load at the dump where the Mexicans were waiting to chop up the carcasses into dog food for the penned animals. As usual, I noticed they kept a few of the fresher cats aside. I wasn't sure what they planned to do with them, but I continued my vow not to eat any more tamales as long as I was in El Paso.

After leaving the dump, I tended my team and wagon and started the walk back to my boarding house, hiking three blocks before I hitched a ride the rest of the way to my place. Back in my room, I showered and changed clothes before I went to the Gem so I wouldn't smell like a scavenger. Annie Williams caught me walking back to my room and asked if I was ready for her to fetch our supper. I told her I had to visit the Gem Saloon and listen for prizefight news, so I would pass. She looked disappointed, so I pulled a couple of dollars from my pocket and told her to treat herself to a good restaurant, so she didn't have to tote food to me or clean up afterward. Back in my room, I slapped on my gun belt, put my badge in my pants pocket, and left the Herndon House for El Paso Street and the Gem. Crowded and noisy, the saloon was as fine a drinking establishment as I had ever entered. Long and narrow, the saloon sported a tile floor, marble columns, leather-cushioned booths, and an elegant mahogany bar with polished foot rails and spittoons. As crowded as it was, I figured I could get by without buying a drink since I would be better at my task sober than tipsy.

Men in suits and bowlers teemed around the corner booth, and I saw my boss amid the throng. As I headed his direction, he spotted me and waved me over, quickly introducing me to seven members of the carnival committee, then pointed to a portly fellow with a handlebar mustache, thin eyebrows, and wavy hair parted just right of center and shining like he touched up his mop with shoe polish. "That's promoter Dan Stuart, who's dreaming big. He's gonna let the country see the prizefight, even if they can't attend the bout."

"Kinetoscope, right?"

Schloss nodded. "You're smarter than I gave you credit for, Lomax."

"No, he's not," came a familiar voice. "He's the lyingest son of a bitch in Texas."

"That's saying something," I answered, turning to face Rip Enreed, still fuming over the Gringo Bandito story that had tarnished his golden reputation.

Enreed clapped his hands together to get the attention of men clumped around Stuart. "This is H.H. Lomax. He can't be trusted. Lied to me about the Gringo Bandito."

His audience laughed. "Perhaps we can't trust you and the *El Paso Times*," said one carnival committee member before downing a jigger of whiskey.

The others turned away, ignoring Enreed until he shouted, "He's the brother of Andy Lomax, the Texas Ranger, likely here to spy on your plans and notify the governor."

The gang around the table fell silent. Then Stuart looked at me, stroking his chin. "That true, fellow?"

"My brother's a ranger, true, but I'm my own man and have nothing against prizefights. Besides, the way I figure it, I might have information that would benefit your cause."

Stuart dropped his hand from his chin and leaned toward me as far as his belly would allow. "Tell me more."

"Nothing in particular, just that the governor'll be

sending another dozen Rangers to El Paso by the end of the month."

"Don't believe him," Enreed cried.

The promoter whistled, then glared at Enreed as he sat back against his cushioned seat and nodded. "The governor's serious about stopping this fight."

"You can't believe him," Enreed shouted.

Stuart pointed a beefy finger at the *Times* newspaperman. "Another outburst like that, and I'll not invite you to my table again."

Enreed tucked his pride back in his pocket and nodded, desperate for whatever news he could scrounge on the prizefight.

"Tell me more, Lomax," Stuart commanded. Everyone looked my way.

"No. Half of you here don't believe me. So, let's just wait and see if the reinforcements show up. I'll be in from time to time so you can thank me once more rangers arrive." I tipped my hat at the crowd, turned, and strode out of the building.

The next day when I returned to the Gem, one of Stuart's cronies asked if the rumor was true that my brother had cold-cocked Constable Selman, and I had loaded him in the back of the scavenger wagon.

"It's my job to clean the filth off the streets of El Paso. Last I saw of the constable he was lying on the trail to the city dump. Looked like he'd fallen drunk off his horse. On top of that, he smelled like he had been wallowing with the hogs."

"That's not how we heard it from Rip Enreed," said Stuart.

"He must've gotten his information from the Gringo Bandito," I replied.

Everyone laughed, except Enreed.

Three days later, a dozen Texas Rangers stepped off the afternoon train in El Paso, vowing to stop the prizefight at all costs. My credibility improved with the carnival committee and Dan Stuart. While the boxing crowd did not embrace me, they listened to what I said, and I eavesdropped on what they were saying to take back to Andy.

Between my job, my time at the Gem, dining with Annie, and occasionally writing letters to Bean, I stayed busy, November trickling away into December and the hot summer heat easing off until it was tolerable to be out and to do my work. But through that time all that Stuart and the carnival committee did was talk and revise their plans for outwitting two presidents, the U.S. Congress, two governors, one mayor, and so it seemed, all the preachers and do-gooders this side of hell.

Then on Christmas Eve, Aaron Schloss instructed me to be at the Southern Pacific Depot the next day at nine o'clock in the morning. He told me to start early enough to pick up a few cats and dogs, but not to worry about any manure before heading to the depot. When I arrived, I saw a Mexican band serenading the empty platform and a throng of men I had previously seen at the Gem, some with their wives. Midmorning the westbound pulled into town, the band started playing Mexican music and a lanky fellow stepped from a passenger car with an African lion on a leash.

Bob Fitzsimmons had arrived. The fight was more than just palaver and dreams.

CHAPTER SIXTEEN

The heavyweight challenger waved to the crowd, but the lion kept the committee members from getting too close to Bob Fitzsimmons to welcome him to Hell Paso. The Mexican band finished a jaunty tune, then went silent for the celebrity's remarks. As porters unloaded his baggage and his retinue disembarked from the train car, Fitzsimmons stepped with his lion toward the crowd and announced his delight at being in a city brave enough to hold the title bout in such challenging times. He thanked Dan Stuart for his courage in standing up against the naysayers and do-gooders to promote the manly arts. Between the porters and the luggage handlers, a mountain of gear arose behind Fitzsimmons. One railroad employee wheeled a bicycle up to the front of the trunks, bags, crates, and valises. As he did, the lion growled and lunged for the railway man, who shoved the bicycle between himself and the beast, then backpedaled from the flashing white teeth. The lion's mouth closed around the front tire and the animal shook the bicycle, dragging the leash and Fitzsimmons to the edge of the platform, the spectators scrambling back from the animal.

"Easy, Nero," the prizefighter called. "Easy, boy!" Yanking on the leash with both hands, Fitzsimmons pulled the lion away from the spectators, then swatted him on the jaw until he dropped the bicycle and its bent front tire. "I know you're hungry, Nero. Give me a few minutes, and we'll get you something to eat." As the animal calmed, the boxer released one hand from the leash and pointed to the crumpled bicycle. "That's what I'll do to Peter Maher or any other fighter that gets in the ring with me. I'll demolish him."

The crowd cheered his bravado as he waved with his free hand. Then he grabbed the leash with both hands and dragged Nero toward a pen the railway men had unloaded from the baggage car. All the porters and handlers backed away; fearful they might wind up like the bicycle. Once Fitzsimmons ushered him in the cage and shut the door, the lion roared, startling me and the other spectators. I flinched when I felt a hand grab my shoulder, then turned around to see Aaron Schloss.

"Glad you made it, Lomax. What do you think about our newest visitor?"

"I'm thinking he's hungry. Maybe I can sell the carcasses to Fitzsimmons."

"Nice idea, but that's already taken care of. One clause in his contract requires that we provide free carrion for his lion. You'll take your daily load to his training camp."

"What about the dogs in the impound? What'll they do for food?"

"They'll go hungry, or we'll shoot them for lion food. Once the crowd clears and they load Nero, we'll feed him what you brought this morning. Every day after that you'll carry your load into Juarez and—"

"Juarez?"

"Yeah, that's where he'll be training to throw the rangers off. You'll drive into Juarez to keep the lion fed."

"That's gonna make for a longer day for me, walking to and from the pound with a daily trip into Mexico. I don't have the money to feed and stable a horse."

"Have you thought about buying a bicycle? It'll get you around. No feed costs and you can keep it in your room."

"From what I've seen, only maniacs use them. Besides, I don't know how to ride one."

"It's as easy as falling off a log."

"Falling's what I fear."

"Head down to the W.G. Walz Company at El Paso and San Francisco streets. They sell bicycles and offer free riding lessons. Buy one with solid rather than cushion tires. It'll make for a rougher ride, but you'll save time and money on fixing flats. They'll be open tomorrow. I'll give you the day off so you can handle it. It'll save us time in the long run."

After the crowd ambled off, most following the prize-fighter's carriage to the Gem for his meeting with Stuart, and once the railroad workers loaded the lion's cage on a freight wagon, Schloss and I maneuvered the scavenger wagon beside Nero and tossed him carcasses through the bars. I would see a lot of Nero in the coming weeks.

The next day I went to W.G. Walz's, and after two hours of instruction, I managed my balance, pedaling, and braking. After finishing my training, the bespecta-cled instructor advised me of city ordinances limiting bicycle speeds to ten miles per hour or less on city streets and prohibiting the riding of bicycles on any sidewalks. I paid seventy-nine dollars for a Columbia bicycle with a steel frame, twenty-eight-inch wheels, and a spring seat which helped cushion the ride of the solid rubber tires. After completing the sale, the clerk gave me a pair of rubber garters to wear on my pants cuffs to keep my britches from getting caught between in the chain and socket.

I mounted my new wheels and pedaled around town until I spotted Schloss on the scavenger wagon making the rounds. Riding up beside him, he looked over and grinned.

"I see you took my advice. Why don't you stow it in the back, and I'll take you across the river and show you where Fitz is training."

"Let me ride along beside you because I need the practice."

We spent an hour attending our duties, me propping my bicycle against a rear wagon wheel at each stop and scooping up dead cats and dogs so Schloss could stay in the wagon seat. After that, we headed toward the Rio Grande and over the wooden bridge into Juarez where Fitzsimmons had set up his training camp inside a walled compound that allowed his people to charge twenty-five cents a day for spectators to watch him train or see Nero chained to a tree. We arrived during a break in the boxer's regimen, and Schloss introduced me to the boxer as the man who would provide supper to Nero. The prizefighter seemed less interested in that than in my bicycle.

"Lomax," he asked, "would you be willing to sell your bicycle? Nero ruined mine and I haven't had time to look for a replacement."

I figured I'd price my bicycle so high that no fool would buy it. "A hundred and sixty dollars."

"I'll take it," he shot back.

"Cash."

"Of course," he replied, whistling and motioning for his business manager to come over.

When the fellow arrived, Fitzsimmons instructed him to pay me the price, and I quickly pocketed twice what I had paid just hours earlier. As the prizefighter's man rolled the bicycle away, I realized boxing could be a profitable, if bruising, profession.

Fitz thanked us for providing food for Nero and said he had to get back to training. The last I saw him, he was jumping rope as Schloss and I drove the scavenger wagon to Nero and tossed the carcasses within his reach. Like Bruno, my Langtry bear friend, Nero seemed to like me, or at least the food I provided.

I rode back to El Paso with Schloss, who dropped me off at Walz's again to buy a replacement bicycle. He also suggested while I was at the store to purchase a wide sombrero and a colorful serape for a disguise when I crossed over into Juarez. Since the city council hadn't approved the disposal of the dead dogs and cats this way, he thought I should hide my identity, just to keep do-gooders from raising a stink.

So, my daily routine now included a bicycle ride to and from work, a trip into Mexico to feed a lion, and frequent baths to remove the aroma of my job before I went to the Gem to see what was developing with Dan Stuart. New Year's Eve came, and the Women's Christian Temperance Union protested the availability of liquor and all the drunkenness that would follow that night. The women pledged to take all the fun out of life, but El Paso and Juarez celebrated anyway with whiskey, fireworks, and gunshots, as well as the arrest of two "disciples of Oscar Wilde," as one paper put it. Still, as the New Year began, the local committee had only one fighter for the fistic carnival Dan Stuart so infamously promoted to anyone who would listen, though he remained coy about the date and location of the match. That left my brother, the Texas Rangers, and the governor worried they were being outfoxed. Tensions tightened the first week in January when Enoch Rector, a partner in the Kinetoscope Exhibition Company, arrived in El Paso with the equipment and crew to cover the prizefight. Either Stuart kept a secret better than a dead man, or he did not know what he was going to do. I could never read Stuart when he held court at the Gem, so I never knew if he was holding four aces or a pair of deuces.

Andy or one of his men visited me daily to glean whatever I had picked up, but I had to tell my brother my stock had fallen among the sporting crowd since I had provided no significant information on the rangers' plans. Andy advised me to pass along word that once a date was set for the match, the governor would send another dozen rangers for reinforcements. Though he didn't want this information shared, he indicated the rangers received permission to shoot to kill the fighters and the promoters if they had no other option to stop the match. Then on the eleventh day of January, I stood in the Gem near the table where Stuart plotted his fight when a commotion started at the front door and worked its way to Stuart's table, as a burly six-foot Irishman with receding hairline parted down the middle, a black handlebar mustache and deep-set dark eyes flashing with anger muscled through the crowd. He elbowed me from his path, then stopped and glared at me.

"Outta me way, boy," then he sniffed twice with his crooked nose. "Ye stink like a gut wagon. Move downwind from me."

That was my introduction to Peter Maher, the disputed heavyweight champion of the world. He had a chiseled build rather than Fitzsimmons's lanky frame, and by appearance the stronger boxer, but I'd go broke or to jail before I would ever root for this loudmouthed punching bag of hot air after he insulted me.

Maher shoved himself past me. I wished I had a hatpin that I could prick his ego with, but as crowded as it was, I'd probably have stuck the wrong man. Once he reached the table, he balled his fists, planted them on the shiny wood, and leaned toward Dan Stuart, who seemed more amused than intimidated. "Ye training grounds don't suit me, Danny boy. I's finding another."

"That's the champion's prerogative," Stuart said, "but you'll find and pay for your own."

"I's done so, Danny boy. I's training in Las Cruces."

"You realize Las Cruces is forty-seven miles away in New Mexico Territory. It won't be easy on the news-papers to cover you, give you as much press as your opponent is getting."

"All the press I's need is after the fight when I's knocked him all the way to the Emerald Isle." With that Maher straightened, spun around, and pushed back through the crowd.

Whether Maher's encounter with Stuart was planned or not, I never knew, but it seemed certain to me that the intent was to confuse those trying to stop the match. With Dan Stuart in Texas, Bob Fitzsimmons in Mexico, and Peter Maher in New Mexico Territory the bout could occur virtually anywhere and anytime, save for a couple day's lead time to get the ring and bleachers set up.

As Maher shoved his way out of the throng, the newspapermen followed, scribbling notes for their next stories. Once they left and the crowd thinned, I looked at the promoter. "There's something you should know, Mr. Stuart."

"From the rangers?"

I nodded. "Once a date is set, the governor is sending in another dozen or two rangers to stop it by any means necessary."

"They're tailing me and my men everywhere we go. We should visit sometime, Lomax, to discuss matters."

"Sure," I said. "Be glad to."

Stuart smiled. "Before we do, take a shower and have your clothes cleaned. The Irish Giant was right. You stink."

"I'm a working man," I responded. "It comes with the job."

Stuart crossed his arms over his abundant chest. "I have nothing against a working man as long as he is also a bathing man." He hesitated, then finished, "A bathing man who uses soap and lots of it."

Tipping my hat, I offered my goodbyes and emerged into the twilight, the noise of laughter and companionship drifting from the red-light district in the still night air. I went back to the Herndon House, showered with plenty of soap, and put on clean clothes. Annie came to see me afterward and announced she had missed our evening meals together. I told her I had as well, but work was keeping me busy between cleaning the streets, feeding Fitzsimmons's pet, and checking on things at the Gem for my brother. Then I asked her if she would mind taking my dirty clothes to the Chinese laundry the next day and buying me some new garb. I gave her thirty dollars to cover the costs. We visited a while with the door open, then she read a couple of scriptures before leaving. I secured the room and retired, unable to sleep, which was fortunate because around midnight I heard a rapping on the door.

"Lomax, Lomax," came a whispered voice, trying not to wake anyone.

Figuring it was my brother as he was the only one that would visit me this late at night, I got up, ambled to the entry, and opened it. "Come on in, Andy," I said, then looked at the barrel-shaped form standing in my darkened doorway.

"It's Dan Stuart," my visitor announced. "Let's talk, but don't turn on any lights." He entered.

I pointed to a table chair in a shaft of moonlight filtering in from the Overland Street window and shut the door, then sat on the bed opposite him.

"Sorry to bother you this late, but I hoped to get away

196

from the Vendome unseen. I'm not sure if the rangers trailed me here or not, but I needed to visit."

"Shoot," I said.

"I'm in a bind and can't figure out how to pull this fight off without getting everyone arrested or worse, as rumors are floating that Texas officials have permission to shoot to kill. Can you help me?"

"Why me? Besides, I don't have any pull anywhere. I'm just a dogcatcher, a scavenger that rankles the nose of everyone I stand near."

"That's true, but your brother is Andy Lomax, a Texas Ranger that can't be bribed or corrupted."

"He's just a lawman, not the governor."

"I'd rather deal with an honest lawman than a corrupt politician any day of the week."

"What are you proposing?"

"Right now, Lomax, I don't have an answer. I've ridden my horse into a box canyon with no way out. I'm trying to pull off the fight without the law getting involved, but politicians in Texas, in the territory, and across the river are dead set against it."

"Andy can't change that," I replied. "Besides, I don't want to tarnish his reputation."

"I won't sully his name, either, though I wouldn't mind if some mud stuck to Governor Culberson in Texas or Governor Thornton in New Mexico."

"Then what are you proposing exactly?"

"I'll never contact your brother but work with you to get information to him. He's not to share it with his superiors. He can send responses through you to me. I'll never share his plans with anyone. It's the only way I see out of this box canyon without someone getting killed. I don't want that. The only men that should get hurt out of this are the two in the ring, but even then they'll walk away from it alive."

"What if Andy won't go along with this? Or what if he doesn't trust you?"

"I'll know I tried, and the law turned me down."

"Give me a day or so, and I'll talk with him. Just us three, nobody else, right?"

"You have my word, and everybody knows the word of a promoter is as good as gold," he said, then paused before breaking out in laughter. I joined him.

As he arose from his chair, he scooted it back and bumped my bicycle, which tumbled to the floor.

"What was that?"

"My bicycle. I don't have any place else to keep it from getting stolen, so I tote it up and down the staircase every day."

Stuart bent over, grabbed the handlebars, and sat my bicycle up against the wall. "Be honest with me, Lomax, and I'll be truthful with you and your brother." We shook hands and Stuart exited, leaving me to ponder if his offer was authentic or just a ploy to throw the rangers off his track. He seemed genuine, though I could not evaluate his eyes and face in the darkness. I pondered his proposal for a day as I did my rounds, then plopped on my serape and sombrero for the trip into Juarez to feed Nero. On the way back into El Paso in my scavenger wagon, I encountered a ranger on the Texas side of the bridge.

The lawman touched the brim of his hat with his finger. "Thomas sends his regards," the ranger said as he pulled in beside me.

As Thomas was my oldest brother, I knew my new acquaintance was representing Andy. "Nothing new to report, but I must speak to Andy soon."

"Anything I can tell him?"

"Nope, just to see me as quick as he can on Cane Hill business."

The lawman nodded, then turned his bay at the next intersection and rode off.

Back at the impound, I unhitched my wagon and tended my team, Schloss coming out to visit. "Dan Stuart wanted me to check on you since he hasn't seen you in a couple of days."

"Tell him I'm working on a project and will get back to him in a day or so."

Schloss nodded and returned inside. I finished my tasks, mounted my bicycle, and rode back to the Herndon House, where I carried my two-wheeler upstairs. I showered and shaved, then went to my room, where I put on some of the new duds that Annie had bought me. Suitably attired, I marched to her office and knocked on the door.

I offered her a smile when she answered. "How about I take you out to dinner?"

Annie patted her auburn hair. "I'm not really made up for it and not in my best clothes, certainly not the match of your new outfit."

Shrugging, I extended my hand. "I don't care. You've gone out with me when I didn't always smell the best, scavenger work leaving its own special perfume."

Annie laughed. "Let me get my wrap, and I'll join you, Henry."

She got a shawl and accompanied me onto the streets of El Paso, where we found a nice restaurant pricey enough to discourage the rabble. We sat and enjoyed each other's company a couple hours through dessert and coffee, then I saw her to the boarding house and her room.

As I reached mine, I slipped inside, turned on the electric switch, and then jumped when I saw Andy sitting in a chair by the table.

"You scared me!"

"I let myself in. My messenger said you needed to see me. That it was important."

"Dan Stuart visited me a couple nights ago, sat where you're sitting."

"He's tossing in his hand, is he? Giving up?"

"No, far from it. He intends to hold the fight but wants to make sure nobody gets hurt. He's willing to advise you of his plans through me as long as you tell no one. Just the three of us will be the only ones that know about this."

"Do you trust him?"

"He seemed like he was desperate enough to mean it."

Andy tugged at mustache as he considered the offer. "It could ruin my reputation if this came out. I've always valued my good name."

"If things go wrong, you can blame me, that I gave you worthless information. My name's never been as pure as yours."

He pulled harder at his whiskers, then licked his lips. "Perhaps it's a way to end this Mexican standoff. The longer this goes on, the more money it costs the State of Texas. Bringing all these rangers to El Paso is draining other parts of the state of needed lawmen."

"What have you got to lose, if this goes wrong?"

"My badge and my job. I'm too old to start over."

"I don't know what to tell you, Andy."

Taking a deep breath and letting out a long sigh, Andy nodded. "I'll go along with it. However, if I find out any information he sends me is wrong, the deal's off, and I'll be looking to get him personally for it."

"I'll tell him, but it's just the three of us. I don't want any of your men taking messages for you. It's you and me. Nobody else."

Andy nodded, then stood up, walked over, and hugged me. I was more surprised than if Lilly Langtry had entered and planted a kiss on my lips. Andy said nothing else and marched out of my room.

The next evening after I'd cleaned and put on fresh clothes, I went to the Gem, where a handful of men clung to the promoter's table. Stuart acknowledged me with a nod and a comment.

"We haven't seen you for a few days," he said.

"Been working on a deal with a friend. He's agreed to go along with a purchase as long as the goods are genuine, not counterfeit." I nodded to let him know the agreement was real.

"Glad to hear that business is picking up, and you're back. Have a drink on me." He slipped his hand in his shirt pocket and handed me a bill folded in half. Once I took the bill, Stuart turned to the fellow sitting beside him and continued his conversation.

I headed to the bar, unfolding the bill to find a handwritten note between the folds. It read: *Tell your friend I'm setting the date for Valentine's Day, Feb. 14th, but that's not the actual date.* I pocketed the dollar and message, then left the saloon. I got the note to Andy the next day, just as the papers announced the fight in three weeks.

The state and El Paso broke into two camps, not for

one boxer or the other, but for whether the bout should be held or cancelled. The governors in Texas and New Mexico were foaming like rabid dogs about the fight. Across the river in Juarez, the mayor ranted about the possibility and the governor of Chihuahua again promised troops. In Congress, they quit talking about outlawing prizefighting in the territories and introduced the bill to make it so. President Cleveland promised to sign the law immediately.

Locally, those for the fight said it would bring needed money into El Paso. Those against said it was tainted revenue, the El Paso Ministers Union raising the greatest uproar. But the sinners among the community countered that if the wicked could be redeemed, why couldn't cash? The Women's Christian Temperance Union said the spectacle would just bring more liquor and intemperance to El Paso, not to mention petty thieves, pickpockets, murderers, tainted women, and a lower class of people. The depraved argued that if Jesus drank wine, so could they. It was a dilemma that had no satisfactory solution, a quandary that would've driven King Solomon himself to drink.

Figuring this was an impasse that a poorly educated fellow like myself could never solve, I just went about my business, providing regular updates between Andy and Stuart. I was especially mad the last afternoon in January as I was stuck on the Rio Grande bridge waiting for an overturned wagon to be righted and its contents re-packed so I could enter Juarez, feed Nero, and return home before dark. To kill the time while they cleared the wreck, I got down from my wagon and walked to the railing, and looked at the murky river waters, which were down so much that a muddy isle had emerged from the middle of the Rio Grande.

Then it hit me. That island was the answer. Langtry was the solution. I had to talk to Andy!

CHAPTER SEVENTEEN

After I finished feeding Nero, I hurried back to the impound, tended the team, and notified my boss I needed the next morning off to attend to personal business. Schloss eyed me with a frown and hesitated to answer like he knew I was up to something. I explained I intended to return in time to deliver Nero's supper in Juarez that afternoon. When Schloss nodded his approval, I thanked him and told him I'd find him somewhere on his afternoon rounds to take over my duties.

The next morning after the sun had first peeked over the eastern horizon, I carried my bicycle downstairs and out onto the street, starting the twelve-mile ride to Ysleta and the Texas Ranger headquarters to talk with Andy. As both foot and animal traffic were light this early in the morn, I pedaled as fast as I could through the streets, turning south toward Ysleta. I was ginning along fine on the macadamized streets but as I neared the edge of town, the improved roads gave way to an uneven and rutted dirt path.

Paying more attention to the path before me than the occasional pedestrian I passed, I heard a shout as I zoomed by a slender man walking with a limp. He cried after me.

"Slow down, you S-O-B. You're breaking the law."

I recognized the voice and glanced over my shoulder to confirm it was Constable Selman.

"Stop, you S-O-B. You're under arrest."

Pedaling even harder, I continued my trek to Ysleta.

"Stop or I'll shoot," Old Selman shouted.

Looking, I saw him point his pistol at me and fire, just as I hit a rut in the road. Losing control of my bicycle, I heard the whiz of the bullet overhead, then tumbled to the hard-packed dirt, lying there dazed for a moment, but staring at my attacker and preparing to yank my revolver and defend myself if he fired again or came closer.

"I got the son of a bitch," Selman shouted, then looked around for any witnesses that might have seen him fire. "Go to hell, Lomax," he spat, then turned about and limped among the adobe houses and structures that dotted the road, glancing back to see if I had moved.

Remaining motionless until he was out of sight, I finally got up, dusted myself off, and picked up my bicycle, which seemed no worse for the fall. Mounting it, I continued toward Ysleta. With my left shoulder, ribs, and knee throbbing from the impact, I pedaled slower to reduce the pain shooting through my side. Along the way, I encountered a pair of Anglo riders, a Mexican shepherding six goats toward El Paso, two wagons, an ox cart, and one stray hog. About halfway to Ysleta, I met a tall rider and recognized my brother by his profile in the saddle. Andy startled when he spotted me. I stopped and straddled my bicycle as he reined up.

"I was coming to El Paso to see you, Henry."

"And me you," I replied, "though I got slowed up. Old Selman took a shot at me on the outskirts of town, claiming I was riding too fast."

Andy drew his right sleeve across his mouth and mustache, then sneered. "That's no reason to shoot at a man."

"He intends to kill me."

"Is that the reason you wanted to see me?"

"It's about the prizefight."

"As for Old Selman, I'll be in El Paso tonight, so I'll send him a message that'll get his attention. Now, what about the fight?"

"I had an idea where to stage it."

"Have you talked with Dan Stuart about it?"

"No. I'm starting with you. If you don't like it, I won't

suggest it to him."

"Go ahead."

"During my stay in Langtry, the judge and I bathed on an island in the Rio Grande. He said it was neither fish nor fowl, neither Texan nor Mexican, and he could shoot me there and get away with it."

Andy nodded. "That sounds like Bean."

"Anyway, perhaps Stuart could stage the fight in the middle of the Rio Grande. Would that get everyone out of this box canyon, as Stuart calls it since nobody wants the fight?"

Tugging at his mustache, Andy thought aloud. "Langtry's across the river from the Mexican State of *Coahuila de Zaragoza*, so that might work, as long as the site remains secret as long as possible, so the governor of Coahuila doesn't step in. This could work, though we'd have to let Bean in on it, but as talkative as the judge is I'm not sure he can keep his mouth shut."

"I could telegraph him."

"No. We're reading all the telegrams to stay ahead of Stuart. A letter would take too much time. You'd need to visit him."

"That would take two or three days. I'm not sure I can get that much time off."

"I'll take care of that with Schloss. Visit with Stuart as soon as possible and see if he's agreeable. If he is, take the first train you can to Langtry and check with Bean. If the old fool doesn't let the cat out of the bag, this might work and remove the governor from our backs and return the rest of the rangers to their proper jobs. Are we agreed?"

"Sure but order your men to quit tailing Stuart at night. The safest place for us to talk is my room, and I don't want your men knowing he's there or it could spoil everything."

Andy nodded. "Fair enough. Now I best be riding on. I'll visit Schloss first thing, tell him you've business to attend to out of town. And I'll send a message to Constable Selman."

"If Schloss is driving the scavenger wagon for a few days, you'll know that Stuart's agreed. and I'm visiting

Langtry."

My brother grinned. "Henry, you may have just saved my job and the reputation of the great state of Texas. I didn't know you had it in you."

"I do what I can," I replied as Andy nudged his horse's flank with his spur and put him into a trot toward El Paso. Turning my bike around, I waited a few minutes to let the throbbing pain in my side ease, then started back to El Paso at a slower pace than I had left as I didn't want to be stopped again for speeding on city streets.

In town I found Schloss making the rounds and relieved him, putting my bicycle in the wagon, and finishing the day with the regular trip to Juarez to feed Nero. I returned to the impound and finished my chores, then rode to the Herndon House and cleaned up in time for my visit to the Gem.

Stuart sat in his accustomed place, eating a boiled egg, and washing it down with a mug of beer, while his men and reporters circled around him. "How's it been going, Lomax? Any news to share from your rounds?"

"Nothing much," I replied, "though I had a new friend come by my room a few nights ago. We had a nice visit. I'm hoping he returns soon."

"I'm sure he will," Stuart answered, then handed me a folded dollar bill. "Get yourself a drink."

"Thanks," I nodded, "but it's been a long day, so I'm heading back to my room to get an early start in the morning."

Stuart nodded. "Sleep tight." Then he took a bite of his egg and resumed talking with the others.

I walked past the bar and out the door, opening the dollar bill to see Stuart's latest missive. It read: *Opening bids in two days for 4,000 board feet of lumber for ring, bleachers. Valentine date a sham, still looking for site.* I would relay the message to Andy the next time I saw him.

Back at the boarding house, I asked Annie if she wanted to go to dinner, but she had a headache and declined my offer. I settled for a nearby eatery and downed a bowl of chili and some soda crackers, then returned to my room waiting for Dan Stuart to show up, assuming he had understood my message. About midnight the gentle rapping on the door told me he had. I turned off the electric light and welcomed him. Slipping inside, he went to the corner table and a chair.

"Tonight's the first time in a spell I didn't feel like I was being followed."

Pulling up the other seat opposite him, I responded. "I asked my brother to call his men off after dark because they might discover you and I were meeting."

"I'm obliged, Lomax. What did you need to see me about?"

"A site for the bout."

In the soft glow of moonlight from the window, I saw Stuart lean forward. "Go on."

"At Langtry, there's an island or sandbar in the middle of the Rio Grande. No one's certain if it's American or Mexican. It borders Coahuila, not Chihuahua. If we can keep the location quiet, we might make it work, though I must check with the kingpin of Langtry."

"Where's Langtry?"

"Almost four hundred miles southeast of here on the Rio Grande. It's a water stop on the Southern Pacific. There's a cantankerous old man that runs the town, calls himself 'law west of the Pecos.' He's an acquaintance I think I can convince to welcome the fight."

"That's a long distance away."

"You got any other options?"

Stuart shrugged. "I guess not."

"My brother's fine with it if you are, but I must visit Langtry to confirm."

"You do that, Lomax."

I extended my hand, and we shook on the deal. Then I turned my palm over. "I'll need money for train fare and an incentive for him to go along with it and keep his mouth shut. Good thing about it, is Bean is a judge. If we get into any trouble, he can save us in his courtroom."

"Bean … law west … Pecos … Langtry," Stuart mulled. "Seems like I heard of him. Something of a character, as I recall. How much will you need?"

"Can't say for certain but give me two hundred and

fifty dollars, to begin with."

Without hesitation, Stuart reached into his coat pocket and pulled out a wad of money, quickly thumbing the amount on the table. "Count it," he said.

"I trust you," I replied. "I'll leave tomorrow after the grocers open."

"Grocers?"

"I need to buy a tin of Wes-Tex Syrup for a friend. I think he'll like it."

"Bean?"

"No, his bear, Bruno."

"Oh, brother, what have I gotten myself into?" Stuart moaned.

"A way out of this canyon you've boxed everyone in," I replied as Stuart pushed himself up from his chair and started for the door, swinging wide of my bicycle leaning against the adjacent wall.

"If Bean and his bear agree, when would you want to hold the match?"

"A week from Valentine's Day, the twenty-first of February. That's another Friday."

"I'll catch you when I return. If it's a go, I'll tell you the bear liked the syrup."

Stuart nodded. "No tricks, right, from you or your brother?"

"Honest injun! Same goes for you."

He left. Now all I needed was Judge Roy Bean's cooperation. And silence!

Arising the next morning at the usual time, I rode to the impound and found Schloss already hitching up the wagon and team. Surprise crawled across his face when he saw me.

"I didn't expect you in today. Andy told me you had to handle some family affairs and would miss two or three days."

"He's right, but I wanted to make sure he reached you."

"Are you okay, Lomax?"

Nodding, I asked, "Why?"

"Yesterday a rumor circulated you'd been killed outside town. I knew it to be false since I'd seen you in the afternoon."

"Old Selman took a shot at me. He thought he'd hit me when I fell off my bicycle, I suppose."

"Then I heard this morning someone took a potshot at Junior Selman last night. Know anything about that?"

"Hadn't heard that," I shrugged, figuring Andy had fired the warning to Old Selman that if something happened to me, his son was in danger.

"This town's getting more dangerous by the day."

"It must be all the riff-raff that's coming here for the fight."

"Maybe so," Schloss responded. "The hotels are full, and the saloons are booming."

"Now all we need is a fight." I turned my bicycle around and headed back to town.

At the Herndon House, I stowed my two-wheeler and grabbed my valise with a change of clothes and my smaller weapons inside. I wore my Colt.45 on my waist and kept my badge in my pocket in case anyone challenged me. On the way out, I stopped by Annie's place, checking if she was over her headache and telling her I'd be gone for two or three days and to watch my room for me. She seemed disappointed that I was leaving, but I told her I would be returning. I left her and marched out of the boarding house, heading to the corner grocer where I bought a tin of syrup for Bruno, paying for it with Stuart's boxing money.

Then I marched to the train depot, stopping in the telegraph office to send a message to Bean that I was leaving El Paso on the next train and needed to visit with him. I bought my ticket and a copy of each local paper I could find so I would have something to read on the long journey to Langtry. The news about the fight speculated it would be in Juarez, especially since Congress had passed the bill outlawing prizefighting in any territory under the control of the United States, and Governor Culberson had sent in another dozen rangers, just as Andy said he would once the match date went public. When I wasn't reading the papers, I dozed off to kill the time and miles between El Paso and my destination. I arrived in Langtry just before midnight and found Bean seated on the platform with Bruno at his side. As I stepped off the train with my valise and the tin of syrup, Bean arose and ambled my way, tugging on Bruno's chain. When he realized it was me, Bruno stood on his hind legs and walked to me, giving me a bear hug, and licking my face.

"He's glad to see you," Bean said. "Me, too."

"Where's Sam? I don't want him ambushing me."

The old judge laughed. "Once I got your telegram, I sent him with some folding money to Del Rio for a couple days. He'll be too busy squiring all the women that'll have him."

"I'm obliged."

"How's my book coming along?"

"That's what I came to talk to you about, but let's do it in the morning. We'll have most of the day before I return to El Paso."

"I figured you'd be tired. Your same room is ready, and Bruno'll stand guard for you."

"For breakfast, I brought Bruno a tin of syrup. It's sweet. He'll like it."

We walked to the back of Bean's saloon, where Bruno and I entered my room. Exhausted, I undressed quickly, and crawled into bed, and would've had a great night's sleep, except for Bruno pulling the covers off my feet and licking my toes. Come morning, I dressed and took the tin with the bear to his cage, where I pried the lid off and sat the amber liquid behind the bars. When Bruno stepped inside, I latched the cage. He looked at me for a moment with betrayed eyes, then sniffed and licked at the syrup. After his first taste, everything was all right between us.

I found Bean at his breakfast table, drinking hot coffee, and eating cold biscuits and sausage patties. Joining him, I explained we had overplayed our hand with Rip Enreed since our tales of the Gringo Bandito were so outrageous that everyone except the newspaperman caught on, making him a laughingstock, which he loathed.

Bean sighed with disappointment. "Perhaps it's a

dream too distant to reach."

"Maybe not," I said, "because I've got an opportunity that might make you the most famous man in Texas, these United States, or even the world."

The white-whiskered judge cocked his head at me and grinned. "Go on."

"You know about the fight, don't you?"

"Who doesn't? All talk and no bout for what's it been, eight, ten months?"

"Yep, the promoter's in a first-rate predicament with no place to host it that won't create trouble or get people killed. But you might succeed where others failed and welcome it here."

His eyes glowed. "In Langtry?"

"They can't hold it in Texas or New Mexico Territory or Juarez or Chihuahua, but you remember that island you marched me to naked to bathe when I first arrived?"

"I do."

"You told me no one was sure it was Texas or Mexico. Why not host the fight there? You'd get plenty of newspaper stories about putting on something no one else in the world could do, and you'd build on your legend, perhaps attracting an author for your biography."

Bean's face brightened like the landscape when the sun first cleared the horizon. He thrust out his chest. "Yeah, I could do it."

"There's just one catch, Judge. You can't tell a soul. If word gets out ahead of time, everything'll go south, and your moment will have passed. Can you keep a secret?"

"Don't know that I ever tried," he answered.

"Not only will you have to try, you'll need to succeed."

"I'll do my best."

That's when I added another incentive. "The promoter will pay you a hundred dollars now and another hundred dollars if the fight goes off without a hitch. Think you can do it?"

Bean licked his lips. "I can pretty near guarantee it."

Then I decided I'd throw in a final incentive, false as it may have been. "From what I hear, Lilly Langtry might even be interested in attending."

The old judge's eyes widened. "Could it really be? Might I actually meet the most beautiful woman in the world, right here in Langtry?"

Shrugging, I answered, "I can't guarantee she'll be here, but if you let the word out early about the fight, I can guarantee she won't come."

"Lilly Langtry," Bean said, his lips grinning as wide as a West Texas horizon. "Here in town. I'll do it! Where's my two hundred dollars?"

"A hundred now, the other hundred later." I peeled off his down payment and explained that Stuart would have to send an advance crew to set up the ring and build the bleachers for the match. His job was to point them to the Rio Grande, show them the trail down to the river and the island, then tell people they were engineers looking at building a bridge across the water. I told him he could tell Bruno, but not Sam or anyone else.

After that, we shared the latest happenings in El Paso and Langtry, me showing him my badge for but an instant so he didn't see it represented the scavenger office and telling him how I was cleaning the varmints from the streets of El Paso.

"There's a lot of bad men in El Paso, I know. That's why there's so many rangers in those parts. Did you have anything to do with John Wesley Hardin's killing?"

"I'd gone to the saloon to arrest him," I lied, "but Constable Selman had the same idea and hated me so much he shot at me and hit Hardin instead. Selman's a terrible shot. I hear he can't even hit a guy riding a bicycle."

Then Bean brought me up to date on Langtry, passing along the sad news that I was now a widower, as my wife for a few minutes just up and died three months after I left.

"It must've been from a broken heart, losing me," I said.

Bean nodded. "She broke a lot of hearts and stools, for that matter. Odd thing, though, not a one of her dozen former husbands showed up for the burial."

"If only we'd known," I replied on behalf of me and her previous spouses.

I spent the rest of the day with Bean and Bruno, reiterating the importance of him keeping quiet about the prizefight if he ever had a chance of seeing Lilly Langtry and getting his remaining hundred dollars from Dan Stuart.

Departing on the evening train, I reached El Paso late the next morning and headed straight to my room, where I cleaned up, put on fresh clothes, and invited Annie to go to lunch. She agreed and we had a fine meal before I escorted her back to the Herndon House and marched on to the Gem, where I waited a half-hour for Dan Stuart to arrive. He strode in and stopped to shake my hand. "How's it been going, Lomax?"

"Fine," I said, "and you'll be glad to know the bear liked the syrup."

Stuart's grip on my fingers tightened. "Have you told anyone else?"

"Not yet, but I will by morning."

"Have another drink on me," he pulled another folded bill from his pocket for me.

This time, I slipped the note into my pocket, stepped to the bar, ordered a jigger of whiskey, downed it, and left for the boarding house. Stuart's latest note said he would decoy his moves with false shipments in the early days of February. When I got back to the boarding house, Annie caught me in the hall.

"I let your brother in your room," she told me. "I hope that was okay."

"It was fine. Just don't tell anyone."

She nodded as I marched down the hall and opened the door. My brother was sitting by the window, studying the traffic on Overland.

Without turning to look at me, he spoke. "I heard you were back."

"Your men are watching the train depots, are they?"

"Indeed. How'd it go in Langtry?"

"It's set," I said. "Paid the judge a hundred dollars from Stuart's pocket with the promise of a hundred more and the possibility that Lilly Langtry might show up if he kept it quiet."

212

Andy laughed. "That should seal his lips."

I handed him the note from Dan Stuart. He read it, then tucked it in his pocket as he stood up and looked at me for the first time. Grabbing my hand, he shook it firmly and even smiled. "You did it, Henry. You saved my job and the reputation of the great State of Texas."

CHAPTER EIGHTEEN

Aaron Schloss greeted me with a rapid handshake when I returned to work, ready to resume feeding Nero. The finicky lion, apparently dissatisfied with my boss's meals in my absence, had broken loose from his chain and killed a couple of goats, creating a stir in Juarez that the big cat might kill someone if he got loose again. Though Bob Fitzsimmons gladly reimbursed the Mexican herder for his loss, the locals avoided the boxer's compound and even called for *Federales* to come to Juarez to protect them from Nero. Peter Maher kept working out in Las Cruces with much less fanfare and newspaper coverage.

As January trailed off into February, the hotels filled as did the brothels, saloons, and gambling dens, either in anticipation of the fight or a speech by Democrat orator William Jennings Bryan, who appeared at the Myar Opera House and spoke on bimetallism with silver augmenting the gold standard. The *Times* quoted Bryan as saying the money question was the most important issue facing the United States. Apparently, the politician had never heard of the Fitzsimmons-Maher match.

The local ministers' union never mentioned the gold standard, but railed against the prizefight, citing the influx of questionable characters, though they didn't mention Bryan by name. Those supporting the fight marched in a torchlight parade, going to all five local train depots demanding lower fares to El Paso, so more men and women of loose morals could visit El Paso to watch two men willingly pummel each other. Across the border, the Mexican government grew uneasy as well, though I wondered if Nero or the fight was the actual cause. The Mexican president reiterated his prohibition of any match on Mexican soil, threatening to close Fitzsimmons's training compound and to expel the boxer and his pet lion from the country. The clergymen of El Paso and the goats of Juarez may have celebrated his warning, but half of the population wanted the fight, and the other half didn't. *El Presidente's* decision eliminated Mexico as a bout site, and then a week before Valentine's Day, President Grover Cleveland signed into law the rushed bill prohibiting prizefighting in the U.S. Territories. That ruled out New Mexico as a site. The Texas governor had long made his position known on the bout so that left a simple sandbar in the middle of the Rio Grande outside of Langtry as the only viable option, provided we—and Judge Roy Bean—could keep it secret.

I went about my business, removing dead animals from the streets of El Paso, shooting mean dogs, feeding Nero in Juarez, and delivering messages between Andy and Dan Stuart so both of them could get out of the mess the prizefight had created. A day after Cleveland signed the territorial prohibition law, I finished my work and returned to my boarding room, cleaned up, and headed to see Stuart at the Gem. With the Valentine's fight date less than a week away, a clump of reporters and supporters clung to the promoter's table like leeches, hoping to learn where the fight would occur. Stuart deflected all the questions, only saying he would announce the location twenty-four hours in advance, once all the arrangements were completed.

As men left or retreated to the bar for refreshment, I worked my way closer to his table. Seeing me, he reached in his pocket and handed me a folded bill. "For a drink," he said.

"How come you always buy him a drink?" one observer complained. "How about the rest of us?"

Stuart smiled. "He feeds Fitz's lion. Anyone else want the job?"

"I'll be damned," said a fellow who looked vaguely familiar and sat at Stuart's right hand. "I do believe it's 'Leadeye' Lomax."

Tucking Stuart's bill in my pants pocket, I grinned at the man who had given me that nickname years ago on the Texas plains while we were hunting buffalo. "Bat Masterson," I answered. "How the hell are you?"

"At least I'm not feeding big cats."

"Hey," I replied. "I carry a badge now." I pulled it from my pocket and flashed it quickly so he couldn't see it was with the scavenger's office.

"Yeah," called another fellow, "he's a dogcatcher."

Bat laughed. "A job suited to his skills. He was such a bad shot with a buffalo gun he must've wasted a ton of lead before we put him to skinning carcasses. That's why we call him 'Leadeye.'"

Everyone laughed.

"We called him 'Bat' because he was batty," I shot back. No one laughed, so I asked him a question. "What brings you to El Paso?"

"Dan here hired me and some of my friends to police the fight."

"Don't you mean fight the police?"

Bat grinned. "I never figured to run into you in a place as tough as El Paso, Leadeye."

"A town this mean needs a man tough enough to clean the streets," I replied, drawing laughs from everyone.

Masterson just shook his head. "You're not known as Leadeye for nothing."

"I've outlasted a lot of tougher fellows."

"You always seem to draw four of a kind in life, but you never win a big pot. Why is that, Leadeye?"

"Some days chicken, some days feathers. I need a drink." I backed away from Stuart's table and headed to the bar, buying a shot of whiskey with the promoter's dollar, keeping the change and the message in my pocket until I was clear of the saloon.

Outside I read the note with Stuart advising me to be home around midnight so he could drop by. Back at the Herndon House, I visited for a spell with Annie in her office, then went to my room, and waited in the dark so it would look like I had retired. When the promoter knocked on my door, I let him in without turning on the light in case anybody was spying on us.

Stuart took his accustomed seat. "Bat says you're a dependable fellow, if occasionally slow-witted."

"It wasn't Masterson that found you a place for your match," I reminded him.

"That's why I came to visit, so I can let your brother know what's going on. I've got to make this work, or I'll go broke. My best hope of making a profit is with Kinetoscope sales after the fight because I won't have a large gate. I'm chartering a train through a third party to keep my name out of the papers, but I can't carry enough spectators to profit from the gate sales."

"The Valentine's date is still a decoy, right?"

"That's correct. Let your brother know I'll be sending two flat cars of lumber and a boxcar with the Kinetoscope equipment into New Mexico the day before Valentine's, but they'll remain on a siding and return through El Paso in the early morning darkness of Valentine's Day. They'll stay in Sanderson for four days, then go on to Langtry as my workers need two days to bridge the river so men won't get their boots wet and to set up the ring and what stands we can make for the spectators."

"I'll let Andy know."

"Advise him this as well. The Rangers will pay their fares. I can't afford to have two dozen of them taking up space I could sell to ticket buyers. I expect it will cost twelve dollars for a round trip. If they intend to watch the fight, it'll cost them another twenty dollars to get inside the fence. We'll raise tarps around the fence to keep freeloaders from watching. If the Texas Rangers insist on being ringside to stop it, they'll have to pay twenty dollars and confront Bat Masterson and his gunmen at the gate. The rangers need to know that."

"Andy says there'll be no need for that if they fight on the sandbar, as the law will consider it out of their jurisdiction."

"You're not expecting me to pay for train fare and fight

217

tickets, are you?"

"I need every dollar I can get, Lomax."

"So do I, Mr. Stuart. Fact is, if my tongue was to slip about the location, you'd be out a lot more than thirty-two dollars."

"Bat warned me you were shrewd, and not above a little chicanery."

"He's right," I said. "Even us slow-witted fellow's got to get by."

Stuart nodded. "Okay, you'll get complimentary fare and admission."

"What's your plan for Valentine's Day?"

"I'll announce I've postponed the match for a week at a location to be determined. Twenty-four hours before the bout, I'll put out notices of which depot to meet the chartered train. Then it's a matter of just getting there. It's a long trip, and it'll be crowded, but the fight'll be worth the wait, one of the greatest in the history of prizefighting, I can guarantee. We'll film it, and fight fans can watch it for decades."

"What about Nero?"

"The cat won't be accompanying Fitz. I've already made that clear to him as I've got enough problems as is pulling this off."

"Why's he keeping a lion, anyway?"

"Fitz likes to wrestle with him as part of his training regimen."

"Nero might eat him if he weren't so skinny," I noted, as Stuart chuckled. "When's Maher returning to town?"

"Forty-eight hours before the train leaves for Langtry."

"Who's gonna win?"

Stuart shrugged. "That's why we schedule bouts."

"Andy wanted you to know that the state adjutant general, the fellow that the Texas Rangers report to, will arrive in town on February twelfth with another dozen lawmen to take command."

"Will any rangers remain elsewhere in Texas once those reach El Paso?"

"Likely not, as there's no bigger threat to the future of

this wretched state than your fight."

"The way I look at it, it's us against the presidents of two nations, three governors, every Texas Ranger alive or dead, and all the suffragists, prohibitionists, and ministers west of the Mississippi and north of hell!" With that, Stuart arose and shook my hand. "Thanks, Lomax, but make sure your brother gets the message and insist he doesn't let the adjutant general throw grit in the gears. I trust you and him, but no one else, especially not a politician from Austin."

"We'll make it work," I replied, escorting him to the door.

The next morning Andy found me at the impound, readying for my daily circuit and I shared Stuart's message. I advised him Bat Masterson and five gunmen had arrived in El Paso to help Stuart secure the fight.

"That's what we heard," Andy said. "I'm not sure we can trust Masterson or his men."

"I'm his acquaintance of longstanding. We buffalo hunted together, or he hunted, and I skinned. He bluffs more than he fights, usually easing tensions with a smile or a quip."

After updating Andy on the details, I asked him if he still thought the plan would work.

"If the adjutant general doesn't jump into the middle of things without looking or listening to me first, it should, but I guess we'll know for certain in ten days."

"By the way, Andy, I never thanked you for shooting at Junior Selman to let his pa know the consequences if something happened to me."

Andy offered a sly grin. "I don't know what you're talking about, Henry." Then he turned his horse and rode away. I finished preparing for a long day and started my rounds, ending in Juarez. Crossing the Rio Grande, I put on the serape and sombrero from the floorboard, following my usual route on the dirt streets to Fitzsimmons's compound. Nearing the stone walls, I saw a hundred *Federales* in their tan uniforms patrolling the perimeter.

As I approached the gate, two Mexican soldiers stepped in front of my wagon and started jabbering in

Spanish. I didn't understand them, trying to explain I was delivering meat to feed Nero so he wouldn't eat any more goats. I pointed to the carcasses in the back of my rig, and they stepped over and looked, holding their noses at the fragrance, then shrugging.

"*Carne para tamales*," I offered, and they both smiled, waving me inside, where I quickly fed Nero and left Juarez as soon as I could get past the guards again. I debated whether to continue providing meals for the lion because I feared him eating me, though now I also worried about Mexican troops shooting me.

Informing Schloss of the problem, I told him I was considering quitting. He begged me to stay on at least until after the prizefight, so he wouldn't have to feed Nero. I had to admit I enjoyed being able to carry my gun around without being subject to arrest, but I knew my time as a scavenger was drawing to a close. I figured to make good money on the fight, putting everything I had on Fitzsimmons. Though physically, he didn't look like much of a challenger to Peter Maher, the Irishman—to my knowledge—had never wrestled a lion. Too, I despised Maher for his insults during our one and only encounter.

Events sped up as Valentine's Day approached with fourteen more determined Texas Rangers and the adjutant general arriving on schedule. The bars and brothels stayed full, and the do-gooders remained incensed. Two days before Valentine's, the Chinese celebrated their New Year. I don't know how many celestials lived in El Paso beyond my laundryman, but they sounded like thousands with their firecrackers and their ting-tangy music. The closer the fight date came, the scarcer Dan Stuart made himself, sending out decoy messengers tailed by rangers and other lawmen trying to figure out where the fight would occur. Of all the newspapermen, Rip Enreed went to Las Cruces and clung to Peter Maher like a leech, figuring that no bout would occur until he left New Mexico, which he didn't. I delivered Nero's supper on Valentine's Day and armed Mexican soldiers surrounded Fitzsimmons to make sure he didn't soil Mexican soil with his pugilistic ambitions.

The next day, Stuart apologized for the unfortunate and unannounced postponement of the bout, saying it couldn't be avoided. He promised the fight would indeed occur the following Friday. Everyone clamored to know where, but Stuart kept the secret, though the rangers had stationed a man in Sanderson to watch the promoter's railroad cars on the siding there, should they be moved. Stuart did promise that he would give twenty-four hours' notice of when the chartered train for the bout would depart, announcing twelve dollars for round-trip fares and twenty dollars to witness this historic boxing match. The merchants and hoteliers of El Paso loved the delay because it gave them another week to empty the pockets of visitors. Unfortunately for the locals, the out-of-towners had grown exhausted waiting for a fight that the authorities—Texan, American, and Mexican—all opposed. The delay also gave the do-gooders more time to protest the barbaric exhibition that would forever tarnish the reputation of El Paso and perhaps expedite the second coming that would separate the righteous from the wicked and put an end to all the city's and world's iniquities. But more and more, they were talking to a smaller crowd of visitors.

I, too, wondered if the fight would ever come about, but Andy assured me it would, that he had tipped the adjutant general off and had received unofficial approval to let the matter pass as long as the fight occurred in the middle of the Rio Grande. Perhaps a flash flood would wash the whole mess downstream, Andy reported him saying. With two days to go before the fight, El Paso looked virtually deserted, compared to the throngs that had arrived for the Valentine's Day event that never happened.

The Wednesday evening before Stuart was to announce his chartered train, I took Annie to dinner at the fancy restaurant Andy had taken me to after we first ran into each other. We ordered steak and potatoes.

"You seem distracted tonight," she noted.

I couldn't deny it. "A lot on my mind."

"The fight, isn't it?"

I nodded. "I'll be going wherever it is."

"Will you be coming back?" She reached across the table and took my hand. I enjoyed the soft touch of her flesh.

"For a while, but I'll be leaving soon after that."

"I feared as much."

"I've wanted to see San Francisco all my life, so I'll head west and hope I get there."

"You ever thought about settling down?"

"A time or two, but it never worked out. Too, I always had a wanderlust that made it hard to settle down. And, I don't care that much for El Paso or this godforsaken state."

Annie let go of my hand and offered me a gentle smile that was betrayed by her sad eyes. "I haven't had success with men, never finding the right one, but Texas is my home and I'm scared to leave what I know."

"I understand."

"But I must thank you for protecting me from Hardin and Beulah."

"And you even got quoted in the *El Paso Times* out of the deal."

"On both Hardin and the Gringo Bandito." She laughed. "How's Gringo doing?"

"I'll have to ask Judge Roy Bean when I see him Friday."

Annie cocked her head and spoke softly so no one else could hear. "So that's where the fight will be."

I grimaced, realizing I had given the site away. I looked about to make sure nobody was watching, then nodded slightly.

"And you arranged it, didn't you? That was what your three-day absence was about last month, wasn't it?"

Again I nodded. "It's gotta stay a secret, though. Lives and jobs depend on it."

"You know what I'll miss most? Our scripture readings, H.H. They've been a source of tranquility for my troubled soul, especially with a male friend that wasn't after something from me. Besides that, you paid your rent early every week."

"Annie, you're the best landlady I've ever had."

We finished our meal and left the restaurant. As we stepped on the plank sidewalk, I came face-to-face with Old Selman. He scowled.

"Bastard," he snarled, then tipped his hat to Annie. "Sorry, ma'am."

"Shot any more bicyclists lately, Constable?"

"Not lately," he replied. "But I might try again if I see you while no one else is looking."

"That could be dangerous for your health and Junior's."

"I got the message, but once my trial's over I'll decide what I plan to do."

"That's only if you're not in the penitentiary. Maybe you can have Hardin's old cell. That would be Texas justice."

"They won't convict me for shooting John Wesley Hardin. He needed killing years ago."

"Several men in El Paso need killing, Constable."

Annie tugged on my sleeve. "Let's go, H.H. I'm getting chilled."

Taking her arm, I steered her around Selman and escorted her back to the boarding house. I stayed with her in her office for an hour, reading scriptures to calm her nerves. And mine.

When we finished, I stood up and kissed her on the forehead, then informed her I would be leaving the next afternoon and would not return for a few days.

"Be careful," she said, "I hear the Gringo Bandito roams those parts and everyone knows how mean he is."

"Especially, Rip Enreed."

We both laughed as I left for my room.

Come morning, I bicycled out to the impound and told Schloss I would not be working the day as I was going to the fight.

"I had an inkling the bout was coming up. Any truth that it's at Fort Hancock or Fort Stockton?"

"Nope," I answered, "farther away than that."

"It'll be a prizefight west of the Pecos."

Schloss laughed. "Watch out for the Gringo Bandito. I hear he's the devil incarnate down Langtry way."

"When I get back, Aaron, I'll likely be leaving."

"You made a good hand, especially getting Butch straightened out. You know he's closed his business and left town."

"I've cleaned up the streets in more ways than one," I replied.

We shook hands, and I rode my bicycle downtown, stopping at the grocery by the boarding house to buy two tins of Wes-Tex Syrup for Bruno. Hanging one tin on each side of the handlebars and riding carefully around the corner to the Herndon House, then toting everything upstairs. I took a late lunch, then wandered over to the Gem where men crowded around the front window where Stuart had posted a notice: *Persons attending the prizefight should report to the Southern Pacific Depot by 9 o'clock tonight. Railroad fare will be $12.*

Returning to my room, I cleaned up, put on fresh clothes, and sorted out my money, hiding some in each pocket and in my boots. I strapped my gun belt around my waist and stuck my badge in my coat to prove I was allowed to carry a weapon. I slipped my dagger in my right boot and my five-shot in my pants pocket, then put on my jacket and hat, grabbed the tins of syrup, and headed for the depot so I would arrive two hours ahead of the crowd.

At the train station, Stuart himself directed fight fans to get in orderly lines to buy their tickets. Seeing me, he pointed to the lead coach of ten passenger cars and told me to board. As I entered the car with my syrup tins, I saw Bat Masterson and his gunmen sitting in seats and reading the afternoon papers. Bat looked over the top of his newspaper.

"Afternoon, Leadeye, glad you could make it. I hear you're the one that figured this all out. You're smarter than I thought you were."

"I've learned over the years," I answered, shoving my syrup tins beneath my seat, "that even a jackass like you can teach me things."

Masterson laughed and resumed reading his paper. Before I could sit down, I saw four men enter from the opposite end of the car. To my surprise, Andy led three of his Rangers aboard, each wearing a revolver and carrying a Winchester rifle.

"Glad to see you, brother."

His comment caught Masterson's attention, and I didn't figure Bat would cause me any trouble for the rest of the trip. Andy introduced me to his fellow lawmen, and we visited for about three hours as the fight fans bought tickets and boarded the train for a destination unknown to most. The crowd applauded as first Fitzsimmons and then Maher climbed into their separate cars. As the platform finally cleared after eleven o'clock, Dan Stuart joined us in the coach.

"I can't believe it," he said as he plopped down in his seat.

Just before midnight, the locomotive whistle cut through the night air and the train inched eastward. The fight would happen after all.

CHAPTER NINETEEN

As the train chugged away from El Paso, Dan Stuart arose from his seat and paced up and down the aisle in the dim-lit coach, stopping occasionally to chat with the Kinetoscope chief, who assured him he had enough film for fifty rounds and his crew would be set by the time the boxing entourage arrived. Stuart blessed him because the film was the only thing that would make his venture a financial success. The longer the fight went, the more profitable it would be. Stuart estimated he needed at least twenty rounds to turn a profit but fretted about Bob Fitzsimmons's platform comment as he marched to his car. The Australian announced if he ever got to fight Maher, there would be just two hits. He would hit Maher, and his opponent would hit the floor. "I'm ruined if that happens," Stuart worried.

To the west, the dark skies occasionally brightened with flashes of lightning from distant thunderheads, as if God himself was siding with the do-gooders against the sporting crowd and the boxing match. Having been in El Paso for the past seven months, I had forgotten rain even existed. The storm clouds gave Stuart even more vexations. "You don't think the river'll rise and wash away the ring and arena, do you?" he asked anybody who would answer. Only Enoch Rector, the Kinetoscope boss, answered. "I'm more worried about the cloud cover reducing our light so we can't film."

During the night, the train crawled from water stop to

water stop. Each time the train took on water, Fitzsimmons and Maher disembarked and sprinted up and down the tracks to intimidate each other and to impress the crowds that had gathered to glimpse the famous pugilists, even in the darkness. At one water stop, we sat for an hour, a delay attributed to a derailing somewhere down the line. As dawn broke, our entourage reached Alpine where three hundred spectators awaited, Fitzsimmons and Maher stepping from the train and taking bows. By their shouts and cheers, the crowd favored Maher. At the water stop in Marathon, I spotted a black bear chained to a stake outside an adobe home a hundred yards from the track. Fitz noticed him too and sprinted to the animal, wrestling with the surprised creature and throwing Stuart into a panic. "The fool," the promoter cried. "What if the bear hurts him? I'm ruined." He put his head in his hands, unable to watch. From my vantage point, it seemed the boxer scared the bear half to death. The Australian survived the bear bout, but I wondered how Fitz would take to Bruno, and if he'd want to wrestle with him before boxing with Maher.

At every stop where there was time and a telegraph, the newspapermen would rush to wire updates to their papers across the country. I overheard Enreed shouting his message at a telegrapher at one place: "*Two engines, ten coaches Langtry bound. All pugs aboard, cars crowded. Two hours late. Threatening weather.*"

About one o'clock the afternoon skies threatened a deluge as the train pulled late into Sanderson for a meal stop. Though the sports had brought whiskey to drink on the trip, few had thought to bring any food, so the passengers stampeded to the eateries by the track, grabbing a quick bite of grub during the fifteen-minute stay. I accompanied Andy and his rangers. The crowd parted to let us and Masterson with his men pass. In the eatery's tumult, Bat angered at a Chinese waiter, grabbing his arm, shaking it, yelling, "Hurry, quickie, quickie, or I'll beat you."

Andy slapped Bat's shoulder. "Release him and don't you dare strike him," growled my brother as it thundered outside.

Masterson's eyes narrowed. He cocked his head as he released his grip on the waiter. "He's just a Chinaman."

"But he's a Texas Chinaman, and I'll broach no insults. Just mind your manners," Andy answered.

For a moment I feared Bat might challenge Andy, but after scowling for a couple of seconds, he broke the ice of his glare with a smile. "Whatever you say, Ranger. I'd hate for either of us to miss the fight."

The waiter brought us a platter of biscuits and fried bacon. We grabbed a handful as we tossed our money on the table and hurried out the door to our ride. Minutes later the locomotive cut loose its shrill whistle and the remaining passengers raced back to the train and boarded. As the train inched forward, then picked up speed, the clouds opened up and dumped rains on the landscape in a deluge, likely the first in West Texas since Noah's time. The downpour drenched Stuart in worry that the waters would wash away the arena or the light would be too low to film. Then he worried if the facilities had even been completed, telling Rector he had hired a sporting man from Dallas to construct the arena and had wired him money to hire forty Mexican laborers. There might be wealth in promoting prizefights, I decided, but there were costs, too, in addition to the consternation and restrictions.

An hour and a half later, we pulled into Langtry, which was as dry as ever but blanketed in low dark clouds. As the locomotive's shrill whistle announced our approach, men stuck their heads out the windows to see the tiny town that for the rest of the afternoon would be the center of the prizefighting world. I observed dozens of people on the depot platform awaiting our arrival. Langtry's population of less than a hundred had swollen to three times that thanks to a train that had arrived earlier from the south, unloading sporting men and a few women from San Antonio, Eagle Pass, and Del Rio.

As our train huffed and groaned to a stop, I reached under my seat and extracted the two tins of syrup for Bruno. Out the window I spotted the justice of the peace dressed in his finest suit, shirt, and tie atop his donkey, waving his sombrero at the passengers scurrying onto the platform.

"Welcome to Langtry," he cried. "I'm Judge Roy Bean, law west of the Pecos and mayor of Langtry. We're glad to have you. Cold beer's available at the Jersey Lilly to wet your thirsts before and after the bout. I'm here to answer your questions and escort any special celebrities to the ring."

I exited the train behind Masterson's gunmen and Andy's rangers, hoping Bean wouldn't spot me until I delivered my gift to Bruno. Scurrying across the platform, I descended the steps and started trotting toward the saloon. There in the cage, I saw Bruno lying down, oblivious to the commotion or maybe not caring to wrestle Fitzsimmons. "Hi, Bruno," I said as I sat the syrup tins down. He looked up and lifted his head as I reached in his pen and patted him between the ears. "I brought you something."

I took the dagger from my boot and pried the lid off one tin, then opened the cage and slid it inside. He made no effort to get up, so I dipped my fingers in the syrup and let him lick off the sweetness. "Sorry you're not feeling well, but I'll see you once the fight is over, which could be a spell if it goes fifty rounds." I latched the cage, then went into the saloon, spat on my hand, and found on the bar a towel to wipe the stickiness from my fingers. Tossing the towel back on the counter, I headed outside in time to catch Bob Fitzsimmons emerging from his sleeping car, hands uplifted to a smattering of cheers.

As the crowd studied the Australian, I watched Andy, with his Winchester cradled in his arm, walk over to Judge Bean. They exchanged pleasantries, then Bean pointed toward the Rio Grande, and Andy motioned for three more Rangers to join them. They marched off to the bluffs overlooking the river as the crowd awaited Peter Maher's appearance. Once Fitzsimmons had cleared the platform with his managers, the Irishman stepped from his railcar and lifted his dukes, shadow boxing for the spectators. They cheered and whistled, more impressed with his physique and attitude than Fitz's. A pause followed his emergence as no one knew quite what to do until Bean returned atop his trotting donkey. He pointed to the west.

"See the Texas Rangers?" he cried, pointing to Andy and his men. "Head their way and you'll spot the ring." That was typical Bean, making it look like the rangers were there to help rather than cancel the match. As he waved visitors toward the river, he spotted me and immediately rode over.

"Howdy, Judge. You're the most important mayor in the world today. Not only that, you kept it secret."

His face beamed, even beneath the dark, low-hanging clouds. "Did she make it?"

"Huh?" I answered, delaying his disappointment.

"Lilly Langtry, did she come to the fight?"

I sighed and shook my head. "She sends her regrets. Miss Langtry has been so rattled by Oscar Wilde's imprisonment, that she just couldn't bear the thought of leaving Britain, even for an event as important as this."

The old judge's spirit clouded like the sky. "This was my last hope," he sighed. "I'll never glance upon her lovely face, at least not in this world." He sighed and turned his donkey toward the river, the animal moving so slowly that I passed them both on my way to watch the fight that I had arranged. Men were already descending the trail down the bluff. At the cliff's edge, I looked below at the site of the world heavyweight championship bout as the boxers and spectators descended the two-hundred-foot trail to the Rio Grande's edge and a pontoon footbridge that linked the bank to the sandbar, where I had taken my first bath in Langtry. In the middle of the island, I saw an elevated boxing ring with a canvas mat centered in what appeared to be a circular circus ten without the top. The fence looked twelve feet high and would screen the spectators on the sandbar from seeing the match, but everyone on the bluff would have a clear, if distant, view of the contest.

The Texas Rangers and a half dozen deputy U.S. Marshals lined the cliff, the strain in their faces dissipating as they realized the fight would come off with nobody getting shot or hurt, save possibly one of the boxers. Andy spotted me, strode over, and slapped me on the shoulder. "You did it, Henry. Now maybe the governor will let us get back to our actual jobs. On top of that, we'll watch the match for free."

"You think it'll go fifty rounds?"

Andy laughed. "We won't be here twenty minutes before the Irishman knocks out that skinny, bow-legged Australian."

"I'll take the skinny one and bet you fifty dollars to the contrary."

"Henry, you've got a bet."

We shook on it. "I'm heading down to watch the fight up close and to find some other suckers along the way." As I turned for the path down the slope, Bean approached on his donkey, his head hanging so low his white-bearded chin sat on his chest. My conscience twitched with regret that I had led him on to help him keep the location secret. "You going down to watch, Judge?" He didn't answer.

I started down the trail looking for gamblers that would bet on Maher. There were plenty who favored the Irishman, so I had no trouble finding takers, so much so that I probably had twelve hundred dollars in bets but only about a fourth of that amount on me by the time I reached the pontoon bridge and crossed over onto the sandbar. I had faith in Fitzsimmons. How could a man that wrestled a lion lose to a dumb Irishman? Then I remembered the thunderstorms and rain upstream and wondered if right now God was sending a wall of muddy floodwaters down the Rio Grande gorge to wash us, sinners, away. It seemed like everyone else had been against this fight, so it wouldn't have surprised me if He opposed it as well.

Stepping onto the sand bar, I followed the others to the opening in the canvas where Masterson and his gunmen intimidated those who complained about the twenty-dollar admission. When I got to the head of the line, the attendant demanded my money, but I informed him the promoter had promised me free admission. He pointed to his helper, who stood just inside the barrier. "He's got the free list," I told the fellow my name, half expecting to be shunned, but he confirmed I was on the list and let me pass.

When I got inside, I spotted Dan Stuart beside himself, pacing back and forth arguing with Enoch Rector. "What do you mean, there's not enough light? It's daylight."

The Kinetoscope man shook his head. "Too much cloud cover. We need bright sunlight to film this."

"Shoot it anyway," Stuart ordered and stormed away.

"It'll look like we shot it in a dark room, just blurred silhouettes," Rector answered, then shrugged when the promoter ignored his response.

Stuart headed to the makeshift dressing rooms and treaded back and forth outside, perhaps regretting he had ever promoted the Corbett-Fitzsimmons fight, much less the Fitzsimmons-Maher debacle, especially after a light mist drizzled from the clouds. After a quarter hour, Fitzsimmons emerged from his quarters wearing a striped robe. He walked to the nearest corner and climbed in the ring as Maher left his dressing room in a green robe. Reaching his corner, Maher tugged on a brown pair of gloves while Fitzsimmons donned a green pair. When the opponents were gloved, the referee called them to the center of the canvas and explained this was the fight the world had been waiting for, but as I looked around, it was obvious little of the world was watching. Because it was a championship bout, the referee said he wanted it decided on fair play and then described what he would call as a foul.

"If either of you violates these rules," the referee said, "you will forfeit the fight and be declared the loser with your opponent the world champion." Completing his instructions, the referee sent the two men to their corners where their trainers helped them out of their robes, Fitz in dark blue trunks with a red, white, and blue belt while Maher wore black trunks with a green belt. The referee invited them back to the center of the ring to touch gloves in a symbolic handshake. As I saw them in their trunks, I had my doubts about my man. With his receding hairline, narrow face, and skinny torso, Fitzsimmons looked like a cadaver while Maher had a body chiseled out of stone and thick black hair and mustache. If the bout was decided on looks, I had already lost. When they separated, a ring attendant yelled "Time!" and banged the gong.

The fight that would never happen began at the sound!

Rather than feel each other out, the two fighters went at it instantly. Fitz struck Maher with a quick left and a quick right, but Maher clinched him and punched the Australian with a right to the cheek during the hold.

"Ain't that a foul?" Fitz bellowed.

Yelling spectators agreed, and the referee issued Maher a warning. "Do that again, and I'll decide the fight against you."

The two boxers moved in close, pounded each other's torsos, then clinched twice, Maher punching Fitz's ribs each time on the side away from the referee. Fitzsimmons complained again, and when he did, Maher popped him in the mouth, drawing blood from a split lip. Both men issued a flurry of punches as they worked their way into Maher's corner. Barely a minute into the fight and my cadaver was bleeding and losing.

Though Maher hit Fitz with light strikes, his heavy ones kept missing because of the Australian's nifty footwork. The crowd chanted, "Maher's got him, Maher's got him." I feared they were right, and I looked upstream, hoping God was sending a flash flood our way to save the day and what money I had on me.

Even as he retreated, though, Fitzsimmons worked the Irishman to a corner, then reversed places with him until Maher had no place to escape. The Irishman stepped toward Fitzsimmons, leading with his left, but the Australian plowed his right hand into Maher's chin. The blow lifted the Irishman from the canvas and twisted him halfway around. Maher tumbled forward like a felled tree and bounced with a thud on the canvas.

"Maher's down," I cried in jubilation as the referee started his count before the hushed crowd.

"*One!*"

Maher lifted his head and shook it.

233

"*Two!*"

His eyes stared somewhere beyond the ring.

"*Three!*"

Then Maher's head collapsed on the canvas. He remained motionless except for his shallow breath.

"*Four!*"

Fitzsimmons returned to his corner, grabbed his stool, and sat down like he had barely been tested as the count continued. His trainer yelled for him to get up to await Maher's assault, as the drizzle changed to a light rain.

"*Five!*"

"He's out for good," Fitz answered.

"*Six!*"

"Get up," his trainer pleaded. "The rain may save him."

"*Seven!*"

"Leave me alone. It's all over, I tell you. He's out." The Australian unlaced his gloves.

"*Eight!*"

Fitzsimmons smirked at his downed opponent.

"*Nine!*"

The Australian remained on his stool as the championship became his.

"*Ten!*"

The new heavyweight champion ripped off his gloves and handed them to his trainer. "Didn't I tell you he was out?"

"But the rain might have revived him."

"Noah's flood wouldn't have revived him today. I hit him solid."

The timekeeper announced the knockout at one minute and forty-three seconds in the first round, much to the disgust of the Irishman's fans. When Maher's men slipped between the ropes and helped him to his corner, Fitzsimmons finally stood up as the referee declared, "Bob Fitzsimmons is the new heavyweight champion of the world. He is now ready at any time and any place to defend his title against any man."

I was ready to collect my money and started finding all those I had bet with. Some paid on the spot, several grumbled they would pay me on the train since they wanted to get out of the rain before it got worse, and a couple said I'd have to wait until we reached El Paso as they hadn't expected to lose. Doing a rough count, I figured I'd collected between five and six hundred dollars with that much more to come. Not a bad day's work, though it had actually been months in the earning. As I exited the arena, I heard Stuart announce that the charter would return in an hour to El Paso.

With the other fans, I trekked across the footbridge and up the bluff to reach Langtry and shelter. The losers grumbled about having to travel to this godforsaken place just to watch their man get whipped in the rain. As for me, I didn't care as I would return to El Paso with more money than I had arrived with and with additional money due me in that cursed city.

At the top of the cliff, I found Andy waiting for me, a grin on his face. "What did you do, Henry? Put a horseshoe in Fitz's glove?"

"Never bet against a man that wrestles lions and bears."

"It didn't last long."

"A minute and forty-three seconds is what they said."

He placed his arm around my shoulder, and we marched back through town toward Langtry. "I'll pay you when we get back to El Paso."

"A lot of others said the same thing."

"The difference is, I really will."

"Keep the money, you're family."

"No, sir. I intend to pay it. You solved a problem that could've gotten me fired, so fifty dollars is a small price to pay for keeping my job."

"I won't argue if you insist. Did you see what happened to Judge Bean?"

"He headed back to the Jersey Lilly. Seemed he lost interest when he wasn't the center of attention."

I knew better than that. Bean mourned that Lilly Langtry hadn't shown up. I regretted I had ever planted the seed in his mind. "Yep, he needs to be the baby at every birth, the bride at every wedding, and the corpse at every funeral."

235

"He's colorful, a remnant of the days when you had to break the law to enforce it."

"Yeah, I had some experience in his court. It's justice on a whim."

"And a fine," Andy added. "Don't forget the fines."

We ambled past the train and headed for Bean's saloon, where dozens of others had beaten us. I followed in Andy's wake as men of questionable character moved out of his way, and we got to the bar ahead of our turn.

"Two cold beers," Andy said to one bartender, then turned to me. "You know to give them exact change or a small bill for a drink, never a large bill because they seldom seem to give you your money back before the train leaves."

I nodded, then startled when the barkeeper slammed my mug on the counter in front of me, sloshing some of my beer out. Then I saw Sam Bean. The judge's son still smarted over me befriending Bruno and taking his gun when I first left Langtry. "Thanks for your fast service," I said smugly. "Have you met my brother, the Texas Ranger?"

Sam grimaced and scurried down the bar, whispering something in his father's ear, and the judge strode over to us.

"So it's true you're brothers, Andy?" he asked.

Andy nodded. "He's my kid brother, though neither of us are kids anymore."

"Henry there's cut from a different cloth than you, likely a cheaper cloth."

"Say what you will about Henry, but he's the one that figured out where we could hold this fight, and he brought you a good payday the best I can tell."

"That he did, but he didn't bring Lilly Langtry like he promised."

Andy looked at me like either Bean or I were crazy.

"I did mention the fight *could* draw her to Langtry, not that it *would*," I admitted.

"By my way of thinking," Bean continued, "that should be a crime."

Andy laughed. "By that reasoning, everything in

Langtry could be a crime."

Bean found no humor in Andy's remark. "That's the way it should be if we're to bring law west of the Pecos."

"And this beer should be cold as promoted rather than lukewarm," I noted.

The judge left us to attend to other customers, and I thought no more of it, drinking a mug of tepid brew. We finished our mugs and headed outside, where I stopped by Bruno who was snoring in his cage, the tin of syrup half gone.

"I called him Judge Roy Bear," I told my brother. "He's the only trustworthy critter in Langtry." We watched the crowd for a few minutes, then heard the locomotive whistle announce the pending departure.

We ambled back to our car and boarded it. I sat by the window staring at the Jersey Lilly, knowing this would be my last time in Langtry. I watched the passengers scurry back aboard, then I saw Bean run out of the saloon, jump on his donkey, and slap him into a trot toward the depot where the judge dismounted. He ran along the platform, looking in the train windows until he spotted me. Then he climbed the coach's steps and came down the aisle, pointing his finger at me.

"H.H. Lomax," he called, "I am hereby placing you under arrest!"

"What?" I screamed. "You're arresting me for what?"

"Theft, fraud, and defamation," he announced for everyone to hear.

CHAPTER TWENTY

"Theft?" I stammered.

"You stole Sam's pistol. The evidence is riding on your hip," Bean announced.

"Fraud?"

"You took two hundred dollars from me to get a book published about my life. I ain't yet seen any results. And you owe me another hundred dollars for hosting this fight."

"And defamation?"

"You defamed the good name of Miss Lilly Langtry, suggesting she would attend a public spectacle as vile as a prizefight."

Dan Stuart, still fuming from his money-losing fight, stormed down the aisle toward me as Andy stood up to assist.

"Get him off of here so we can start the train rolling to El Paso," Stuart shouted.

Bean grabbed my arm, and Andy gripped Bean's. "Hold on, Judge."

"I'm the law west of the Pecos," Bean reminded my brother.

"As a Texas Ranger, I'm the law everywhere, Judge." He turned to me. "Is that his son's pistol?"

Answering with a reluctant nod, I replied, "Sam tried to kill me."

Andy released Bean's arm and asked me another question. "Did you take two hundred dollars from Bean to get his biography published?"

"I did."

"And did you use the name of Lilly Langtry in vain?"

"I did mention she might attend the fight."

"Okay, Henry, I can't help you." He turned to Bean. "He's yours, Judge, but if you don't treat him right, and he isn't back in El Paso by day after tomorrow, I'm coming to find out why, and let me assure you I won't be smiling."

Bean nodded. "His trial will be over in thirty minutes, Andy, if the train can wait."

"The train's not waiting," Stuart growled.

"I've still got bets to collect on the train," I pleaded. "If I don't get them now, I'll lose hundreds of dollars."

"Small change," Stuart grumbled. "I've lost thousands. Get him off of this car so we can go home."

Bean dragged me down the aisle. I could've broken his weak grip, but the gesture would've been pointless as no one would come to my aid, not even my brother. I eased along the aisle and then down the steps onto the platform as a gentle rain peppered me. Barely had I stepped on the slick weathered planks than the train inched away from the depot for the return trip. At least this time, I wasn't being pulled naked to court. I figured I had about nine hundred dollars on me. No telling how little I would have left once Bean finished fining me.

Once the train picked up speed so I couldn't catch it afoot, Bean released my arm and pointed me toward the Jersey Lilly. "We'll try your case this evening." He mounted his donkey, and we headed for the courtroom.

"I can't believe your accusations, after all I did for you, bringing a heavyweight title match to your doorstep."

"You didn't get my book written, much less published. You didn't pay me the hundred dollars you owed me. You didn't bring Miss Langtry here like you promised. You left my son defenseless when you stole his gun."

"I brought Bruno two tins of syrup."

"Bruno's been down lately. He's getting old like me."

As we reached the saloon, Bean pointed to the door. "Get inside and wait for the judge, once he stables his steed."

I didn't consider a donkey much of a steed, but I didn't argue the point either, figuring I'd be fined if I did. Stepping onto the porch and out of the rain, I took off my hat and shook it, then brushed water off my coat. I entered the building and turned right into the saloon, where Sam was straightening the place after the fight crowd's departure.

Sam smirked when he saw me. "You'll pay," he snarled, "for stealing my pistol. Just wish we had a tree nearby big enough to hang you."

"Maybe if you had more shade in Langtry, your brain wouldn't be so sun-addled." I retreated from the saloon into the hallway and quickly pulled as much money as I could from all my pockets and stuck the bills inside my long johns, hoping Bean wouldn't strip me buck naked again looking for my cash.

Just as I finished, Bean entered by the back door and saw me buttoning my britches. He looked at me, then at the puddle beneath my boots. "I hope that's rain, not piss on the floor."

Bending over, I dipped my trigger finger in a dollop of liquid and touched it to my tongue. "It's only water, Judge."

"Good thing," he said, "or I'd be forced to fine you. How much money are you carrying, Lomax?"

"Can't say with certainty, since I won a plenty betting on Fitzsimmons."

Bean smiled and pointed to the door into the saloon. "Go on in. Court's in session."

The judge walked around the counter, grabbed a mallet, and pounded it against the bar as Sam continued to clean up the debris left by the sporting crowd. "Court will hear the matter of the State of Texas against H.H. Lomax, who is accused of theft, fraud, and defamement."

"I demand a jury," I responded.

"Request denied. We don't have time for a jury if you are to be back in El Paso by day after tomorrow. Now, empty your holster, pockets, and boots before this court."

Stepping up to the bar, I pulled Sam's Colt.45 from my side and placed it before Bean, who picked it up, examined it, and declared, "Stolen goods. Fifty-dollar fine."

Next, I extracted everything else from my pants and coat pockets, including the five-shot revolver, a handkerchief, a dollar thirty-seven in change, and my Herndon House room key.

"What, no bills? That's another fifty-dollar fine."

"You're fining me for not having money?"

"No, for carrying a concealed weapon."

Reaching into my shirt pocket, I pulled out my badge and slammed it on the bar. "I'm a lawman. I can carry a gun."

Sam bolted across the room and grabbed the badge. "Let me look at that." He studied it, then shook his head. "This represents El Paso's scavenger office. He's nothing but a street-sweeper, a dogcatcher."

"I'm still permitted to carry concealed weapons."

Bean nodded. "Fine dismissed."

Sam threw the badge on the counter, and it skittered over the edge, Bean stopping the proceedings to pick it up and place it with my other belongings.

"Empty your boots," he next ordered.

I complied, dumping the dagger and my cash with my other possessions on the bar. Bean thumbed through my money, counting out three hundred and seventy-three dollars on the counter.

"Now that I know your assets," Bean informed me, "we can conclude the court proceedings."

"In the matter of the theft, you are fined seventy-three dollars and are to hand over all other weapons you carry. Keep your badge."

"What about the handkerchief, key, and change?" I asked.

"Certainly, but only after you put your boots back on. Something stinks in here."

"It's the court proceeding that smells."

"One more remark like that, and you will be held in contempt. Now, as for the charge of fraud, I'm fining you two hundred dollars, an amount equal to what you were given to see the book published, bringing your total fines so far to two hundred and seventy-three dollars

241

plus the hundred dollars you still owe me for keeping the fight location secret. That comes to three hundred and seventy-three dollars."

I nodded, thinking I might actually come out okay from my court proceeding, especially with all the cash tucked in my long johns.

"Now as for the most serious crime, the defamement of Miss Lillie Langtry, this court has decided that a fine of one thousand dollars is in order."

"What?" I screamed "A thousand dollars!"

Bean banged the mallet on the counter. "Order, order, Lomax, or I will hold you in contempt."

"But a thousand dollars?" I whimpered.

"That is a minor fine, considering the seriousness of the charge," Bean explained, "but in light of your kinship to Texas Ranger Andy Lomax and his desire for you to be back in El Paso by day after tomorrow, this court is suspending the fine."

Sam grumbled from across the room, "Lomax is the only thing that should be suspended, by the neck until dead."

"on the condition that H.H. Lomax never again defame the name of Miss Lilly Langtry. Do you accept the conditions of the suspension, Lomax?"

Relieved, I quickly nodded. "I do."

"Good," Bean said, "these proceedings are adjourned." He banged the gavel against the bar and picked up my fine money. "How about a beer?"

"I need a whiskey instead."

"That'll cost you."

"Okay, a beer."

Sam left the courtroom disgusted that his father and I were sharing a drink together. Bean and I visited until bedtime, then he put me up in the same room I'd stayed in before, even bringing Bruno to sleep by my bed. As I lay on the mattress, I dropped my arm over and stroked Judge Roy Bear's head until he dozed off. I awoke in time to eat some tortillas and eggs with Bean and catch the morning train to El Paso, paying my fare with the money I'd stuffed in my union suit. Breakfast was the last time I ever saw the justice. He lived another seven years, dying without ever meeting Lilly Langtry. A year later, the papers reported that Miss Langtry stopped in Langtry to honor Bean's memory. The grateful citizens, so the papers said, gave her his Colt revolver, which I suspected was the one that I had taken from Sam and Bean had taken from me.

After an almost four-hundred-mile train ride and multiple delays, I arrived back in El Paso well after midnight and walked to my hotel, feeling edgy since I was weaponless and Old Selman was still on the loose. Back in the room, I retrieved that second Colt.45 I had left Langtry with originally. I still owned a revolver and a bicycle, but I decided to leave Hell Paso for San Francisco, so I could walk where my pa had gone during the California gold rush. I spent the next day looking for but finding none of the men who owed me fight money. That night I read scriptures with Annie. When she closed her Bible, I told her I would leave once I settled my affairs, and I wouldn't say goodbye when I did. I paid for another week of lodging even if I wasn't going to use it and gave her fifty dollars as a parting gift for all her favors.

The next morning, I rode my bike to the impound and handed Schloss my badge and the.22-caliber revolver he had issued me for shooting dogs. He gave me my sombrero and serape I kept in the wagon for when I ventured into Juarez. I shucked my other hat and stuffed it in my coat, then pulled on the serape to cut the chill of the northern that had blown in overnight. I yanked the sombrero over my head. From the impound, I rode south to Ysleta to find Andy's office. I enjoyed a peaceful ride through the barren countryside, finding a tranquil Mexican village without the hectic pace of El Paso, though even that city had calmed once the fight business had finished.

Ranger headquarters was a wooden building, one of the few that wasn't adobe in the community dominated by a catholic church. I parked my bicycle and opened the door, which moaned on thirsty hinges. A pair of rangers sat at desks opposite me. They both looked up and nodded, not recognizing me until I removed the large sombrero.

Andy popped up from his desk and strode over, throwing his arms around me and giving me a hug. "Things mustn't have been too bad with Judge Bean."

"I got away better than most with a three-hundred-and-seventy-three-dollar fine and a lecture never to defame Miss Lilly Langtry again."

"It seems I still owe you fifty dollars," Andy said as he broke his grip on me.

"I was going to let it slide Andy until you abandoned me in Langtry to face the law west of the Pecos."

"Couldn't be helped, Henry. I had reports to write to the governor. He wouldn't wait until Bean finished with you, but I was heading to Langtry tomorrow evening if you hadn't shown up by then. I hadn't forgotten you, but I had other duties first."

"Tomorrow I'm leaving for San Francisco because I've wanted to see it ever since hearing Pa's stories about the Gold Rush."

"Pa always was a vagabond at heart. You've lived the life he probably would have preferred over farming."

"And I have little to show for it, no wife, no children."

Andy grimaced. "Life dealt me a bad hand as well, losing my wife and boy. That's why I've stayed with the rangers. They're my family."

"I can't claim anything for family and likely never will."

"Come on, Henry, let's go for a walk." He turned to the other Ranger. "I'll be out for a while with my brother." He grabbed his hat and coat, and we walked outside together, like the brothers we were.

We spent the rest of the morning visiting, then sharing lunch at a Mexican eatery where they served a spicy chili con carne with tortillas. As I ate it, I couldn't help wonder if it was dog or cat meat I consumed. Even so, I paid for it with all the change in my pocket, as Andy had paid upon our boxing bet. Andy and I reminisced about family, the good times we had shared before the war, and the brothers we had lost during the conflict. We had both made it home once since the war and regretted not having returned more, but that was the life we chose and led.

About an hour before dusk, we said our last good-byes, knowing we'd likely never see each other again. Then I got on my bicycle, waved *adios* to my brother, and pedaled back to El Paso as the evening chill turned cold, driving most people indoors for the warmth of their stoves and fireplaces. I expected to go straight to my room so I could get up in the morning and catch the Southern Pacific westbound, but as I neared downtown, I spotted Constable Selman striding along the sidewalk. Figuring the sombrero and serape would be enough of a disguise for me to settle a score, I trailed him to the next block, where he stepped from the walk to cross the street. Seeing my chance, I stood on my bicycle and pedaled as hard as I could, going as fast as I could despite the ten-mile-per-hour limit. I bet I was going at least twenty when I plowed into the unsuspecting lawman, knocking him down as me and my bicycle plowed over him, then flipped on the road. Though momentarily stunned, I had known what was coming and recovered quicker than Old Selman. I jumped up and scrambled to his side like I was trying to check on him. As I squatted down, I pressed my knee against his neck and grabbed his cane. Before a handful of spectators could gather around, I conked him on the skull with the head of his walking stick. He groaned, then went limp. I pulled his gun from his holster and tucked it under my serape.

As a handful of pedestrians walked over to help, I stood up, still holding his cane. "I no see him," I cried, trying to sound like a Mexican with poor English. "Must get to doctor." Jumping up, I ran to my bicycle, grabbed it, and climbed aboard, still toting Selman's cane.

From there, I pedaled quickly through town to my room and sprinted inside, carrying the bicycle upstairs and wondering if Old Selman would ever figure out who ran over him. Inside my place, I packed my two valises, so I was ready to leave the next day. That morning I arose to clean up and dress in fresh clothes, then put the last items in my bags and closed them. Next, I shoved the serape

245

and sombrero under the bed. Unlocking the door, I left the key in the lock so Annie would know I had departed. While my heart said I should tell her goodbye, my brain told me if I did I might never leave and see San Francisco. Grabbing the two valises and the cane, I headed down the hall and out into the midmorning chill, hoping to avoid anyone I knew. Barely had I stepped outside than Rip Enreed, who was leaning against the brick wall, accosted me.

"Lomax," he said matter-of-factly, "I've some questions for you."

"I've got a train to catch."

"Are you the one that arranged Langtry for the boxing match?" he asked, as he fell in beside me.

"Ask Dan Stuart."

"He's left town."

"Then you're out of luck."

"Another question, did you run over Constable Selman last evening with your bicycle?"

"Don't know what you're talking about?"

"It looks like you're carrying his cane. Is it his?"

"I found it on the street."

"Some witnesses say it was you that ran over him."

"What did the fellow look like?"

"They couldn't tell, except he was wearing a big sombrero and a serape, ones that matched your disguise when crossed the river into Juarez to feed Fitzsimmons's lion."

"Sounds like a Mexican to me. Maybe you need to find the Gringo Bandito and ask him?"

"Go to hell, Lomax."

"There's a better class of people in hell than in a newspaper office. *Adios*, Enreed."

I strode away to the music of his profanity with the confirmation that you could never trust a newspaperman. In the next block, I passed the Acme Saloon and on impulse stopped, dropped my two valises, and flung Selman's cane on the establishment's roof, figuring John Wesley Hardin would have approved and even more so two months later when the papers reported Selman had died in a shooting with another El Paso lawman during a poker game.

Grabbing my bags, I headed to the Southern Pacific Depot, purchasing my ticket, and waiting an hour for the train to arrive. Once it did, the agent called for passengers to board. I grabbed my bags from the warm waiting room and stepped onto the frigid platform.

As I strode to my passenger car, a newsboy approached, offering me a newspaper. Though he wore a thin shirt in the chilly breeze, I recognized the little Mexican as the scamp who had not given change when I first arrived in town. He smiled and offered me a paper. I checked the date that it was actually the day's edition and then reached into my pocket, pulling out a dollar since I'd used all my change at the Ysleta eatery.

The lad grinned even wider, stuck the bill in his pants, and darted off, calling over his shoulder.

"*Adios, estupido,*" he cried as he ran away laughing.

I boarded my car for San Francisco with my belief further confirmed that you couldn't trust anyone associated with a newspaper, not even the newsboys.

A Look At: Preston Lewis
Western Collection, Volume 1

SPUR AWARD WINNING AUTHOR PRESTON LEWIS BRINGS YOU FIVE TIMELESS WESTERNS IN ONE!

Get swept away by five western heroes all on a bout of good versus evil. From fighting for freedom in the Texas Revolution to fighting the demons and secrets that have been holding one hero back, Lewis will have you captivated the whole time.

In Choctaw Trail, retired U.S. Marshal Doyle Hardy is called back into service to track down the culprit in a brutal double murder in Indian Territory. The no-nonsense lawman working out of Fort Smith, Arkansas, returns to the trail to track down the murderer, who he doesn't want to admit is his own son...Hardy must confront his own son and tough family truths that he had tried to avoid in all his years as a lawman.

The Preston Lewis Western Collection, Volume 1 includes: *Blood of Texas, Lone Survivor, Choctaw Trail, Tarnished Badge and Sante Fe Run.*

AVAILABLE NOW ON AMAZON

About the Author

Growing up in West Texas and loving history, Spur Award-winning author Preston Lewis naturally gravitated to stories of the Old West and religiously read his father's copies of True West and Frontier Times. Today he is the author of more than 30 western, juvenile and historical novels as well as numerous articles, short stories and book reviews on the American frontier.

Preston Lewis is a past president of WWA and WTHA, which in 2016 named him a fellow. He has served on the boards of the Ranching Heritage Association and the Book Club of Texas. He and his wife Harriet live in San Angelo, Texas.